Reforming Jake

by
Leslie Kelly

Prologue

AS FAR AS Leanne Weston knew, the typical duties of a maid-of-honor included helping the bride with her train, ensuring the flower girl didn't pick her nose at the altar, holding the bouquet during the vows, and making a toast that was warm, funny, gracious, and entertaining. Having read every word she could find in bridal magazines and on blogs, she'd felt sure she could nail it, and had promised her best friend, Eve, that she'd be the best maid-of-honor ever.

She had not, however, anticipated one unexpected duty: having to wrangle an obnoxious guest and drag him out of the reception before he could brawl with the groom.

Yet here she was.

"You absolute jerk! How could you?" she snapped as she shoved her index finger into the chest of the groom's half-brother, Jake Montez, who had been invited to the wedding, but who nobody had really expected to show up.

As an illegitimate black sheep, whose father had once paid his ex-mistress to hide his existence, Jake had a chip on his shoulder about the size of a bowling ball. His bad behavior was expected, according to Eve, and even understandable. Who wouldn't be resentful at having been raised in a poor, run-down house while his two-days-younger, legitimate brother had always sipped from their father's silver spoon? Anybody could forgive Jake's feelings...but Leanne wasn't about to forgive him his actions. Not today's, anyway.

"You should be ashamed of yourself."

"It was just a little kiss," Jake said, continuing to back across the patio of the country club where the reception was being held. He lifted a hand and rubbed his square jaw, which already bore a faint bruise. "Damn, my baby brother really knows how to throw a punch."

"Sam should have done more than that." Leanne continued to push and poke him until he backed against a frozen-over fountain. The two of them were the only ones out here, braving the bitterly cold December day while inside all was warm and romantic. At least, it had been, until the groom's brother had behaved so obnoxiously. "Typically, kissing the bride does not include tongues, or grabbing her bottom."

He gaped. "Her *bottom*? Who are you, Miss Proper Noun?"

Leanne's eyes narrowed.

"Besides, I didn't grab her ass, I just pinched it. And I've been suitably repaid."

"I might agree if your jaw were broken."

"Okay, you're Eve and Sam's bodyguard?"

"I'm Eve's best friend, and the person who's not going to let you ruin her wedding day."

Jake blew out a breath, scoffing at her indignation, and she caught a whiff of scotch.

She scowled. "You're drunk."

"Nah, not even close."

"Yes, you are. I'm going to have someone call you a cab." A few too many drinks was the only explanation for his behavior. No normal, sober person would grab a brand new bride, in front of her husband, and kiss her so inappropriately.

"I didn't even finish my first drink," he insisted, and the steadiness of his gaze, not to mention his voice, made her believe him.

But then, why would he have been such a jerk?

The reception had been winding down, Eve and Sam getting ready to depart for their honeymoon. Leanne had followed to help Eve get ready. She had walked around the corner into a back hallway just in time to see the groom's brother land a very inappropriate kiss on the bride's mouth. The kiss had lasted a few seconds before Sam wrenched his brother away and punched him, cracking his head back hard enough so that Jake stumbled against the wall.

Jake hadn't fought back, instead chuckling with wicked satisfaction at having achieved his twisted goal of causing trouble. His amusement had been enough to inflame the situation, and Sam appeared ready to leap on him. Which was when Leanne and Eve had jumped between the men, Eve calming her new hubby, Leanne dragging out his jackass of a brother.

"In any case, I think it's best if you just go," she said.

"You're kicking me out?"

"Yes, Mr. Montez, I am."

"You mean I can't stay and throw rice?"

She gritted her teeth. "We'll be throwing birdseed. Now, please leave."

He sighed heavily and ran a hand through his thick, shoulder-length dark hair—a stark contrast to the closely-shorn, blond-haired groom. The brothers couldn't look more dissimilar, each of them apparently taking their looks from their respective mothers. Even their physiques were different, with Sam being more stocky and brawny, while Jake was a smidge taller and leaner. The only place they resembled each other was in the eyes. They shared their father's brilliant green-gold irises, which were a natural fit for Sam, but looked startlingly bright on his swarthier half-sibling.

Not for the first time, she had to admit just how attractive the trouble-making cretin was. There were those eyes, of course, plus that long, gleaming black hair. His face was lean, stubbled, with a jaw that looked like it could be as stiff as granite. Considering it hadn't broken under Sam's powerful punch, it might well be.

"It's not like I crashed the place. I was invited to the wedding," he finally said.

"You've worn out your welcome."

"You're a fierce one, aren't you?" he said, a crooked smile tugging at that mouth.

A surprising pair of dimples flashed in his cheeks, and Leanne sucked in a breath, taken off guard. Because, when he smiled, well, his sexiness level went right off the charts. She would never have expected those dimples, not with his whole badass, motorcycle-riding, black-leather-jacket wearing persona.

She straightened, steeling her spine, knowing better than to let a sexy guy charm her. Been there, done that, still bore the scars on her heart. "Fierce enough to do whatever it takes to make sure you leave."

"Whatever it takes, huh?"

She was nodding before she noticed the twinkle in his eye. Once she did notice, she froze, wondering if she'd just made things worse.

Then he stepped close, cupped her cheek in his hand, and tilted her head up. "Okay then. One kiss."

Leanne's jaw fell open in shock. She'd definitely made things worse.

"You can't be…"

"I'm serious," he said. "One kiss from you, and I'll go away."

She rolled her eyes, about to tell him he was crazy, but before she could do anything—slap his face, shove him away, turn and run—his mouth was on hers and he was kissing every one of her brain cells into helpless submission.

He dropped his strong hands to her hips and pulled her close to his tall, hard body. Leanne was unable to find any will to resist. His mouth was so warm on hers, his lips soft, persuasive and delicious. And when his lips parted and his tongue demanded even more, she could only gasp…giving him the access he desired.

He tilted his head, holding her more tightly, the kiss getting hotter, wetter, and deeper. He explored the recesses of her mouth, claiming her with the kiss as nobody had ever put a claim on her before. Leanne found herself reaching up to cling to his back, her fingers digging in to his jacket, her hands clenching the material.

The air was frigid, icy drops of freezing rain beginning to fall against her cheeks like a snowman's tears, but inside she was a raging ball of flame. The man's mouth tasted of scotch and sin, heat and hedonism. She was furious, she was on fire. She was loving every second, she was ordering herself to put a stop to the insanity.

She was being kissed the way every woman should be kissed at least once in her life… by someone who she couldn't stand.

She didn't know how long it would have gone on, if she would eventually have come to her senses and shoved him away, but it turned out she didn't have to. Slowly, his every move feeling reluctant, he ended the kiss and drew his mouth from hers. He stared down at her, his bright green eyes now darker, swimming with emotion. Heat. Leanne stared up at him, her lips numb, her heart thudding, her thoughts whirling in her head.

Nothing like this had ever happened to her before. She truly had been kissed speechless.

"Damn, princess, you sure do know how to use your mouth. If that was how you convince me to go, I'd love to see how you'd entice me to come."

She swallowed hard, mortified, catching his innuendo. Icy raindrops notwithstanding, her cheeks suddenly felt hot, and so did the rest of her. And not in a good way.

Fierce anger surged through her. The guy was unbelievable. He had kissed his brother's wife, started a fight, and then done the same to her? And his smirky self-confidence afterward just made the whole thing worse.

She didn't hesitate. Moving close, she lifted her foot and then slammed it down, as hard as she could, onto his. Her spiked heels were narrow and sharp, and they came down right on his toes. When he groaned and staggered back, almost falling into the fountain, she shoved her index finger in his face one more time.

"Go, Mr. Montez, and while you're going, you'd better pray to God that I never see you again, or you're going to get more than a bruised foot."

And then, without waiting to see if he obeyed her, she swung around and stalked back into the reception, sending up one prayer of her own.

That she never had to see Jake Montez again.

Chapter 1

As FAR AS jail cells went, this one wasn't bad.

The mattress was lumpy, but so far didn't appear to be infested with bugs...at least not the fifty legged ones like those Jake had killed with his bootheel during his only other stay in jail years ago down in Mexico. The floor was concrete, rather than packed dirt, and the walls weren't encrusted with mold or riddled with bullet holes. Above the washstand there even hung a mirror, a warped plastic one that distorted his features making him look like a circus clown. But a mirror nonetheless.

Jake felt right at home.

Reclining on his back on the cot, with his head resting on the arms he'd curled on top of the pillow, he continued to stare straight up. He wondered, for the twentieth time, who had bothered to reach high overhead and use some unknown tool to scratch an obscene message in the ceiling tile. Whoever it was, the guy couldn't spell. Nor was he very imaginative.

Jake's shoulders ached, though not enough to make him straighten his arms and allow his head to actually come in contact with the pillow. Relatively clean cell or not, he wasn't stupid enough to allow his hair to come anywhere near linens used by previous residents.

"You're sprung, Montez," a cop said as he paused outside the cell.

Jake continued staring up at the ceiling. He'd just been able to fully read the graffiti as the sun broke over the edge of the building and allowed light to slant in through the barred windows. His curiosity had been nagging him through the night hours as he tried to figure out whether the letter at the beginning of the last word was an "f" or a "t".

"Did you hear me?" the officer asked as he punched in a code on the control panel and the cell door slid open.

"F," Jake muttered as he finally lifted himself up and sat on the edge of the cot. He shrugged his shoulders, rolling them back to work out the kinks from the night spent in the cell. Not really a night…he figured it had only been about six hours since the cops had dragged him in from The Slaughter House. Seemed like days. He was definitely ready to go home and take a forty-five minute shower. He felt grimy from the wasted time spent the previous evening in a smoky bar, not to mention the time in the jail cell.

He sure hadn't expected that agreeing to do a favor for an old Army buddy would result in him spending a night in lockup in one of Philadelphia's downtown precincts. As far as he was concerned, the gratis investigative work Jake had done on Tommy Jerome's behalf, and the not-so-comfy night in the cell, canceled the debt Jake owed him. Not that Tommy would think so. Jake imagined he was destined to hear about the time Tommy had come to his aid when he was jumped by two hoods for the rest of his days. Especially now, with Tommy's current gang trouble, which was the reason he'd called in the old debt Jake owed and asked him to see what he could dig up on the ringleaders.

"You like it here so much you want to stay another night?" the officer asked as he impatiently tapped the cell door with his night stick. "You've made bail."

"I guess my brother got my message," Jake said, a small grin curling his lips upward. He wondered how Sam had reacted when he heard Jake's voice mail during the night, asking him to come down to the 27th precinct and post bond. "Bet he wasn't too pleased."

The cop fell into step one pace behind Jake as they walked down the short hallway that ran between the holding cells. "I don't know your brother, but unless he's one hell of a drag queen, he ain't the one bailing you out."

Jake paused and looked over his shoulder at the short, stocky man. "Gorgeous woman?"

"Oh, yeah," the man said, a smile crossing his jowly face.

Standing to the side, Jake waited while the heavy door leading into the processing area of the police precinct swung open. He wondered why Sam's wife Eve was the one bailing him out. After the stunt he'd pulled at their wedding two weeks ago, he'd figured she'd just as soon let him rot. He'd imagined Sam would, too. But he'd still been unable to resist placing his one phone call to his brother, the famous author.

Sam needed a little shaking up every now and then. Otherwise he might sink too far into a life of respectability. Of course, he had his stunning new wife to keep him on his toes, but Jake had gotten too used to playing Sam's Achilles' heel to give it up entirely. He'd been doing it since the night they met, just five-and-a-half years ago.

Jake didn't resent Sam anymore, and, other than the wedding incident, he didn't think Sam bore any ill will toward him, either. They'd both finally realized neither one of them was responsible for the actions of their parents. The fact that their father had gotten two women pregnant, and those women had given birth to boys within two days of one another, was certainly not their fault.

Not that Jake had acknowledged that originally. He wasn't too proud of how he'd acted when he'd first come face to face with his younger, golden-haired, *legitimate* brother. But, to his credit, Sam had never appeared to really hold it against him. It was only their father Sam had blamed, and rightly so.

"Sign for your stuff, exit through there," the officer said as he held a clipboard toward Jake.

Quickly scrawling his signature, Jake grabbed his wallet, and keys, and thrust them into the pockets of his soft, worn jeans. He swung his leather jacket over one shoulder and prepared to walk away.

"Aren't you going to check your wallet?" the other man asked, a look of suspicion on his face.

"If you can't trust Philadelphia's finest, who can you trust?" Jake asked.

The officer frowned. "Thought a night in the cell might have helped you watch that mouth of yours. If it had been me you took a swing at, you wouldn't be so cocky."

Jake slowly stared at the man, who stood belligerently next to his desk, twenty other cops within spitting distance. He allowed his gaze to travel down the officer's portly form, wondering how many dozen donuts the guy had to put away to develop such a pear-shape. "If it had been you I took a swing at, I doubt I'da missed."

Not even bothering to watch while the cop sputtered and scrambled to come up with a retort, Jake walked out of the processing area into the main precinct.

Though it was not even eight a.m., a cacophony of noises greeted him. Angry shouts came from one corner where a man stood nose to nose with a cop, insisting he be allowed to see his lawyer immediately, if not sooner. Three other overnight visitors, probably drunk and disorderlies judging by the rumpled clothes and bleary eyes, sat on a bench, forced to wait for their breathalyzers to prove they were sober enough to be let back on the streets. A burly detective typed, hunt-and-peck style, at a computer console at a nearby desk. Two others poured coffee. The phone rang incessantly. Could have been any Saturday morning at any police precinct in any big city in America.

Jake quickly glanced around, looking for Eve. For a second, he thought he spotted her, standing with her back to him next to a soda machine, but quickly realized he was mistaken; the height and hair color were wrong. He stared at the woman anyway.

She was obviously out of place in the raucous room. Her long, charcoal-gray, wool coat should have concealed her figure, but was tailored to outline it very nicely, instead. From the looks of it, she had curvy hips that would fill up a man's hands just perfectly.

For some reason, he found himself thinking of that other woman he'd met at the wedding.

The one he'd kissed.

The one he'd had a hard time getting out of his head.

Damn, he'd behaved like an absolute ass. Sure, he'd had his reasons for starting a fight with the groom. Reasons involving his father, the very man he'd tried so hard to avoid, who'd confronted him throughout the reception, wanting to bond, or talk, or fight, or some shit. When he'd followed Jake to the men's room, the final straw had landed too hard on Jake's back. So he'd done something stupid— grabbing his new sister-in-law and kissing her—just to start a fight and get away from the old man.

Sam would forgive him. He probably already had. His two-days-younger brother had had his own run-ins with their incredibly pushy, stubborn, self-important father.

Yeah, he'd send Eve flowers or something to apologize, and to thank her for the bail-out.

Of course, he didn't really have an excuse for the way he'd behaved with the hot bridesmaid who'd rightfully called him on his bullshit. There *was* no excuse, except for the fact that he was a greedy bastard who took what he wanted. And he'd wanted one kiss from those perfect lips, wanted to shock the primness out of that luscious mouth.

He shook his head hard, forcing the memories away. The sexy

blonde would never speak to him again, that had been made clear by her furious exit, not to mention his mangled foot.

So he instead turned his attention to the brunette standing by herself in the station house. She wore slim-fitting leather gloves and she clutched her purse against her hip like it was an extension of her body. Her entire form was rigid, as if she expected to be accosted at any moment. Obviously not a prisoner, she must have come down to bail someone out. Lucky s.o.b. Because it definitely wasn't *him* she'd bailed out—she wasn't Eve. The curls visible in her sophisticated, twisted-up hair-do, were not Eve's pure, sunshine-blond. They were darker, honey-brown-tinged-with-gold. And this woman was a good six inches shorter than his sister-in-law.

She turned her head, gazing curiously at several laughing women who entered from the processing area. Jake caught a brief glimpse of a perfect profile. Straight, elegant nose, high cheekbones, smooth cream-colored skin. She looked familiar to him, though he couldn't immediately place her. He wanted a better look, but she turned her head away too quickly.

He wondered who she was here to bail out. Whoever it was, he was one lucky bastard.

Reluctantly taking his eyes off the woman, he looked around for Eve. No one else came close to fitting the description of his brother's beautiful wife. Just as well. He hadn't meant to drag her down to the police station early on a Saturday morning, just her husband. She had probably dropped off the bond money then skipped out, not wanting to run into Jake at all.

Shrugging, Jake pulled his leather jacket onto his arms and over his shoulders. Whoever had posted the bond, he was glad to be getting out of here. Unable to resist, he glanced once more toward the soda machine. The beautiful woman was watching him, and he caught her eye.

Instead of coyly looking away, embarrassed to be caught staring, she raised her eyebrow quizzically. Jake responded with a quick grin and a wink. He watched the color rush into her pale, perfect cheeks, then she frowned and crossed her arms over her chest, her leather bag swinging freely in front of her. She resembled nothing less than a school teacher confronting a misbehaving child.

Disappointed that she didn't offer so much as a tiny smile in response to his flirtation, Jake walked to the door. He paused to zip up his jacket, trying to remember where he'd left his bike. He didn't know exactly where the precinct was in relation to the bar he'd been at last night before the trouble started, and hoped it was within walking distance.

"Are you even going to say thank you?"

Somehow, before he even turned around to see who was speaking, Jake knew it was the woman he'd been eyeing. Her words were precise, her voice smooth and refined, but with a hint of huskiness that had to accompany someone with a body like hers. No one else in this place could have sounded like that...like high-brow culture and hot sweaty sex rolled into one.

Unable to resist checking to see who she was talking to, he cast a quick glance over his shoulder. She stood right behind him and was looking directly at Jake.

"Were you talkin' to me?"

The woman's eyes narrowed and her jaw clenched. "Of course I was talking to you, Mr. Montez."

Jake took one step to the side, allowing the bright morning sunlight to shine through the windows by the front door and fall on her face. He wanted to get a better look at her.

She pursed her lips disapprovingly, and Jake thought he'd die right there on the spot. God, the woman had the sexiest mouth he'd ever seen. Her lips were perfect, full, made for kissing...and other pleasures. Hot thoughts flooded his mind and he couldn't say a word.

Because he suddenly remembered her. How could any man ever forget that mouth? Having once tasted it, explored it, no person with an ounce of testosterone could forget it.

She looked different—her hair color was a big change, that's what had thrown him—but there was no doubt he was looking at his new sister-in-law's best friend. She was the sharp-tongued, but sweet-lipped bridesmaid.

He should have realized it sooner, considering she'd occupied his thoughts more than once since he'd last seen her, but that hair, and the utter incongruity of her presence at a police precinct, had thrown him off balance. Or it could have been the blow to his head during last night's fight that had done it. Whatever the case, he was thinking straight now.

For some reason, though, he wasn't quite ready to let her know that. She'd been so bossy, so self-confident at the wedding, when she'd been telling him off, at least until he'd ruffled her feathers with that kiss.

"I just bailed you out of jail." She tilted her little jaw up and waited, expectation in her gray eyes. "Don't you have anything to say?"

"Yeah," he said, suddenly wanting to ruffle her feathers again. Hiding his smile, he asked, "Who the hell *are* you?"

OF ALL THINGS Leanne Weston had expected to hear from the man she'd just, essentially, rescued from a cell, this wasn't one of them. She'd expected excuses, apologies, thank yous, anything else one would typically say to the person who'd bailed them out of jail.

And you don't even remember me?

Leanne stared dumbly up at Jake, wondering if he truly didn't remember. Because she sure as heck couldn't have forgotten him. No woman could have.

Jake Montez was walking, talking, one-hundred percent pure male sin. He was surly, he was rude, he was flirtatious, he was charming, he was a complete contradiction. And, she had to concede, he was also the most drop-dead sexy man she'd ever seen.

He wasn't dressed in a suit today, as he had been at the wedding, but that was okay. This rough-and-ready look suited him much better. His black jacket looked like it had been around for years. Its faded, smooth texture molded every bump and bulge of his thick arms and broad chest. He wore loose-fitting jeans that looked like they'd been around even longer. The soft denim cupped powerful legs, a taut backside, and...other places. She half expected the worn seams to give way.

Leanne cleared her throat and looked away, wishing she hadn't been tormented by long, erotic dreams about that crazy kiss they'd shared. She'd found herself looking at fabric swatches, trying to find one that was the same swirly mix of green-and-gold as his eyes. In short, she'd been crazily affected by the man.

And the asshole didn't even know who she was.

Maybe that isn't such a bad thing.

Because, again, he was sin. Pure. One hundred percent. Therefore, someone she needed to stay away from, for fear she'd be tempted into sinning like poor Eve with that juicy apple...the biblical one, not her best friend.

But something wouldn't let him off the hook that easily.

"I'm Leanne Weston. Eve's maid of honor. Remember Eve? Your brother's wife?" she said, questioning his memory and his skills of observation.

She didn't mention their argument on that cold, wintry day. Or the kiss. Hopefully he'd had been drunk enough that he'd forgotten all about it. Though, honestly, she'd believed him when he said he hadn't had more than one drink. She still couldn't figure that one out.

"You changed your hair color."

Okay, so maybe he was a little observant. "So you do remember?"

He gazed at her mouth. Those eyes narrowed, assessing, heated.

Oh yeah. He remembered.

"Of course I do. I was just messing with you. I'm hung over and banged-up, not brain-dead. But it did take a minute. You were a platinum blonde two weeks ago. Now you're a brunette." A lazy grin spread across his lips. "Pretty in pink Leanne. I guess I also didn't recognize you without the bows and lace and that big bunch of flowers you had busting out of your *blond* hair."

She glared at him, even though she'd felt the same way about the awful stylist who'd fixed her hair on Eve's wedding day, and had, somehow, mistaken her head for a vase.

"I wanted a change," she admitted, wondering whether he thought the hair-color shift was a good thing or a bad one. She also wondered why it had taken this man, who barely knew her, minutes to notice the change when it had taken Ned, the man she'd been dating, two days to mention it.

"I also seem to remember you trying to shove me into a fountain," he continued, his words slightly tinged with a drawl that brought images of old western movies to Leanne's mind. "Of course, my memory could be faulty. I wasn't at my best that night."

"Are you ever?" she snapped, knowing he was intentionally avoiding any mention of that kiss. Which only made her think about it more.

"Come on, you're not going to hold one mistake against me, are you? I got a little rowdy. Where's the crime?"

"Eve told me she thinks she knows why you did what you did."

"Enlighten me."

"Apparently, you yelled at your…at the father-of-the-groom," she bit out.

"He wouldn't get out of my face."

"The day wasn't about *you*."

"I know," he admitted with a heavy sigh. "I should've just kept walking away."

"Yes, you should. Instead, you got even with your father by demanding a kiss from the bride. A very inappropriate kiss."

"For which I was suitably punished," Jake replied. He lazily rubbed a hand on his jaw, as if remembering his brother's reaction.

"It serves you right," Leanne retorted. "Sam shouldn't have stopped with one punch. He should have thrown you out altogether."

"That's what you did, if I'm not mistaken," he said, narrowing his eyes. "Well, you didn't exactly throw me out. But you persuaded me to go."

"If that's how you want to look at it."

He stared at her, his green eyes studying her figure so intently she drew her heavy coat even tighter around her body. His attention seemed to linger for the longest time on her hips, and then her chest, before he settled on her mouth. A strange, confused look crossed his face. "Maybe I really was drunk. Well, no, I wasn't, but maybe Sam's punch rattled my brains or something."

Leanne had no idea what he was talking about.

"Cause, damn, lady, how could I have kissed that mouth of yours and then left, when the one thing I wanted to do was kiss you again until you forgot all about trying to make me go and instead took me to the nearest bedroom?"

Leanne took in a breath, shocked into silence. Jake stared at her face, a definite twinkle in his eye. Not conscious she was doing it, she sucked her lips into her mouth, biting the bottom one with her teeth. He frowned disapprovingly and made a tsk'ing sound.

Not one other man Leanne knew would have said something like that to her. Oh, she received compliments, she'd been told she was beautiful by men hoping she'd end up in their beds. Professionally, she'd heard smooth assurances that her clothes were stylish, her taste and eye for color impeccable. Since she'd focused every ounce of her attention on her career, however, she'd never met a man who looked at her as if imagining she was using her mouth on him.

She told herself she was offended. But the sound of her blood rushing through her veins as her heart beat faster made it clear she was fooling herself. He might be crude, and too darn confident, but there was just something so charming about his crooked grin and the cute laugh lines around his eyes.

And oh, that sin. It did appeal to the most feminine parts of her.

"Don't act all uptight, darlin'," he said with a chuckle. "I'm just calling it as I see it. You've got a body that would make a man beg. You must have had a drug in your lipstick to make me stupid enough to give up without taking another shot."

Her eyes widened as she tore her attention away from those cute laugh lines. The guy just pushed every limit. No wonder he was always in trouble, if he was in the habit of saying every single thing that was on his mind. She didn't imagine the words *tactful* or *discreet* were listed in his mental dictionary.

She didn't know whether to tell him he was a pig, or just spin around and walk away. Another part of her, the part she kept buried deep down inside, so deep she almost didn't know if it was there anymore, threatened to send a chuckle past those lips he seemed to admire so much.

The impulse was something of a shock to Leanne. She'd worked long and hard to build up the veneer she showed the world, both in her career and her personal life. Smooth, cultured, in control...all the outward trappings of a confident young woman quickly climbing up the ladder toward success.

Those trappings disguised the original Leanne—the one who'd been taught as a kid to fake a communicable disease whenever the landlord came knocking. Or to pay one admission price to a movie and spend the entire day in the theater, watching every feature until she and her laughing mother were chased out by the manager.

That Leanne had no place in her current existence. She was not at all pleased that Jake Montez had been able to find her so quickly, with just a few obnoxious comments.

The realization that he was slipping past the shell she'd shown the world for so many years hit her like a splash of cold water in the face. She needed to get away from him. Now.

Squaring her shoulders and lifting her chin in haughty dismissal, Leanne attempted to brush past him to leave. There was no point talking to the man any longer. He was completely impossible. She'd learned the best way to handle impossible men was to refuse to associate with them.

Before she could go, however, she heard a shrill woman's voice say, "Hey, look, it's my knight in shinin' armor!"

Leanne paused, her hand on the knob. A tall, pale-faced woman with hair an improbable shade of cherry-red gave Jake a big grin. She wore a short, bright blue leather skirt with matching bustier, and spiky black high heels that Leanne couldn't have walked in even if she'd ever have the nerve to wear them. Which she wouldn't. The redhead beckoned to two other women, who wore similarly revealing outfits.

"I don't ever forget a favor, sweetie. Anytime you want repayment for helping me out last night, you just look me up, okay?" the woman gushed as she leaned closer to Jake, pressing her more than ample boobs into his upper arm.

To give him credit, Jake looked uncomfortable. He caught

Leanne's eye over the woman's head, and sent her a pleading glance. Before Leanne could say a word, the woman's two friends had him circled. A blonde in a halter top and obscenely tight stretch pants shouldered Leanne out of the way in her haste to get close to him. And another wearing knee-high boots and a fuchsia mini skirt pushed her arm across his chest, blocking his access to the door.

It sounded like the opening to a joke: A blonde, a brunette and a redhead walk out of a jail cell....

"Well, looks like everything's under control, Mr. Montez," Leanne said with an evil grin, planning to leave him to extricate himself from the three clinging women.

"Oh, honey, don't you go being too hard on him now," the redhead said when she finally noticed Jake had not been standing alone. "He was a real hero."

"I'm sure you're right," Leanne said, her tone breezy even if her mood was turbulent. As she watched, Jake managed to detach himself from the blonde. He ducked beneath the outstretched arm the brunette held across his chest and reached for the exit. His hand met Leanne's on the doorknob, and even through the fine leather of her glove, she felt the strength of his fingers. She stared dumbly at her own hand, wondering why she suddenly felt so warm inside when it was such a cold day.

"You ladies take care of yourselves now," Jake said as he twisted the knob and ushered Leanne outside.

"We'd rather take care of you," one said with a leer.

Leanne gave an unladylike snort that was half amusement and half disgust as she walked out the door. A cold blast of air hit her face, and she pulled the collar of her coat up around her cheeks. Walking down the icy cement steps, she held tightly to the rusted railing so her high-heeled boots wouldn't slip out from under her. Before she even knew he was following close behind her, Jake took a firm hold on her elbow, guiding her down to the sidewalk below. She immediately tried to pull free, but he didn't appear to want to let go.

"Goodbye, Mr. Montez," she said firmly, yanking her arm out of his grasp so hard she nearly fell backward onto the steps she'd just descended.

He steadied her, this time grabbing her shoulder, and smiled broadly, as if he understood why she was so skittish around him. How could he not? She bet the man had women falling at his feet all the time, especially if the three in the police precinct were any indication. "Thank you," she muttered as she twisted her arm and turned to leave.

"You going to let *me* say thanks to *you*?"

She paused, cocked her head to the side, and waited. He just looked down at her, his eyes once again zeroing in on her mouth, which she self-consciously tightened. He didn't say a word. Finally, after a long silence, she sighed and prepared to walk away.

"No, wait, I'm sorry," he said. "You did me a favor, bailing me out. I need your address so I can send you the money I owe you."

"Just give it to Eve and Sam," Leanne replied. "I'm sure you'll be seeing them soon. I imagine Sam will be looking you up when they get back from their honeymoon."

"They're still on their honeymoon? Didn't figure little brother had it in him."

"The wedding was only two weeks ago. Remember?"

Jake grimaced, rolling his eyes as if he didn't want to hear another word about the infamous wedding.

"They're due back tonight," Leanne explained. "I'm taking care of the cat…"

"They still have that demon cat from hell? Figured Eve would have put her foot down by now and said the cat goes or she does."

Leanne liked animals, but even she couldn't argue that one. Because, frankly, Sam's cat was a demon. Somehow, though, Eve had won him over. That didn't mean Leanne had, however, and Quigley had either ignored her or else tried to stalk and scratch her every time she went to feed him.

Not that she was going to rag on Sam's cat to his obnoxious brother.

"Yes, well, anyway, I stopped by their apartment early this morning to feed him before I went to work. They also asked me to check their messages, and I heard yours."

"Work? Thought school was out on weekends."

Leanne lifted a questioning brow. "What do you mean?"

"Well," he explained with a twinkle in his eye, "you're Eve's friend, and she teaches. Plus, you've got that whole disapproving teacher stare down to an art form."

She almost gave him one of those stares before she thought better of it, but forced a look of calm disinterest to her face. "I'm sure you've seen your fair share of those."

"No," he said with cocky assurance, "the last teacher I dated always wore a big ole smile."

Probably when he was in high school. Or middle.

Leanne turned abruptly. "I'll have to take your word for it," she said as she walked down the street toward her car. She expected him to stroll off in the other direction. Obviously, the two of them had nothing in common and not one good reason to exchange another word. He'd said his thanks, sort of, and that should be the end of that.

He obviously didn't agree. "Can I hitch a ride?" he asked as he fell into step beside her.

She wanted to say no, but it was a bitter morning. And his leather jacket might look sexy when he wore it with his faded jeans, but she doubted it did much to keep out the cold. She told herself she was agreeing only because he was Sam's brother, a black sheep one, admittedly, but his brother nonetheless. "All right, Mr. Montez."

She unlocked her Lexus, and walked around to the driver's side while he got in. Jake had to slide the seat back to accommodate his long legs, and she found herself watching him get comfortable. The seat had never had to go any further back for Ned, its usual occupant. Leanne thrust the thought out of her mind, angry with herself for thinking such a childish, traitorous thing. So what if Ned wasn't much taller than she? What he lacked in height next to Mr. Recently Bailed Out Of Jail, he more than made up for in terms of social standing and position. Not to mention bank account.

As for sex appeal? Well, she wasn't even going to think about that. Few men could measure up to the one sitting beside her.

"My ride should still be parked behind The Slaughter House," he informed her as she started the car.

"The Slaughter House," she murmured. "Lovely."

Following his directions, she turned a few corners away from the precinct, quickly finding her way into a seedy area of north Philadelphia. Leanne bit the corner of her lip as she spied the old, sooty, brick buildings, complete with boarded up windows and graffiti-covered signs for stores long since closed. Her hands instinctively tightened on the steering wheel. She found herself staring at the forlorn chains hanging from old rusted swing-sets, their seats broken or stolen ages ago. She had to force herself to focus on the road.

"Don't panic, lady, most of the ax murderers don't come out til at least noon."

Leanne cast a quick look at Jake leaning back in the seat. He stared at her with judgment in his eyes, as if he had already pegged her as an upper middle class, society type, who would never be caught dead in an area such as this.

To hell with what Jake Montez thought. She knew more about

areas like this than she cared to remember. Hadn't she'd lived the first several years of her life in similar neighborhoods?

Her father had been a one-night stand who her mom swore was a famous rocker...though she couldn't remember which one. And her mother, though a fun-loving and caring parent, had never been very good about things like paying bills, or being responsible. Nor had she much liked working a regular nine-to-five job. She'd had lots of dreams...grandiose, creative ones, but never the ability to stick with a steady job and bring in a regular paycheck. By the time she was ten, Leanne and her mother had moved a dozen times, sometimes into neat two bedroom apartments in shabby but respectable neighborhoods. Sometimes into holes in the wall her mother found for them while she scraped together some cash for her next project.

Leanne had never blamed her mother for her upbringing. Though she might have served boxed macaroni and cheese for dinner six nights out of seven, Janie Weston had also instilled in Leanne a strong sense of creativity, and a love for color and texture, and beautiful things. What she couldn't purchase for Leanne, like pretty clothes, curtains, or pictures, she'd help her create, using photos from catalogs and magazines they'd "borrow" from office waiting rooms.

That eye for color, and the skill at creating, had paid off. Leanne's career as an interior designer was flourishing. She thanked her mother, who had finally settled down and married a nice, hardworking man when Leanne was a teenager, for giving her the drive to succeed.

She knew who she was, knew where she came from. And she would never let herself forget. To forget would mean letting her guard down, and only by being constantly on guard could Leanne be assured of never returning to such a world such as the one that now surrounded her.

"So, if you're not a teacher, what do you do, Miz Leanne?" Jake asked as they waited at a traffic light.

"I'm an interior designer," she replied absently, glancing to the right and left at the deserted road. There was no activity at this time of morning, but she imagined four or five hours ago, the streets had been jumping.

"Isn't that a fancy way of describing somebody who picks out curtains?"

"Yes, Mr. Montez," she said, her tone as dry as bread crumbs. "I pick out curtains."

A few moments later, Leanne swung the car into the abandoned parking lot outside a dilapidated wood frame, single story building. A sign advertised the bar Jake had described. "Did you say you were parked here?" she asked, knowing her tone was dubious.

"Almost. I never would have left my baby outside the gate. The owner's a friend of mine, and he always lets me park in back." Jake pointed to the back of the building where she noticed a padlocked, high fenced area.

"You have a key?"

"Nope."

She wondered for a second how he was going to get to his bike, but didn't think she really wanted to know the answer.

"Thanks for the ride. And for the bail-out. I'll be sure to give Sam the money when he comes to tell me off for what happened at the wedding."

The man looked pleased at the prospect; she saw a glint of good humor in his green eyes. She wondered at that, knowing there was a history of bad blood between the brothers, who hadn't even known the other existed until five or six years ago. "You don't seem too disappointed at the prospect."

"Nah, riling up Sam is one of my few pleasures." A genuine smile crossed his features and she had to smile in response. He looked like a man who was remembering a fine meal, or a particularly good cigar.

"That's a rather perverse thing to say."

He slanted a glance at her out of the corner of his eye, and she could have predicted his words before he said them. "Well, maybe I'm a rather perverse sort of person."

"That's a fairly accurate description, from what I hear," she said. "You seem to delight in ticking people off, Mr. Montez."

He chuckled. "There's some truth in that, I have to admit. But maybe the reality is, I just give people what they expect to see."

She wondered just how much of his persona was part of his give-them-what-they-expect philosophy. Considering his quick wit and obvious intelligence, she had to suspect there was a lot more to this man than met the eye.

"Sam delights in frowning at me," he added. "How can I disappoint him?"

"I guess it didn't hurt that your father was there to witness it at the wedding."

The smile faded from his lips, as, deep down, she'd suspected it would.

"The old man can get his laughs somewhere else," he finally replied. "He's got plenty of people he can pay to amuse him."

She heard the bitterness in his voice and she supposed she couldn't blame him. From what Eve had told her, she knew Jake had been raised far away, never even knowing who his real father was. When she saw the closed-in look on his face, she almost wished she hadn't brought up the subject.

"Thanks for the ride," he said as he reached for the door handle. "And for the bail-out."

"Tell me one thing, Mr. Montez," she said before he could step out of the car into the cold air of early morning.

"Jake," he replied. "Call me Jake."

"Tell me why you were arrested, Mr. Montez," she asked, determined to keep a formal distance between herself and this disturbing man.

"I threw a punch at a guy."

"And for that you were hauled away to jail?" Leanne heard the skepticism in her voice, and knew he heard it too.

"Well, how was I supposed to know he was a cop?" Jake asked, disgust lacing his tone.

She nodded, understanding. "You assaulted a police officer."

He shook his head. "Never landed the punch. I didn't know his partner was there until he tackled me from behind."

"So, you were brawling with two officers at The Slaughter House. Dare I ask why you felt it necessary to throw a punch at him to begin with?"

He shrugged. "He looked to be harassing a lady. I was just trying to stand up for her."

"The redhead back at the station?"

"Umh-hmh."

"Oh, I can see why you'd think she was a lady in need of protection."

"How was I supposed to know she was a working girl being busted?"

Leanne raised an eyebrow in disbelief. "I guess the leather, chains, and screw-me shoes weren't obvious clues."

Jake reached out his hand and took her chin in his fingers, turning her head until she stared right at him. He eyed her intently, looking at her face, her mouth, her hair, then down her body. Leanne forced herself to remain calm and relaxed throughout the perusal, which required an effort. His hand was warm and strong, and a thrill of excitement raced through her at his touch. She didn't feel threatened—the touch was tender, not menacing—and she couldn't help but wonder if those strong fingers were branding her jaw, if she'd feel the brush of his skin against hers long after he'd stepped out of the car and out of her life.

She feared she would. Just as she'd continued to experience that kiss for days after it had ended.

"Outward appearances can be deceiving," he murmured. "If I were to judge you simply on outward appearances, I'd say you were a cool, collected professional woman who had never had a decent lover in her life."

A pause. A breath. A charged moment of electricity passed between them. She felt her heart pick up its tempo, beating quickly as her blood rushed through her veins and caused her pulse to pound. Because he was crude. Because he was daring.

Because he was right?

"That's none of your business."

"Hey, lucky for you, I don't judge by outward appearances. I see by the spark in those gray eyes, and in the way you lick those lips of yours when you think nobody's watching you, that you know all about passion." He smiled. "Especially after that kiss."

Leanne self-consciously tightened her mouth as he stared. He shook his head ruefully, frowning at her as she tried to suck her bottom lip tighter against her teeth. She couldn't manage to say a single word as he slid one thumb up from her chin to her mouth, allowing its callused tip to smooth her lips open. A shock of sensation shot from her mouth clear down her body, settling with a hot fire in the pit of her stomach.

The air in the car thickened and she suddenly couldn't manage to fill her lungs. She felt lightheaded, dizzy, more than a little confused. Not even aware she was doing it, she closed her eyes. Leanne felt as if the rational world she'd struggled to build for herself had just exploded into flames. All from the touch of his finger. God help her if he ever kissed her again.

"Thanks for everything," he whispered.

He sounded…closer. Not all the way on his side of the car. Her eyes flew open, and she realized he'd leaned over the seat. To her horror—and, okay, a little bit of mingled excitement—she realized what he was about to do.

She tried to brace herself for it, which was really like trying to brace herself against a tsunami. But to her shock, Jake didn't capture her mouth with his. Instead, he merely brushed his lips against her temple in a soft thank-you kiss, and murmured, "Bye Miz Leanne," in that slow, sexy drawl.

She couldn't say a word, could only stare as he winked at her, those green/gold eyes alight with mischief, before letting himself out of the car. She watched him leap nimbly over the fence, and then, finally, managed to release her long-held breath. Considering it took several moments for her to calm down enough to put the car into gear and drive away, she found herself very thankful he hadn't immediately gotten the gate open and appeared on what was undoubtedly a big, powerful motorcycle.

Because she greatly feared that, right now, she might be stupid enough to follow him just about anywhere he wanted to lead her.

Chapter 2

IT TOOK DAYS for Leanne to put Jake Montez out of her mind. She tried, but the wickedly enticing man kept creeping into her thoughts at the most inopportune times. Ever since Saturday morning, she'd found herself remembering his words, his touch, the knowing sparkle in his eyes. His lazy drawl so at odds with his dark, brooding looks. Not to mention that hard body made for sin. He was one unforgettable man.

After shaking herself out of the lethargic, sensual spell he'd cast Saturday in her car, she'd taken off like she was being pursued by a tyrannosaurus. She hadn't slowed down—or calmed down—for a good four blocks, and was lucky she hadn't gotten pulled over. Having tried so desperately to keep her eyes on the prize, and never again let a man have enough power to hurt her the way her last lover had, she couldn't help wishing Jake had gotten busted one day later so she'd never have had to see him again.

"Stop thinking about him," she reminded herself several times a day.

To make herself forget, she threw herself into her work, preparing for the upcoming trade show at the Pennsylvania Convention Center. It was a hugely important event, where not only homeowners, but also buyers, designers and wealthy shoppers from New York converged. Many careers had been made and broken in past years at that one show. This year's event was especially important, because it included an additional contest for Pennsylvania companies, who could compete for the chance to redecorate some rooms in the governor's mansion in Harrisburg. Her boss wanted to win one of the plum assignments and one of the cash prizes, and there was much to do.

Her company had paid a small fortune for a space big enough for a master bedroom suite, complete with bathroom, and Leanne had been given the task of suitably accessorizing it. She would rather have furnished it. But no way would Ned hand over that plum task. He was the boss, after all. The company bore his name—well, his mother's name—and he was in charge.

"Are you sure lemon yellow is the right shade for those accent pillows?" he asked, a note of skepticism in his voice as they went over the plans one more time in his office on Wednesday afternoon. "I just don't know if that sunny color will fit with the dark cherry four-poster."

Leanne sighed, wondering why a man who'd grown up with the incredibly creative Eleanor Longotti didn't understand how to blend shades and textures. Everything she'd ever seen him design had been safe, each color perfectly complemented, with never a hint of contrast. He dressed the same way. Conservative, dark suits, expertly cut to fit his frame. Safe. Respectable.

"Ned, we've been over this. We want different, new and exciting. Heavy dark furniture with a heavy dark duvet or comforter equals just that—heavy and dark. We've got to lighten the room, only with sunnier colors can the real elegance of that *beautiful* furniture you chose be seen."

She hated having to placate him, but the subtle flattery on his choice of furnishings was necessary. He gave her a quick smile. He did have a sweet smile, though he seldom flashed it these days. Everyone was feeling stressed about the show.

"I suppose," he told her, still looking doubtful. "If the lighting's bad in the convention center, we might want something like this."

Exactly what she'd been saying for weeks.

Once again, Leanne had a quick vision of how differently she'd have done the room. A bleached oak, delicate pieces and colors that would whisper at sunny days and warm pleasures. Yes many big city dwellers were tired of the slick and modern, and Ned's design reflected the backlash against the modernistic, chrome and glass look of the last century, with a return to dark, heavy antiques. But Leanne strongly felt the key to the future was light, bright, clean, and warm.

She had even come up with some drawings, had gone so far as to search through catalogs and contact furniture dealers who could come up with the pieces she had in mind. She'd found some perfect light oak furniture, and coordinating bathroom fixtures. But Ned wouldn't consider her suggestions. He'd glanced at her drawings dismissively, then assigned her the job of accessorizing. That, she had to concede, was more than some of the other staff might have expected. One of the other designers, Noelle, had been with the firm a little longer than Leanne, and thought her seniority entitled her to the project. The owner hadn't agreed; Eleanor Longotti generally liked Leanne's ideas better and assigned her to work with Ned. Noelle had been highly put out and had glared daggers at Leanne for days after the announcement was made.

At least now, thankfully, things seemed to have smoothed over. Noelle had found another job with a competitor and had resigned. Leanne wished the other woman well. Part of her was often tempted to put out feelers, too. Because in Longotti Lines, the only people who got ahead were named Longotti.

Of course, one day she might be asked to be one of them.

She wasn't sure how she felt about that. She didn't love Ned, and knew he didn't love her either. But he'd said more than once that they made a great team and he could see the two of them running the business once his mother was no longer involved. He'd mentioned marriage, discussing it like a potential business merger. Considering they'd never slept together, that sounded about right.

Could she do it? Could she trade love for friendship, give up passion for a great working partnership? She honestly didn't know, and that really surprised her. Considering all she'd ever wanted growing up was a real home, with security, filled with people who *stayed*, she should have leapt at the chance. But her heart didn't sing at the prospect. It didn't even flutter. In fact, her blood pressure barely hiccupped whenever Ned Longotti took her in his arms.

Can you handle a lifetime of that? She just couldn't say.

"Are we still meeting at Josephine's tonight?" Ned asked.

"Sure." Knowing Ned preferred dining late—though she hated it on work nights—she asked, "Eight?"

He nodded. "Don't forget to change into a dress."

She held back a sigh, wondering what she'd have done if he'd suggested they spend their Wednesday evening at a different restaurant or hadn't reminded her to change out of her tweed pants and cute bolero jacket. Probably faint. Ned was nothing if not predictable.

Safe. That was the word. Safe, respectable, admired, everything she'd wanted so much to be during her childhood. Everything she'd always told herself she'd have in a man one day. Nothing like the other men Leanne had dated in her adult life. Nothing like the men her mother had chosen before she finally settled down with Leanne's step-father.

The thought brought Jake Montez strongly to mind. Her mother would have adored him. Before her marriage, she'd always fallen for tough guys, the ones who compensated for their lack of intelligence or ambition behind a surly attitude and some well-toned pecs.

Leanne felt a quick flash of remorse. She wasn't being fair. She didn't even know the man. He could be a Mensa candidate for all he knew, and she'd definitely noticed the quick wit that hinted at a quick mind.

Still, that attitude, the cockiness, and the huge chip on his shoulder all painted a picture. She just hadn't seen enough to know whether that picture was a reflection of the real Jake, or merely a role he liked to portray to the world. He'd admitted he intentionally showed people what they expected to see. What, she wondered, would he show a woman who expected to see the real man beneath the façade?

"Must run," Ned said as he straightened and smoothed his jacket. He leaned down and brushed a kiss against her temple. "Don't forget about the dress."

Right. She had to change into a dress, because he didn't like taking her out if she was wearing slacks. Freud would probably have something to say about that—maybe Ned was trying to establish who would wear the pants in their marriage, should it ever come about. Meaning, because of his short-man syndrome, she got to freeze her calves off.

"I'm meeting mother at her club in an hour," he added as he breezed by. "See you later."

"Right," she mumbled, wondering if Eleanor even knew that Leanne and Ned were dating. Had, in fact, been seeing each other outside of work for weeks. Somehow, she doubted it.

It was probably just as well, she realized. She and Ned were not, by any means, involved in a passionate love affair. Their evenings together were based more on mutual interests rather than real attraction. Leanne had trouble even imagining becoming Ned's lover. Which might make it awfully hard to become his wife.

"No, it wouldn't," she mumbled, trying to convince herself. "A marriage based on friendship, common interests, and a shared career sounds just fine." Much better than a roller coaster ride of emotion with a charming devil who would break her heart in the end.

For some reason, instead of seeing the face of Sloan, her ex, the guy who'd dumped her for a vapid party-girl, Leanne had a sudden visual image of Jake Montez. Sexy, wicked Jake who would never stand for a marriage of convenience. A guy like him wouldn't even dream of dating a woman for a month and never going beyond requisite kisses goodnight. He was probably used to having any woman he wanted out of her clothes within a day.

Remembering the brush of his hand on her face, the way she'd melted inside when he'd stared at her mouth, as if imagining her using it on various parts of his body, and that kiss—oh, God, that kiss—she figured a day was overestimating. The man could probably get a woman flat on her back in an hour.

"But not you," she told herself. *Never gonna happen.*

Getting back to work, she forced Jake's image out of her mind, determined not to let him back in. The rest of the afternoon flew by as she worked on a few projects.

Early that evening, as the office emptied out and silence surrounded her, Leanne finally put her work down. She glanced out the window, noting how quickly darkness had descended. Grabbing her purse, coat, and briefcase, she locked her office door and made her way through the center hallway of the building. No one else was around, and she imagined the staff had taken the opportunity to cut out at a regular time since Ned was gone for the day.

Having a little time before dinner, she called Eve to say she was going to stop by to drop off her house key and take a peek at the honeymoon pictures. She exited the building, an old 1920's three-story house that Eleanor Longotti had bought and re-built a few years before. Offices for Longotti Lines occupied the two bottom floors, and the top was used for storage. The entire building, lovingly restored and tastefully decorated, was an advertisement for the business.

Leanne was walking around to the gravel parking lot on the side of the house, her keys in her hand, when she felt a tug on her arm. Before she could turn around, something hit her back, between her shoulder blades, sending her flying forward. She instinctively put her hands out to stop her fall, dropping her keys and bags as she stumbled. She landed on her knees, right beside her car. For a moment, she was too stunned to think, much less move. She knelt, mentally doing a quick check to see if she was injured as she wondered what had hit her.

Astonishment was quickly replaced by anxiety, if not downright fear. Someone had shoved her to the ground in a darkened parking lot. No other cars were parked nearby. *Don't panic,* she thought as her gut tightened. Digging into the surface gravel with her fingers, she ignored a sharp pain as she tore off a nail. She collected fistfuls of gravel, planning to defend herself vigorously. If she could roll over and fling the tiny rocks into the assailant's eyes, she might be able to make a break for her car.

Preparing herself, she glanced up, catching a glimpse of a person dressed all in dark clothing. She bit back a tiny screech when she saw the figure had no face, but quickly realized it was because he was wearing a ski mask. Which would make hitting his eyes a little more difficult. But damned if she'd give up without a fight.

Before Leanne had a chance to launch her meager stockpile of weapons, however, the attacker scooped up her purse. He also grabbed her satchel that contained a lot of documents but, thankfully, not her laptop, and took off at a hard run down the street.

Her racing heart continued to cartwheel in her chest, but after a few seconds, when she realized she was no longer in physical danger, she breathed a deep sigh of relief.

"Thank God," she whispered, her breath creating puffs in the frigid air. "Just a mugger."

The fact that she was relieved probably said a little too much about city life. Considering she'd grown up in areas that would make a grown man think twice about walking alone, though, Leanne was used to danger. She'd been jumped a handful of times walking to and from school as a kid. This time, she wouldn't shrug it off and figure it was part of life in the projects. Because, if criminals were targeting the area, and her unsuspecting co-workers might be hit next, she had to do something about it. Which was why, instead of using the keys she still held to get into her car and drive to Eve's for a much-needed glass of wine, she instead went back inside and called 911.

She locked up tight, turning on every light. She also called Eve to let her know what had happened. Ned, she'd been unable to reach, but she left him a message.

Help came quickly, and a half-hour later, she was nodding wearily at the young police officer who'd taken her statement. He'd done a thorough job of scouting the parking lot and the alley. Now they sat on a sofa in the lobby.

"It was lucky you had your keys in your hand, and not in your purse, Miss Weston. Otherwise it wouldn't be just your banking and credit card information you'd have to change—you'd be having to have your car, office and home locks replaced."

She hadn't even thought about that. "You're right. And I'm also lucky I didn't have my laptop or any important files with me."

That would have been a catastrophe. One of her design notebooks, a thick, ancient one currently locked in her desk, contained dozens if not hundreds of creative sketches and ideas, dating back to her teenage years. Calling it her dream-book, she'd have been devastated to lose it—even more so than her money and credit cards.

She usually carried it with her, but had known she wouldn't have time to work tonight, with the visit to Eve, followed by dinner, so she'd left it here. *Thank the lord.*

Before he could reply, a loud knocking sounded on the front door of the building. The officer immediately stood, coming to attention and making Leanne feel more confident in his abilities, despite his youth. "You expecting anyone?"

Leanne shook her head and followed him to the door. Peeking out the window, she saw Eve's worried face staring back at her. "It's my friend. I called her to tell her what happened."

The officer nodded as Leanne opened the door.

"Lee are you all right?" Eve immediately asked as she entered the building. She grabbed Leanne's shoulders, gave her a quick once-over and then pulled her in for a tight hug.

As Leanne bit back a smile at Eve's exuberant greeting, she glanced up to see that her friend had not arrived alone. "You," she said softly.

Jake Montez nodded. "Everything okay here?"

Leanne took a step back, nodding warily as she wondered why Jake, of all people, would show up at her office. She had figured she'd never lay eyes on the guy again.

He looked only slightly more respectable than he had the last time they'd met. He still wore faded jeans, and the black leather jacket, but his jaw was shaven smooth and his hair pulled back in a short ponytail. The style emphasized the strong bones of his face, making him look very virile, very male. He certainly wouldn't be mistaken for a businessman, but at least he didn't look so much like a recently-bailed-out-of-jail ex-con.

"Jake was at my place waiting for Sam when you called," Eve explained. "He drove me, which was probably just as well because I was shaking like a leaf. How could you just say 'I was just mugged in the parking lot and the police are on their way' and then hang up?"

"I'm sorry. I should have given you more details. I was nervous and didn't want to tie up the phone," Leanne said, offering her friend a smile of apology.

Eve frowned, giving Leanne one of those disapproving school teacher looks Jake had mentioned at their previous meeting. That was okay, since Eve actually was a school-teacher.

Glancing toward him, she saw a sparkle of laughter in his eyes and knew he was remembering the exact same thing. The moment of shared memory felt strange to Leanne, because, after all, she barely knew this man. Still, something deep inside her warmed at the unexpected connection.

"Well, now your friends are here. Perhaps they'll follow you home, Miss Weston, just to make sure you're okay," the young police officer said.

Leanne had nearly forgotten his presence and turned to thank him. The cop seemed distracted, and Leanne watched as he cast surreptitious glances toward Eve. She couldn't say she was surprised. Eve Barrett—now Kenneman—was a traffic stopper. A nearly six foot tall former model with a long cascade of golden blond curls, she always attracted attention.

"You're that model who was in *Men's Life*, aren't you?" the police officer finally worked up the nerve to say. "I remember seeing your picture."

Eve responded kindly to the young man, obviously well-used to being recognized by the public once again. She didn't appear to mind, even though she'd sworn to all of them that she was perfectly happy working as a teacher and would never consider returning to modeling full time.

Looking toward Jake, Leanne wondered whether even he, with his cocky assurance, got a little tongue tied around his beautiful sister-in-law. He wouldn't be the first man Leanne had known to become a blithering idiot around the statuesque blonde. She'd seen men make complete fools of themselves over Eve since the day they'd met, back in college nearly ten years ago. She glanced over at Jake, almost holding her breath to see how he was reacting, and found him staring not at Eve, but at herself.

"Why don't you tell me what happened?" he asked softly as he took her arm and led her toward the couch. His tone told her he was not asking as much as ordering, and Leanne followed him, not protesting as he pulled her down to sit beside him. He didn't sit on one end, leaving an appropriate width of cushion between them. Invading her personal space, he sat so close to her that his long, lean, jean-clad thigh was pressed into hers.

Trying to distract herself from the feel of his leg, and the minted scent of his breath as he spoke, Leanne quickly found herself telling him exactly what had gone on in the parking lot.

"So, is it normal for you to come outside by yourself after the office is empty?"

"Well," she replied, "generally I leave the office around six or seven, but there are often still people inside."

He nodded, remaining silent, then slowly turned his head to look around the lobby. "Not tonight, though?"

"No. I was the last one here."

Leanne clenched her hands in her lap, immediately wincing with pain as she was reminded of how hard she'd hit the ground.

Jake obviously noticed. His eyes narrowed in concern. "Are you hurt?"

"Just some scrapes and broken nails."

"Did you hit him?" he asked.

"No. I didn't get the chance," she replied coolly.

Before she could protest, Jake took her hands in his, gently coaxing her fists open. He stared down at her palms, frowning at the small cuts which were crusted with dried blood. She must have scraped herself up a little worse than she'd thought when she landed on the ground.

Softly, so softly, he ran the tip of his index finger across the fleshy part of her hand, just below her thumb. The unmistakable gentleness of his touch was completely unexpected and seemed out of character for the man.

"I'm sorry that happened to you," he said, his voice low. He was looking down at her hand, and she couldn't read his expression, but his tone and the clenching of his body next to hers said he was angry on her behalf.

He didn't immediately drop her hand, merely continuing to stroke it, softly, tenderly. It should have been comforting, sweet. But no. The heat of it seared her. Just that simple brush of skin on skin was enough to make her heart tumble wildly in her chest. She found it hard to think, or even to breathe normally. Finally, confusion and tension made her pull her hand away.

He stared at her, concern still visible in those vivid green eyes. "You should go wash up. Maybe splash some cold water on your face. You're flushed."

She wondered if she'd heard a tone of mockery in his voice, if he'd realized his closeness was making her heat up. "I'm fine, really."

"Okay. By the way, I've been meaning to tell you something," he said, his gaze shifting and a smile tugging at the corners of his mouth.

"What?"

"I like your hair."

She sucked in a surprised breath at the sudden change in tone, wondering where *that* had come from. "Really?"

"Uh-huh. Why'd you do it?"

She shrugged. "New Year, new look. I was tired of it and figured, why not?"

"Good call," he said, his smile widening. "I like people who aren't afraid to shake things up—including themselves."

"Probably because you're one of them."

He chuckled and nodded in concession of that fact. "I'm the king of shaking things up. Just ask my brother."

Before she had a chance to respond, he stood and walked over to engage the police officer in conversation. Leanne watched, feeling warm, confused, and not a little bit puzzled. He seemed different. He still had that swagger, and obviously his appearance screamed danger to any woman foolish enough to be sucked in by his knowing stares and raw masculinity. But tonight she saw something else.

He'd been tender, considerate. His worried stare, and that visible tension in his thickly muscled body, had told her he was concerned about her, a woman he barely knew. And his comments about her appearance had been easy and only a little flirtatious, as if he just wanted to distract her from thinking about everything that had gone on tonight.

Funny, how his comment about her hair made her feel—warm and a little girly. Unlike when Ned had noticed it. Jake had admired not only how she looked but why she'd done it. Ned had frowned, said he liked her better blond, and then conceded the darker hair might make people take her more seriously on the job.

That's not fair. You can't compare two men who are so utterly different.

True. But she was still left realizing there was more to Jake Montez than she'd ever imagined. And wondering whether she would have been better off never knowing that. Because, she greatly feared, it wouldn't be easy to put him back out of her mind now that the mystery of the man had become even more intriguing.

JAKE LISTENED CLOSELY as the young cop, probably not long out of the academy, told him the few details of Leanne's encounter with the mugger. Jake knew the routine. The cops would come out, ask a few questions, make the victim feel more secure. Then they'd add this one to the long case of unsolvable muggings that occurred in every big city.

Knowing it was probably pointless, Jake reached into the inside pocket of his jacket and pulled out a business card. "Keep me posted if you get anything on this, okay?"

The cop took the card, glanced at it, then looked back at Jake. A slow smile spread across the younger man's face. "You on this case?"

Jake shrugged. "Just helping a friend of the family."

He saw Leanne's eyes widen in surprise, and glanced over to see a similar expression on Eve's face. Then he realized what he'd said. Friend. Family. Two words he seldom used, when he wasn't speaking of his mother or his younger half-sister Terry. He'd certainly not expected to use them when referring to Sam or his wife. Now that he'd said it, though, he didn't mind it so much. But he'd be willing to bet Sam would choke on his beer when Eve told him about it later.

"You have a real reputation around town, Mr. Montez. Doesn't always make everybody at the precinct happy, though."

Jake gave a short laugh. "Not surprising." He cast an assessing look on the confident young officer. "If you ever get tired of the political b.s. in the ranks of Philadelphia's finest, give me a call."

After the officer left, Jake turned his attention toward Leanne. As expected, she looked flustered, not quite all put together as she'd been the last time he saw her. Still, she wasn't hysterical, or weepy, like some people might be after being robbed. She'd kept her head, kept her cool. He liked that.

Sitting together on the sofa, the two women were an interesting contrast. Eve was blindingly beautiful, the bombshell type who would draw the eye of any man within sight range. But her friend Leanne had a different kind of appeal. She was smaller, rounder, more soft and vulnerable. Her streaked hair was pulled back, accenting her pale, heart-shaped face. A genuine smile creased her lips at something Eve said, and Jake watched her gray eyes widen with pleasure.

She seemed like a different woman. At the wedding, she'd been fiery and protective, and oh-so-sexy. The other day at the jail house she'd been all business, all self-righteous, indignant professional female. At least on the outside. He'd seen glimpses of a dry humor, evidence of hidden warmth, but it was only here with her best friend that she truly seemed at ease.

For some reason, he suddenly wanted to see her smile like that at him. *Yeah, that'll happen!* he told himself as he remembered just how crude and obnoxious he'd acted toward her the last two times they'd interacted. He couldn't regret the kiss—never that—but did wish he'd been a little better behaved on Saturday when she bailed him out. After the night he'd had, it had just been easier to maintain his role as cocky, tough guy than to show his genuine appreciation for what she'd done for him.

In the years since he'd come to Philadelphia from Houston, he'd been himself only around a few friends. With his long-lost biological father he'd been combative. With his half-brother Sam he'd usually been snarky and rude. It had taken him a while to realize what an idiot he'd been, at least as far as Sam was concerned. Sam was as innocent of the machinations of their parents as Jake. But that hadn't stopped the intensity of Jake's feelings the first time he'd seen his brother.

Jake had never even known his father's name until almost six years ago, when his stepfather died. His mother's husband hadn't given a damn about Jake, he'd made that pretty obvious all his life, but he hadn't wanted Jake's mother telling Jake the truth about who his father was. He'd been shocked to learn he was the illegitimate son of one of the richest men in Pennsylvania. A man who'd bankrolled Jake's stepfather to take care of his mistress and young son.

After his mother admitted that fact, Jake had taken leave from the force and traveled to Pennsylvania to meet his father, the famous Jacob Kenneman, for whom he was named. He'd caught up with him at a party. Not knowing what he was walking into, he'd followed the family butler's directions to a local country club, and showed up, just in time to see a huge birthday cake wheeled out in honor of Sam Kenneman, the golden boy, Jacob Kenneman's prodigal son.

It was a Saturday night, and the crowd was celebrating Sam's twenty-sixth birthday, two days early, apparently. By some strange twist of fate, that same night marked Jake's twenty-sixth birthday, too. He was exactly two days older than this cocky, self-assured young man who charmed everyone in the room with his easy confidence.

Jake had stood in the doorway, watching as the father who'd paid someone to take *him* off his hands offered a pride-filled toast to his other, legitimate son.

The bitterness Jake felt at that moment was something he'd never experienced before and hoped never to again.

Looking back, he wished he'd acted differently. He'd caused a lot of heartache that night, particularly to Jacob Kenneman's wife, Sam's mother, who'd been the innocent victim in the entire sordid affair. The consequences of the bombshell he'd dropped in the middle of the infamous birthday party had been far-reaching and permanent. Sam had left his father's company and gone on to become a successful writer. Sam's mother had moved out of the family mansion and they'd since divorced. And all of it had been on Jake's shoulders. His father had committed the original crime; Jake had been an accessory after the fact.

"What did the officer mean when he asked if you were on the

case, Mr. Montez?" Leanne asked, interrupting his musings.

"Oh, Jake's a private investigator," Eve explained. "Didn't I tell you? I'm sure you saw the articles about his firm in the paper last month when he broke that gallery theft case right under the nose of the police."

Jake frowned. He hadn't liked the intense media coverage after that particular case, because it had made the police look like real idiots. They hadn't been happy about it, not at all.

"I didn't realize," Leanne said, studying him in amazement. "I mean, I never imagined you..."

"What? You never imagined I was anything but a motorcycle-riding hood?"

"Well...I mean, no, of course not," she stammered.

Jake chuckled. He was used to the reaction. Leanne wasn't the first person who'd taken stock of him based purely on appearance and attitude. Then again, remembering how he'd behaved toward her at their previous meetings, he couldn't blame her in the least for believing the worst of him. He hadn't given her any reason to believe otherwise.

"Do you think there's any chance they'll find the person who did this?" Eve asked.

"It's doubtful," he admitted. He saw a quick frown cross Leanne's face. "But I don't think you have to worry too much. This guy got what he wanted, your cash. Your other stuff will probably turn up in a dumpster near here. Just be thankful he didn't get your keys."

"That's what the officer said," she admitted. He watched as she cast a quick glance out the window to the dark street beyond. He narrowed his eyes as he followed her stare, wishing he could get his hands on the guy who'd robbed her, who'd had the audacity to shove her to the ground and steal from her. "It might take a day or two for me to go from feeling furious to feeling lucky."

"I don't blame you. God, I hate thugs," he muttered.

He'd grown up with one, and detested strong men who used their physical powers to threaten those around them.

His stepfather had been free with his belt when Jake was growing up, though only to his stepson, not to his wife or Jake's baby sister. Of course, his vicious tongue had been hurtful enough to Jake's mother. Jake himself had reached the point where he could let the man's spite roll right off his back.

Then, in the Army, he'd met more men like his stepfather. Men who couldn't out-think, so they'd out-punch. As a young M.P. in Afghanistan, he'd encountered more than a few beefy, brainless jackasses who'd needed a lesson in civility. He'd been happy to oblige. And his three years on the force in Houston after he'd left the service had continued the lesson.

Jake knew bullies came in all shapes in sizes. There were those who bullied physically, and those who used words to do their damage. Some, like Jacob Kenneman, his biological father, just used their money to do their pushing around.

He detested them all equally. And he'd do whatever he could to never become like them. Which meant he did not need to get any further involved with a woman who lived in that kind of world...a woman like Leanne Weston.

LEANNE WATCHED JAKE stare out the window and wondered what had put that dark frown on his face. Could it be he was still angry over what had happened to her? Maybe he had a white knight streak that would have made him feel the same way about any woman. But she wasn't completely sure about that. There had been a certain tension, an intimacy between them from the moment they'd kissed, as much as she'd been trying to deny it to herself.

"I want to thank you both for coming down here," she said. "But

I am fine, and I think we ought to go now."

"Do you mind if I take a walk around the office, just to be on the safe side?" Jake asked as he walked across the lobby to join the two women.

"Do you think that's necessary?" She hadn't considered that anybody else might be in the building. The thought made her squirm uncomfortably.

"Don't think it could hurt," he said. "Although, I don't suppose any mugger's going to be too worried about stealing whatever curtains you've got stashed in here." His words were light and teasing, with no evidence of mockery in his tone. "Can you come along and show me where your office is? I want to see how visible it is from the outside."

"All right," Leanne said. When he extended his hand to help her up, she took it, noting again its callused strength.

Her breath came faster. Jake seemed to notice. His stare rested on her parted lips, and he didn't let go of her hand.

Oddly nervous, Leanne said, "Eve, you're welcome to come along." She hoped her friend would agree. She suddenly didn't want to wander around the deserted offices with Jake Montez. Though he was being cordial, solicitous, in fact, she still didn't trust the man. *Get real,* she told herself. *You don't trust yourself around him!*

Leanne didn't stop to analyze that thought. Sure, her stomach was rolling around, and her heart was pounding hard enough to explode out of her chest, but that had to just be because of the scare she'd had earlier. No way could it have anything to do with the warm strength of this man's fingers entwined in hers. Impossible that it should be because of the concern in his eyes and the tender, knowing smile on his sensuous mouth.

Jake held her stare for a moment, then glanced toward his sister-in-law. "Eve, maybe you should call home and let Sam know where we are. I'd just *hate* for him to worry himself sick wondering where I've dragged you off to."

Jake's wry grin and the twinkle in his eye made a lie of his words. He'd obviously like nothing more than to get his brother riled up, leaving Sam wondering where Jake had disappeared to with his wife. Eve gave him a sour look, grabbing her cell phone.

Leanne shrugged helplessly as Jake pulled her along behind him down the hall toward the back offices. Never had the old house seemed so large, nor so deserted, as it did right then. All Leanne could hear was the tapping of Jake's heavy boots on the polished hardwood floor, and her own heart sending blood rushing through her veins. As they rounded the corner, out of sight of the lobby—and Eve—the silence swallowed them up and they could have been the only two people in the world.

"In there," Leanne said breathily as they reached the door to her private office.

He nodded. "You're not scared are you?" Jake asked as he un-locked the door, pushed it open and entered her office, pulling her along behind him.

"Why should I be scared of you?" she asked defensively, before thinking better of it.

He paused, his hand in mid-air as he reached for the light switch on the wall. The room was lit only by the overhead fixture in the hallway, but even in the semi-darkness Leanne could see the surprise on his face.

"Of me? Why would you have any reason to be scared of *me*?"

Leanne grimaced, realizing he'd been merely asking if she was scared because of the earlier mugger. How foolish she'd been to voice her thoughts out loud.

Of course she wasn't scared of him. She was *aware* of him. That was all. Aware of his smile, his sensuous lips. Aware of his body; that hard form would put indecent thoughts into the mind of even the most happily married woman. But how could she possibly explain that? She couldn't very well look up into his confident green eyes and tell him that her hand had never felt so warm, and her pulse had never pounded so swiftly in the presence of another man. Couldn't possibly admit that the thought of being alone with him, in the dark, had sent a purely feminine rush of heat through her.

"I meant, I'm not scared at all. I'm fine. The guy's long gone, I'm sure," she said, knowing she was babbling but unable to stop.

"Well, that's a relief," Jake said softly in the darkness. He leaned closer to her, so close his breath fell on her hair as he spoke. "A *big* relief, Miz Leanne."

Her mind told her to take a step back. He was too close, every six-foot tall, masculine bit of him. Before she could do it, he stepped closer so that his chest brushed hers. Her body reacted, her nipples hardening against her bra.

She froze. How could she be frozen when her body was flooded with heat, when a current of feeling was darting from her brain to her stomach to her thighs and elsewhere? She swayed slightly, but his hand was there, sliding against her blouse to her hip, steadying her.

"Because I'd hate to think you were afraid to be alone with me. In the dark." His words were a whisper, and he bent closer to utter them. "All kinds of crazy things can happen to two people alone in the dark."

Several of those crazy things filled her imagination as Leanne was hit with a rush of raw lust, so powerful and unexpected, her legs shook. She couldn't tear her attention away from his face as he stared down at her, as if trying to read her mind. He slowly drew in a deep breath, and again she caught the slight smell of mint and noticed the sensual curve of his mouth. She had a sharp memory of what it had been like to kiss him, how she'd curled her tongue over that lower lip and tasted him completely and thoroughly.

How badly she wanted to again.

"It's a good thing it's just me you're with," he continued. "And not some dangerous guy with lustful thoughts on his mind. Who knows what could happen in the dark."

His words said one thing, his closeness—and his tone—said another. Leanne was torn between reaching up to flip on the light...or wrapping her arms around him to pull him even closer.

In the end, he took the decision out of her hands.

Chapter 3

J AKE COULD HAVE backed off, and considering Leanne's close call this evening, that's probably what he should have done.

But he didn't. Instead, he lifted a hand to her jaw, tilted her head up, and looked into her startled eyes. He gave her one second to pull away, and the fact that she didn't told him everything he needed to know. So he bent down and covered her mouth with his.

She gasped, her lips parting on the tiny, shocked sound, and he took advantage, slipping his tongue against hers. Another gasp. But she didn't pull away. Oh, no, instead that soft form melted against him.

Jake didn't need any more urging. He dropped a hand to the small of her back and pulled her even closer, until their bodies were practically fused. She was so curvy, so sexy, he groaned a little at the feel of those feminine thighs pressing against his. His cock reacted predictably, and when she noticed, she didn't gasp, she actually arched even closer.

Leanne might be dressed in a buttoned-up office outfit, but he caught the scent of fruity shampoo and a deeper, earthier fragrance that reminded him she was every bit a woman underneath. She tasted so good, just as he remembered, her delicious tongue smooth and a little tentative as it thrust back against his own. He was losing focus, able to think of nothing else—not time, place, or circumstance—the longer the kiss went on.

She, however, appeared to regain her senses. Because, to his disappointment, she suddenly pushed at his chest and jerked her head away, ending their kiss. Without a word, she spun around and slapped her hand against the wall switch, flooding the office with light.

Jake was unable to contain a sigh of disappointment. "Guess it's not dark anymore," he said.

She shook her head hard. "No. It's not." She nervously touched her throat, then ran a smoothing hand down her jacket before tucking in her blouse.

He watched her, his stare following her hand on its quick trip over the silky fabric, and her curvy body. He wondered if she noticed that her hand lingered too long here, skittered too quickly there. He would have done a much more thorough job had it been his hand making that smooth journey over those curves. Much more thorough.

"Curse that Thomas Edison," he said under his breath. He saw by the beating of the pulse in her temple, and the way her chest heaved, in and out that she'd been just as affected as he. Damn, the two of them set sparks off each other quicker than he'd ever imagined possible.

She wasn't his type, he mentally insisted. He liked flashy women, with tall, lean bodies and matching attitudes. Not curvy bundles of sophisticated female like this one. Not women who could freeze a man with a stare from those cool gray eyes. Though, he had to concede, he'd long fantasized about a woman with a mouth like hers. And those shapely hips…and that perfect, smooth face.

Quickly brushing aside the sudden rush of heat that had sparked between him and the cool Miss Weston, Jake made a survey of her office. It was neat, all put together, just like its occupant. A requisite plant stood in a corner next to a work table on which piles of drawings were neatly stacked. The antique, heavy wooden desk was immaculate. A valance over the mini-blinds in the window was coordinated to match her desk blotter. Even the trash can was some glassy looking thing with delicately painted roses swirling around the outside. The entire office screamed showroom.

He supposed it suited her. The part of her that frowned and kept her back rigid and her tone cool. But it didn't fit the other part. Not at all. She had a sharp wit, a quick comeback for many of his remarks. Her eyes sparkled with intelligence and humor, when she wasn't trying to be all cold and disapproving.

Jake really wanted to pick up a thick black marker and draw graffiti all over her calendar.

"I don't think anyone could have been watching me in here," Leanne insisted, interrupting his thoughts. "I closed the blinds when it started getting dark."

He followed her glance and noted the covered windows and realized she was right. No one could have stood outside watching her. That was a relief, making the attack seem much more random. "All right, Miz Leanne. I think you were just unlucky tonight."

Leanne nodded, obviously relieved, and she quickly stepped out of her office into the corridor. Jake followed, flipping off the light switch and shutting the door to her office behind him. He cast a quick look down the hall, saw nothing but artsy statues, photos of some old looking furniture, and lots of flowery paintings. "So this is where you do it, huh?"

"Do what?" she asked with a guilty start.

He watched her clench her hands in front of her. For such a put-together lady, she certainly did embarrass easily. It was almost too easy to get a rise out of her, Jake decided.

"I meant this is where you pick out curtains. Right?"

"Among other things," she murmured.

"Must be a lot of people in Philadelphia who need some pretty expensive curtains," Jake commented, taking note of the décor in the building as they walked back toward the lobby.

"We do very well," Leanne explained. "Eleanor Longotti was one of the most sought after designers in the north-east, until she retired. And Ned is following right in her footsteps."

"Ned?"

"Longotti. My…boss."

He heard the hesitation and wondered at it. What had she been about to say? Before he could ask her, he looked up and saw Eve approaching.

"Well, Jake, you have managed to get Sam completely riled up once again. He's insisting that we wait here until he arrives, with your bike. I told him not to, but he cut me off!"

"My bike?" He tensed. "Tell me your husband is not riding my custom Harley over here!"

"I know, I know," Eve said, dismay evident in her tone, "He might get hurt. He hasn't ridden a motorcycle in years."

"Hurt, hell! He might dent my fenders!"

Leanne gave him a sharp elbow in the ribs, shocked that he could be so insensitive when Eve was obviously concerned about her husband. His chuckle drew her attention, and she saw he'd been intentionally baiting his sister-in-law. Eve obviously saw it, too, because she glared at him, turned her back, and walked away from them.

"You do that on purpose," Leanne snapped.

"Absolutely," he replied with a smug smile. "Shall we go wait for my brother?"

THE HALF HOUR in the lobby of the office building was one of the longest Leanne had ever experienced. Jake remained at the receptionist's station, looking large and incongruous at the delicate Queen Anne style desk. Leanne sat with Eve on a sofa, listening to Eve's stories about her honeymoon. But she couldn't hear a word her friend said. Jake, curse his hide, knew it quite well. Every once in a while he'd catch her staring at him and give her a knowing smile, telling her without words that he knew she was bothered by his presence.

She didn't know why that was true. After her brush with danger in the parking lot, she should have been relieved that an extremely competent professional was with them. But Jake wasn't exactly the type to put her at ease. If anything, she felt even more disturbed than she had before he'd shown up.

"Didn't you say you had somewhere to go tonight?" Eve asked, forcing Leanne to tear her attention off the man flipping pages in a fabric catalog as if he was truly fascinated by the difference between chintz and Indian cotton.

"I was supposed to meet someone for dinner." Eve knew who. For some reason, Leanne didn't want to get more specific with Jake so close by. "I left him a message and told him I couldn't make it." She saw Jake stiffen slightly. He continued staring at the catalog, but Leanne knew full well he was listening to them.

"So why isn't he here?" Eve asked.

Jake nodded, as if silently asking the same question.

"I didn't tell him I was mugged," she quickly said. "Just that I couldn't join him tonight."

She didn't elaborate, not wanting to explain why she hadn't told Ned about the attack. To herself, she could admit that she hadn't wanted to deal with his reaction. Knowing Ned, he would display more concern about the building—and criminals lurking around, potentially scouting it for a future robbery—than he did about her. She couldn't say for sure that's how he would have reacted, but it was a strong possibility. And she just wasn't up to that kind of scene, or the hurt that would have come with it. No, they weren't serious, but any woman would feel a little dismayed at finding out just how little she actually meant to the guy she was going out with.

Maybe she was being unfair. Maybe he'd be completely solicitous, concerned, and tender. But maybe he wouldn't. And she just wasn't in the mood to find out.

"When is the Tuesday Margarita group going to meet this guy, anyway?" Eve asked.

"No men allowed, remember?"

"Well, no men on Tuesdays. But there's nothing that says we can't all check him out some other night!"

Leanne sighed. It had never occurred to her to introduce Ned to Eve and their two other best friends. The four of them met at least one Tuesday night a month at their favorite Mexican restaurant. Leanne looked forward to those Tuesday nights the way some people might look forward to holidays.

With Eve, Diana and Ruthie, Leanne could be completely at ease, knowing she didn't have to perform, didn't have to maintain the role she'd been playing in her professional life. With the three friends who knew her better than anyone else in the world, she could laugh too loud, gripe about her boss, eat so much she had to unbutton her skirt, and be completely unladylike if she felt like it. Everyone, Leanne decided, needed at least one friend with whom they could be completely unladylike. She was lucky she had three.

"We'll see," she finally murmured.

Before Eve could comment, they heard a screech of tires spewing up gravel, and the rumble of a powerful engine.

Jake frowned. "If he so much as dinged the paint, I'll…."

He didn't continue as Eve stood and hurried to the front door. She yanked it open and shouted, as loud as a fishwife, "Sam Kenneman, you get off that motorcycle right now!"

Leanne heard Jake's chuckle, and bit the inside of her cheek to prevent herself from laughing as well. The two of them stood and followed Eve outside. As they watched, Eve marched down from the porch, her arms waving wildly as she ordered her husband off the bike before he broke his crazy neck. Her husband didn't seem to care. As Eve reached his side, Sam grabbed her around the waist and pulled her to sit in front of him on the oversized, padded leather seat of the Harley. He cut off her tirade by catching her mouth in a kiss that had so much heat Leanne felt it from where she stood on the porch.

Leanne sensed Jake standing right behind her, also watching as Eve completely gave up her anger and slid her arms around her husband's neck to pull him even closer. Jake's warm breaths fell on the side of her face, and Leanne shivered. She wrapped her arms around her waist, conscious of the cold, night air, and the warmth of the large, solid man standing right behind her.

Daring a glance up at him out of the corner of her eye, she saw a small smile playing about his mouth. When he caught her look, he said, "So much for *101 Ways to Avoid Commitment*."

Leanne chuckled, knowing immediately what he was talking about. She still couldn't quite believe that Sam and Eve were married—were together at all—especially because of the way they'd met.

Leanne, Ruthie and Diana had challenged Eve to get herself introduced to Sam, the famous author of an obnoxious men's book, just to get him to fall for her so she could dump and humiliate him. That anti-commitment book Jake had mentioned had been the hottest selling paperback in the country for a while. Leanne knew one of Eve's reasons for going along with the scheme had been because of the way Leanne's boyfriend had dumped her, touting Sam's book.

Now here it was, eighteen months later, and Sam and Eve were blissfully in love, newlyweds. The last time Leanne had seen Ruthie and Diana, at the wedding, Ruthie had been in tears, claiming Sam and Eve's relationship was the perfect example of the power of true love. Diana had said they were so lovey-dovey it was enough to make a person barf.

Leanne had just been pleased her best friend, who'd been through a lot in her younger years, had finally found some happiness. She'd found it with a man who wanted the same things she did out of life— love, laughter, and family. Not to mention, from what Eve said, amazing sex.

Not that Leanne could even remember what *that* was like.

Possibilities flooded her mind, and she stiffened, very aware that Jake stood directly behind her. They weren't touching, but were separated by only a thin layer of cold night air that did nothing to cool off her heated imagination. Because when it came to amazing sex, she had the feeling the man standing beside her could teach a master class on the subject.

Just not to her.

Most. Definitely. Not.

JAKE STOOD BEHIND Leanne, wondering why he couldn't stop grinning as he remembered Eve's strident voice ordering Sam off the motorcycle. And why the sight of the two of them wrapped in each other's arms so tightly a crowbar couldn't have separated them should make him feel so pleased. But it did. Maybe he really was accepting Sam as a member of his "family" as he'd said earlier that evening.

Jake had once looked on the other man as merely a spoiled, arrogant prick, a brother forced on him by uncontrollable circumstances. But now, seeing the look of exhilaration on Sam's face as he grabbed his wife for a kiss, Jake realized he would have chosen the other man for a friend, anyway.

It was hard not to like a guy who didn't let anything get to him.

And it had been impossible for Jake to hold on to his unreasonable anger toward his half-brother in the face of Sam's constant good humor. Even at the wedding, when Sam had been punching him in the jaw, Jake had seen by the twinkle his green eyes that Sam wasn't truly angry. He'd known why Jake was being such an ass.

When he thought about it, he guessed the real moment of change for the two of them had been when Sam had come to Jake for help. The prodigal son came to the black sheep to track down Eve, the woman he loved—who'd run away and couldn't be found. Sam had broken down the wall Jake had erected, not that Jake wouldn't have done it sooner or later himself. He'd been working up to it, he told himself, continuing to try to rile up his brother as a means of keeping the lines of communication open; doing it more because it was expected than because he wanted to anymore. They hadn't become best friends or anything sappy like that, and Jake had still gotten in digs wherever he could—like at the wedding—but there had been a definite shift in the relationship.

And now, well, Sam didn't need a two-day older brother to keep him on his toes anymore. Sam had as his wife a gorgeous, feisty, former model who left behind a trail of goggle-eyed men wherever she went. Sam was going to be kept quite busy being married to Eve.

Finally, the pair on the motorcycle broke apart. He watched Eve try to work up another scold, but Sam's huge white grin and quick kiss on her nose forestalled it. Eve finally shrugged and gave up.

Sam helped Eve off the seat, then slid his arm around her waist as they approached the porch. "The next time you drag my wife out of my house, at least have the decency to leave your leather jacket for when I come charging after you. It's too damn cold to ride around without one."

"The next time you decide to take a joy ride, find someone else's bike, little brother."

Sam gave Jake an assessing look, and Jake watched the emotions cross the other man's face. His green eyes, so much like Jake's he sometimes felt he was looking at his own reflection, had widened with pleasure at Jake's comment.

Then he narrowed them and tossed Jake's helmet up into Jake's middle hard enough that Jake let out an oomph. "Actually, the next time *you* decide to go chasing after bad guys, leave my wife at home!"

"There was no way he could have left me behind," Eve said. "Leanne needed me."

Leanne sighed. "I'm fine. It was no big deal."

Sam looked at her intently. "You're sure you're all right? You weren't hurt?"

"No, just a bit scared," she insisted quietly. "And I'm ready to go home. I need a long hot bath."

A sudden image of bubbles and candlelight and Leanne Weston's long bare leg lifted out of silky water shot through Jake's mind with the power of a thunderbolt. He shook his head, hard, shocked that such a precise, detailed vision could appear out of nowhere. He surreptitiously shifted his eyes down, wishing he could see the legs hidden beneath her warm winter slacks. Her strappy high heeled shoes were a surprise. He hadn't noticed them earlier. Somehow, he'd have expected the all buttoned up Miss Weston to wear sensible pumps, color coordinated to match her outfit. Instead, she wore sexy, thin-strapped high heels. Not exactly what he'd call *do-me* shoes, but they were not bad. Not bad at all. Another contradiction, another chink in the sensible career woman demeanor. He was glad he'd noticed.

"So, Eve, have you forgotten Mack and Carla are coming by tonight?"

A stricken look crossed Eve's face as she quickly looked at her watch. "Oh, crud. I did forget. Sam, would you...do you think you could hold down the fort? I don't want Leanne going home alone."

"Don't be ridiculous," Leanne said. "I'm fine, for heaven's sake. You don't need to go home with me."

Eve tried to protest, but Jake cut her off. "She's right. You don't need to go home with her. Because I'm going to."

Leanne didn't think she'd heard him correctly. Surely Jake Montez hadn't just said he was coming home with her, not when all she'd been able to think as they stood on the porch was that she couldn't wait to get away from this man who caused all kinds of unsettling sensations to soar through her. "That's completely unnecessary."

He ignored her, staring at Sam. "You two go ahead. We'll lock up, then I'll follow Miz Weston home."

She turned her head slowly. "Did you hear what I just said? I am fine. I don't *need* you following me anywhere!"

He shrugged. "I'm sure you don't. But I *need* to do it. Sam, Eve, see you later."

Jake didn't even wait for them to reply as he turned on his heel and walked back into the building. Leanne watched him, her mouth hanging open. She was tempted to stomp her foot in frustration, particularly when she saw the smile on Sam's face as he watched from the bottom of the steps. She settled for a glare of disdain when Jake returned, carrying Eve's coat and purse. He saw it and laughed, making it clear she had no say in the matter.

Sam and Eve were no help. Leanne had seen the look of relief on her friend's face when she realized Jake was not going to be refused in his offer to see her home.

Sometimes the other woman worried about her too much. After Leanne's breakup with Sloan, Eve had become quite the mother hen. Leanne hadn't confronted her about it—yet. But after Eve got into her car with Sam and pulled away with a cheery wave, leaving Leanne alone with the bossy Mr. Montez, she decided she was going to.

Soon.

"THERE'S REALLY NO need for you to follow…"

"Look, if you don't shut up," he said as she locked the front door of the building, "I'm going to put you on the back of my bike and drive you home myself."

Oh wonderful. She could just imagine the picture that would make, her sitting behind him astride the powerful vehicle, with her thighs stretched around his lean hips.

Images flooded her mind. And heated flooded her body. Because it wasn't embarrassment she envisioned. It was pure, utter want.

She had been trying to lie to herself about her feelings for Jake Montez. But the truth was, she wanted the guy like she hadn't wanted anyone in as long as she could remember. This wasn't about just acknowledging he was hot. It was lust, surging through her, reminding her of all the warm, womanly places in her body that had been neglected for far too long.

Stop it. Get it out of your head because it's never going to happen!

By focusing on her annoyance at being treated like a child, she did manage to stop picturing him naked. But it wasn't easy.

She needed to get away from the man, pronto, which was why, as she drove ahead of him down the quiet street, she decided to lose him. It was shitty, particularly since he was going out of his way to make sure she got home all right. But self-preservation demanded it. Because, if he followed her to her building, the wicked little urchin who lived inside her might just be tempted to invite him up to her apartment. And then into her bedroom.

"Never," she snapped at herself, even as she watched him in her rear-view mirror.

He looked completely at ease on the big motorcycle, his black-leather clad body blending into the chrome and metal of the powerful machine he rode. He at least had the sense to wear a helmet, so she couldn't see his face. But his body was distracting enough. Again and again Leanne had to force herself to look ahead, watching the road, rather than allowing her eyes to seek out his reflection.

The fact that she kept stealing glances at him was another good reason for losing the guy. She needed to focus on driving. She'd had a scare tonight that had left her a little shaken, even now, and couldn't afford any distractions. That man was one hell of a distraction, and if she didn't stop trying to peek at him, she was going to have an accident.

As they approached an intersection, Leanne remembered a trick she'd once seen in an old movie. Slowing down as she saw a yellow traffic light, she bit her lip, studied the intersection, then hit the gas just as the light began to turn red.

"Ha!" she cheered when she saw he'd stopped at the intersection, a little surprised it had worked. She'd have thought minor inconveniences like red lights wouldn't be of much concern to a man like Jake.

When she heard the strident blare of a familiar-sounding siren, she suddenly had a sinking suspicion she knew why he hadn't followed her. A glance in her mirror confirmed her fears. Turning right, into the intersection she'd just blown through, was a city police car. She said a quick prayer, but her hopes that the officer hadn't spotted her traffic maneuver were dashed when his blue lights came to life directly behind her.

"This just isn't my day."

Reluctantly slowing down, she pulled over into an empty parking space on the side of the road and rolled down the window. The police car parked behind her. Leanne wondered if Jake would stop, as well. As she waited for the officer to approach her window, she saw Jake's motorcycle slowly drive past, continuing up the street. His shoulders shook with laughter as he drove by, and wished she had something to pitch at his helmeted head.

"License and registration, please?" the officer asked when he reached the side of the car and held his flashlight up to peer in at her. It wasn't until he asked for them that Leanne remembered the mugging. *Could things get any worse?*

"Uh, I'm sorry, officer, but, actually I don't have my license. You see, I was robbed this evening and my I.D. was in my purse."

He looked skeptical. "Do you own the car, ma'am?"

Before she could reply, she heard the distinctive rumble of Jake's motorcycle again. He had made a u-turn at the next block and was heading back toward them. Her heart leapt, even as she wondered why she wanted him to stop and help her get out of this new mess, particularly considering her anger that he'd insisted on following home. Then again, if he hadn't been following her, she wouldn't have run the light. So, in a way, this was partly his fault.

Jake pulled his motorcycle into the space in front of her car and Leanne saw the police officer stiffen immediately. His rigid stance eased, however, as Jake stepped off the bike and removed his helmet.

"Hey Montez," the officer said, a wide smile breaking over his face. "Working tonight?"

"Flanagan," Jake nodded as he walked toward the car. "I'm tailing a crazy lady," he said, looking pointedly toward Leanne.

She gasped. "Why, you…"

"Crazy lady with a lead foot," the officer said with another pointed glance at Leanne. She gave him an apologetic look and sunk lower into the driver's seat of her car.

Somehow, some way, Jake managed to get her off the hook. She listened to some of the conversation between the two men, realizing here was another Philadelphia cop who did not dislike Jake Montez. In fact, listening to them, it was easy to hear the admiration in the other man's voice.

"Now, you take it easy, ma'am," the officer said as he finally turned his attention back toward her. "I know you are shaken up about the robbery, but you don't need to go causing any accidents. Mr. Montez here will make sure you get home safe and sound."

Leanne gritted her teeth, holding back her opinion of that plan. "Thank you very much, sir," she said. "It's so *comforting* to know Mr. Montez is right there behind me."

"And trust me, I will be," Jake said. "All the way to her front door."

JAKE SHOULD HAVE just let her get a ticket. That's what he'd planned to do when he drove by her car, looking at her biting the corner of her lip as she tentatively watched the police officer behind her. Then he'd remembered she didn't have her license. He didn't have all night to wait for her to get that mess sorted out, and had turned around and gone back.

Not that she appreciated it. If looks could kill, he figured he'd be six feet under the pavement of Chestnut Street.

After the officer left, Jake and Leanne exchanged a long look. Her gray eyes were downright frosty. "Ready?" he asked.

"You enjoyed that, didn't you?" She clutched the steering wheel hard, and he imagined she was wishing it was his throat she had between her hands.

He was unable to contain a grin. "You've got to learn to control your temper, sweetheart. That tantrum almost cost you a hundred and eighty bucks."

She glared at him. "Excuse me for not bowing down to thank you for talking my way out of that ticket. Especially since it's your fault I almost got one to begin with."

"My fault? How do you figure that?"

"If you hadn't been following me, I wouldn't have run that

light."

"Correction. If you hadn't been trying to *lose* me, you wouldn't have run that light." Jake bent down to lean in the driver's side window of her car. When they were nearly nose to nose, he said, "Face it, Leanne, I've followed enough people in my day to know all the tricks. Saw that one coming a quarter mile before we hit the intersection."

He saw her eyes widen as he moved in close to her, close enough that he caught the scent of her perfume and saw the pulse pounding in her temple. The teasing laughter died from his lips as he let his eyes study the smoothness of her face, the curve of her cheek and the soft glow of her loose hair around the collar of her wool coat.

"You know me already, do you?" she asked softly. "From a few brief meetings, you know how I'll react, what I'll say?"

Jake didn't reply. Of course he didn't know her. But he had known plenty of women like her. Trying to ditch him on the way home had been in her nature. She was all business, all independent career woman, and she sure as heck wouldn't take kindly to some man trying to play protector. He would have been surprised if she *hadn't* tried to lose him.

But, for some reason, he had a hard time remembering that right this minute. He suddenly couldn't figure out why he'd ever thought her cold and uptight when she had the warmest glow in her eyes, and the sweetest curve to her amazing lips.

Leanne continued holding his gaze steadily, then shifted her attention lower. He took in a slow, deep breath as she stared at his mouth, still saying nothing. Jake swallowed hard under her perusal. He didn't know what was going on in her mind, but damned if he wasn't curious about what was causing the warmth of her expression.

She finally spoke again, whispered, really, a sultry whisper that bounced around in his head. "Let's see if you know what I'm going to do now."

He didn't. He truly had no idea. But he found himself hoping she was going to follow up her visual study of his mouth with a close, physical inspection—with those lips of hers that had been driving him mad since the first time he saw them. This certainly wasn't the time or place for a kiss, but he didn't care. He wanted it, anyway.

She was the wrong woman for him, and he was definitely the wrong man for her. She was all uptown girl and he was rough-town man. Still, he wanted to taste that mouth, one more time.

The rising car window beneath his arm didn't register at first. But the sparkle in her eyes did. She smirked as she held the button to close the window, almost trapping his forearm and head inside the car. She didn't seem to care too much that he had to yank out of the way to avoid getting stuck.

"Now you're just bein' mean," he muttered, a rueful smile tugging at his lips as he backed away from the car. She revved her engine, gave him a glance over her shoulder and shrugged, as if asking what was taking him so long. Jake hurried to his bike and had time to yank his helmet on and jump into the seat before she pulled away from the curb. He found himself chuckling all the way to her home.

She lived in one of those old renovated downtown buildings that had been turned into big, expensive apartments for the upscale yuppies who worked in the city. It wasn't exactly Society Hill, but it was pretty darn nice. Pretty pricey, too, Jake noted, as he followed her down a side alley to a private parking lot behind the building. Pulling into a space next to her car, he ignored the "reserved" sign and cut the bike's engine.

She didn't hesitate to try to give him the brush as soon as she stepped out of the car. "Thank you for seeing me home. As you can see, I'm fine."

"What was that?" he asked. "I can't quite hear you—I think I've lost half of my right ear. Maybe it's sticking to your door frame?"

She had the grace to cast a quick, guilty look at his head to see for herself that he was all right. Then she squared her shoulders and looked at him with the cool haughtiness he'd come to expect from her. "You don't appear injured. Perhaps your inability to hear is because you don't seem to be able to listen. Like when I told you I could get home all by my lonesome. No accidents, no mishaps."

"Luckily, no tickets, either," Jake said evenly, reminding her of her brush with Philadelphia's finest. Under the bright glow of an overhead floodlight attached to the back of the building, he saw a blush rise in her cheeks.

"Thank you for that," she murmured. "Now, goodnight."

Jake thought about just doing as she asked, getting on his bike and riding away from this prissy female who couldn't gracefully accept a favor. And hadn't cared that she could have crushed his windpipe with her damned car window. But he couldn't. The mugger might not have gotten her keys, but he had her i.d., including her license, and could easily have come to her apartment, anyway.

"Look, you want me to leave, and I'm more than ready to go. But I'm not going to until I make sure you get in your apartment safe and sound." He saw her frown and open her mouth to protest. "Humor me, would you? Just in case somewhere along the line, when you valet parked, somebody grabbed a copy of your house key or something?"

"That's just not...." Her voice trailed off, her face suddenly losing its color.

He tensed. "What is it?"

"Oh, I'm so stupid," she muttered, lifting her fingers to her mouth.

Realizing she'd remembered something important, he stepped closer and put a hand on her shoulder. "Tell me."

"I had a spare key made for Eve. After I took care of their cat, they offered to do the same for me for an out-of-town trip next month, and I planned to give her the key tonight."

"Lemme guess. The spare key was in your purse?"

"My satchel," she admitted. Nibbling her lip, she said, "But it was just a key all by itself, tucked into a zippered pocket. It wasn't on a ring, wasn't identified. You don't think…"

"No," he said, slowly shaking his head. "I mean, it's doubtful. The guy was probably just looking for cash and ditched your purse and satchel in the nearest dumpster."

He hoped, anyway.

"You really think so?"

"Sure. But still…"

"Yeah. But still." She swiped a gloved hand through her hair. "The robbery was almost two hours ago. Enough time to look at my address on my license, and come up here to see if that key fit my front door."

"Exactly."

She sighed heavily. "I hate feeling so exposed. Violated, almost. Even if everything's fine, I'll have a hard time sleeping tonight."

"Well, you won't be sleeping here, not unless you have about five extra deadbolts on your door that don't work off that key."

"No such luck," she mumbled.

"It's okay," he said, hearing her desolation. "We'll check things out and then I'll follow you back over to Eve and Sam's. I'm sure they wouldn't mind you spending the night."

"Except they have company."

"Another friend then," he said, not allowing any crazy suggestions to spill out of his mouth. Suggestions like: *You can stay with me.*

"I suppose," she said.

"Don't worry, we'll figure it out. Let's just make sure all is well inside."

"You don't mind walking me up?"

"I wouldn't leave if you ordered me to." He smiled slightly. "Or if you ran a red light to get rid of me."

She licked her lips—*God, those lips, that soft, silky tongue*—and cleared her throat. "Again, I'm sorry about that. I appreciate everything you've done."

"That wasn't so hard, was it?"

Her eyes narrowed, the overhead parking light catching glints of blue in the depths of those gray irises. "Don't push your luck."

"I won't. Let's go up to your place."

"I'll pay you…"

"Don't be ridiculous," he said, falling into step beside her as they headed into the building. He noted that there was a security buzz-in system for the building. He also noted that it wasn't operating. Leanne just yanked the door open. For the life of him he couldn't understand why people installed security systems but didn't bother to use or maintain them.

"I can afford it."

"It's not a problem. Besides, I'm trying real hard to get back into Sammy's good graces after the wedding…thing."

She snorted at the description.

"All right, the wedding *fiasco*," he admitted with a sheepish grin. "Me seeing you home will make Eve feel better. And you know the saying. Happy wife, happy life."

"So you really care about Sam's happiness?"

He didn't answer right away. Jake didn't actually know the answer to that question. Still, not knowing for sure how it had happened didn't change the fact that he meant what he'd said. He was glad Sam was so happy, and he wanted to continue to improve his relationship with his brother. Of course, he would still be making sure Leanne got home safely even if Eve hadn't asked him to do it. But she didn't need to know that.

"Yeah," he finally replied. "I guess I do."

They rode up the elevator to Leanne's floor in an uncomfortable silence. Jake saw that she looked everywhere but at his face. He figured she must have a real fascination for men's boots, because she kept her eyes glued to the toe of his the entire time. When they reached her floor, she hurried out into the hallway without even waiting for the doors to slide completely open. Even from several feet away, he heard her sigh of relief when she saw her door was closed and everything in the hallway appeared normal.

"I hate to break it to you," he pointed out, "but some thieves might know how to shut a door."

"Can you blame me for a little wishful thinking?"

"I guess not. Now, let me go in first and take a look around."

"I can go first."

"You afraid I'll see you're a slob and your apartment's a mess?"

The teasing laughter died from his voice when he saw a look of confusion on her face. She stared down at the doorknob which turned easily in her hand. Leanne hadn't put her key in the lock.

"Wait," he ordered, stepping forward, immediately on alert.

Before he could stop her, she pushed the door open. "Maybe I forgot to lock it," she said.

He was reaching for her arm to pull her away when he heard her squeal of dismay. He reached for his weapon, pushing her out of the way and stepping in front of her to look through the open doorway.

So much for her hopes that the mugger hadn't found her spare key. Because, to her obvious dismay, and his own anger, her apartment was a shambles.

"I don't suppose I was right and you're just a slob?" he asked, already knowing the answer to the question.

She slowly shook her head, watching as he reached for his cell phone to call the cops "No, I'm afraid not."

He didn't think so. Which meant that whoever had mugged her earlier tonight had, indeed, found the key and come up here to rob her home. Jake's fury, which had been simmering since he found out she'd been attacked, erupted into a full boil.

She might not want him around, but one thing was without doubt.

He was going to find out who did this. And while he figured it out, he would do whatever it took to make sure Leanne Weston remained safe.

Chapter 4

L EANNE HAD SPENT more time with the cops tonight than she
ever had in her adult life.

There'd been the nice young guy who'd come to the office after
the mugging, and then the one who'd pulled her over. Lastly, a
friendly duo who came quickly after Jake's 911 call and spent a few
hours looking around her apartment, walking through the building
and the grounds, questioning her and her neighbors, and filling out
paperwork.

Being a crime victim was exhausting. Especially when it happened
twice in one evening.

By the time the men left, it was well after eleven o'clock. Leanne
had been operating on adrenaline and anger since she realized her
home had been robbed. Now she just felt weary, and very sad.
Tomorrow would be a day of dealing with insurance claims and
replacing whatever stolen items could actually be replaced—like her
small amount of nice jewelry, and her laptop—and mourning that
which couldn't, like some of the files on that laptop. Frankly, she was
more upset about the files than she was about the computer.
Electronics could be replaced. Some of her creative ideas could not.
Thank God she still had her dream-book.

"How are you holding up?"

Leanne didn't even glance up as Jake returned from escorting the
officers to the door. She'd collapsed onto the sofa, her head back,

wondering who she'd wronged in another life to have a day such as this one.

"I've been better. I want a hot bath, a glass of wine, and my bed."

Looking up at the sexy man who'd stayed with her all evening, and getting those crazy butterflies twitching in her stomach, she wished she hadn't mentioned any of those things. Because bath, wine, and bed all screamed romance in her head. And while she might be ready to admit—at least to herself—that she was hot for Eve's brother-in-law, tonight she felt about as romantic as a hedgehog with the flu.

"You *really* want to stay here?"

She immediately caught his point. Because, truthfully, no, she did not want to stay at home. She'd never be able to sleep. It wasn't because she was scared the thieves might come back—well, not entirely. The main problem was, she felt so violated. Knowing someone might have gone through her underwear drawer, sat on her furniture, touched the bottles in her medicine cabinet, perhaps opened her refrigerator and sampled her food, made her physically nauseous.

"Maybe not," she admitted. "Even if they're long gone, the thought that somebody out there has a key to my front door certainly wouldn't induce a good night's sleep."

He walked over and sat down on the chair opposite her, bent over, his elbows resting on his knees. "If you want to, I can rig something up for the door, and I'll sleep on the couch to make sure you're okay."

Her mouth fell open and she could focus only on one part of his statement. "You mean…you want to stay here? With me?"

Those eyes twinkled, as if he knew exactly where her mind had gone. "Did you miss the part about the couch?"

The couch on which she was half-reclining? Yeah, couch would work. So would floor. Up against the wall.

She couldn't believe her imagination was taking her to all these wicked, erotic places, but, honestly, given the day she'd had, was it any wonder she wasn't herself? Didn't she have reason to feel a little reckless? Would one night's indulgence, as compensation for her horrible day, be so bad?

Get a grip, Leanne. You know you can't just have a one-night-stand with this guy.

Right. First, she wasn't really the one-night-stand type, only ever having had one in her life. And actually, it had turned into about a one-month stand because the guy had, to her great surprise, called the next day, wanting to see her again.

But, by its very definition, a one-night-stand was supposed to be something you indulged in that you wouldn't have to think about again. It should be a pleasurable little secret you'd never have to worry about, regret, or deal with after that one night.

Jake…well, she would have to deal with him. He was Sam's brother. Their paths would definitely cross. Meaning hot sex with the guy for one unforgettable night was right out.

Too bad.

"Leanne?" he prodded.

"The couch is pretty comfortable," she mumbled, stalling for time while she tried to get her brain back into gear.

"So you're saying you do want me to sleep on the couch?" he asked, sounding a little surprised that she hadn't put up an argument at his suggestion.

"Not on the couch," she mumbled. Then quickly sat up straight. "I mean, you don't have to stay here with me at all. I've put you out enough today."

"I don't mind," he insisted. "And I'm not leaving you here alone."

"Don't be silly…"

"That chain on your door wouldn't keep out a kindergartner trying to break into the cookie closet."

"Man. Why did you have to go and say that?" He looked repentant, as if sorry he'd scared her. So she quickly clarified, "I could use a cookie closet right about now." Comfort food would go well with her wine. "If the thief were in front of me right now, I'd slap him across the face for the loss of my Double Stuft Oreos."

He snickered. "I don't remember seeing empty boxes of Oreos strewn all over your kitchen floor."

"I'm going to have to throw-out every bit of opened food in my kitchen," she explained with a shudder. "Honestly, I wouldn't be able to take a bite of anything without wondering if somebody had touched it or done something gross to it."

"Yeah. Let's clean out your pantry," he said with a wince.

"And wash all my clothes, linens…and every surface of this place."

"I'm game if you are."

"You're kind. But I meant tomorrow. I'm not up for all that tonight." She swallowed hard, thinking about the chores that faced her, wondering if she would ever really feel this place was *clean* again—not just of germs or dirt, but of associations.

His square jaw thrust out. "I hate that you are going through this."

"I guess everybody's touched by crime sooner or later."

He stared into her eyes, then looked away. Exhaling deeply, he mumbled something under his breath.

"What was that?"

A sigh, as if he already regretted the mumble. "I said, I have Girl Scout cookies at my place."

Leanne laughed softly. "Lucky duck."

"I know. Neighborhood kid was selling them—I have about five boxes of the mint ones in my freezer."

"I think I hate you. Stop rubbing it in."

"What I'm trying to say is, you don't want to stay here, and I don't want you to stay here. I would suggest you go to Sam and Eve's, but it's almost midnight, and I already know you well enough to know you won't call them this late."

"Yes, you're right about that," she said, glancing at the wall clock. Nor would she call Ruthie or Diana. Maybe if it were a weekend, but it was a work night. They all had busy lives and schedules and didn't deserve to get dragged out of bed to make-up a guest room for somebody who was too freaked out to stay in her own place. "But I can always go to a hotel."

Shaking his head, apparently hating to point out an unpleasant fact, he reminded her, "You have no I.D. or, I assume, credit cards."

"Shoot," she said, rubbing a weary hand over her eyes. "Nor do I have any cash, or my ATM card."

Fortunately, she had been able to call from the office and get all her cards cancelled. She'd have replacements soon. Just not soon enough to help her tonight.

She could probably get a room at Ruthie's family's hotel, the Lancaster, but, this late, she'd need to get Ruthie to vouch for her. Which would entail a conversation with chatty Ruthie, who would want to hear every single detail.

"I'd be happy to pay for it, to set you up in a room. I mean, I owe you the bail money anyway. I hadn't had a chance to give it to Sam and Eve yet. But to be honest, at this time of night, in this city, it might not be so easy to get a room where you'd feel any safer in than you do here. So my place might be the best option."

He was right. Every word he said was true. But the fact that he was right wasn't making the idea of staying at his home any easier to picture. Especially because it was far *too* easy to picture being alone with him for an entire night. It was like putting a woman on a diet in a Ben & Jerry's factory overnight, with a giant spoon and vats filled with every flavor of ice cream ever invented, and saying, "Don't eat." Hating yourself the next morning because your jeans were a little tight couldn't outweigh the deliciousness of all the Caramel Sutra and New York Super Fudge Chunk you could eat.

"I really couldn't impose like that."

"It's not an imposition. I have a two bedroom townhouse. My baby sister comes from Texas for a long summer visit every year, and I keep a room for her. It's yours."

"It's very nice of you to offer."

"Nice? That's not a word a lot of people use about me," he admitted with a wry chuckle.

"The redhead you rescued at the Slaughter House thinks you are," she said, casting him a mischievous glance from half-lowered lashes.

He barked a laugh. "Yeah."

"She called you a knight in shining armor."

"My armor's pretty tarnished. The truth is, I'd want to help out anybody who'd had a day as bad as yours…the fact that it's *you* just makes it more important."

"Why?" she whispered, almost afraid to ask. Afraid he'd say she meant something to him. More afraid he'd say she didn't.

Don't be stupid. What can you mean to someone you've only known for a few weeks? Someone you have sniped at almost every time you've been together?

"Let's just say I'm doing it for a friend of the family."

"Oh."

He was still trying to get back into Sam and Eve's good graces. And taking her in like a stray kitten might help. She knew she shouldn't feel deflated by that, but couldn't deny she did.

"And if you don't trust me, let me assure you, there is a lock on the spare room door."

Hmm. *Is there one on yours?*

Suddenly nervous, she licked her lips. Although she was still weary and mentally shaken, she couldn't deny that a surge of interest—excitement—was rushing through her. Leanne had been sitting here telling herself she couldn't have a one-night-stand with this man, but the idea that he just saw her as a sad case he had to protect had put her in a different mood. She felt…challenged, almost. Leanne wanted him to see her as something other than a crime victim in need of protection. She wanted him to perhaps look at her mouth the way he had the first few times they'd interacted. Wanted him to kiss her again. And more.

But no sex.

Right. Sleeping with him would take things to a level neither of them could afford. Still, there were several rungs on the ladder between a platonic sleepover and a full-on monkey-fuck-party. Many, *many* rungs.

Which was why, rather than argue, as he probably expected her to, Leanne simply nodded, rose from her seat and said, "Okay then. Let me grab a few things."

His brow shot up. "Really?"

"Were you serious about the invitation?"

"Of course. I just didn't think you would…"

"Say yes?"

"Well, I knew you'd eventually say yes. You're a smart woman and you don't have many other options."

True.

"But I figured I'd have to argue you into it."

She offered him a small, secretive smile. "Maybe you don't know me as well as you think you do."

He stood as well, staring down at her, studying her face as if trying to see what, exactly, she was up to. Considering she couldn't say herself what she expected to come out of this night, she probably didn't reveal anything with her expression.

"Maybe I don't," he finally murmured, and his eyes, those amazing green eyes, shifted to her mouth. That familiar heat flared up between them, and she knew he was at last seeing the woman with whom he'd flirted so shamelessly, the one he'd kissed at the wedding. Not the victim. Not his brother's wife's best friend.

No.

He was looking at her like a woman he wanted.

And suddenly, Leanne wondered if she had bit off more than she could chew. Was she really equipped to handle a man this hot, sexy and powerful? If he gave her what she wanted—a little bit of heated pleasure to erase this bad day from her mind and soul—would she ever be able to draw any kind of line in the sand and not cross it? Or, hell, drag him across it?

She didn't know. She only knew she was no longer feeling like a sad, lost kitten being taken home for cream.

She was feeling much more like a fully grown adult cat desperate for some heavy petting and scratching.

JAKE HAD NO idea what had prompted Leanne's mood change, but, as they arrived at his place, about ten miles from hers, he began to wonder if he'd made a tactical mistake.

Because having a one-night-stand with his sister-in-law's best friend probably wasn't going to do the job of mending fences with his brother.

He couldn't say for sure when he'd noticed Leanne wanted him more than she'd probably like to admit. Once he'd noticed, however, it had been hard to see anything else. Even before the cops left, she was casting sidelong glances at him. And when he talked about taking her to his place, her silvery-gray eyes had gone darker, becoming mysterious, like snow-filled winter clouds. The sound of her breaths easing over her moist, parted lips had become audible in the silent room. She'd brushed her own fingertips across the hollow of her throat and down her body—maybe not even realizing she was doing it.

All those things told him everything he needed to know.

She wanted him. She might even have decided to take him.

But unless he wanted a furious argument with his brother and sister-in-law, he couldn't even dream of hooking up with Eve's best friend. She was vulnerable and a little broken tonight, understandable for a double-crime victim. He'd deserve the title of creep if he let himself have her, and wouldn't be able to use some bullshit excuse to justify his actions.

Besides, they were totally wrong for each other, complete opposites. She had probably been raised in a mansion, while he'd scrabbled to survive. She was educated, elegant, and always proper. He had a GED and a lot of years carrying a gun, rarely wore anything but jeans and his leather jacket, and, as evidenced by his behavior at his brother's wedding, wasn't the proper sort.

Nah, they were total opposites.

Meaning he had to resist her.

He could do it. He *would* do it. He was no Neanderthal. He was a thirty-one year old, mature man with lots of self-control and willpower.

Those assurances consoled him right up until he glanced through the half-open door of his spare bedroom and saw her pull out a silky, filmy nightgown from her overnight bag. He groaned out loud, knowing his urge to play hero was going to bite him in the ass.

Because having her spend the night under his roof, knowing she was wearing something as deliciously sexy as that nightie, was going to utterly crush his already-weakening self-control.

She apparently heard. Startled, she glanced out, catching him standing there in the small hallway between the two bedrooms. Those unusual eyes of hers widened, and her mouth fell open on a tiny, surprised gasp.

He expected her to shove the gown back into the bag, stalk over and slam the door in his face. He waited for her to do those things. Mentally urged her to do those things.

Instead, to his shock, she kept the gown gripped in her fingers and approached him, stepping out into the hallway. "Bathroom?"

Jake felt the silky fabric brush against his bare hand, and knew for certain that the nightgown could never be as soft as the skin of the woman who would soon be wearing it.

He couldn't speak. His vocal cords had thickened, his mouth was desert-dry. So he merely jerked a thumb toward the door behind him, gesturing toward the room in question.

"Thanks."

"There's, uh, only one, sorry," he muttered, immediately thinking of how personal a thing that was, sharing a bathroom. In fact, his whole house, which he'd bought last year and was trying to upgrade and fix-up, suddenly felt about the size of a doll house. Mainly because the two of them, together, filled up every inch of the space, even when they stood in only one corner of it. There was nowhere he could go in here that would remove him from the sound of her, the smell of her, the thought of her.

"It's okay."

Glad he had kept his neatness habit from his military days, meaning the bathroom was immaculate, he said, "Towels and stuff are in the linen closet if you want to take a shower."

"I'd love one," she admitted, stretching her shoulders and sweeping a hand through that long, silky hair. "I'm pretty achy from my fall."

He frowned, not liking to think about the attack. "Actually, you're welcome to take that bath you mentioned."

Although he knew she might need one, Jake immediately kicked himself because it would be torturous enough to lie in his bed on the other side of the wall, listening to the shower running. If he had to try to go to sleep to the sounds of her soft splashing, picturing her naked and glistening with bubbles in his tub, he would have to take measures into his own hands. Literally. Hell, he was already half-hard for her, his cock stiffening with every breath he took, since each one was perfumed with her womanly scent. Jake might not be the Neanderthal type, but he had enough testosterone to immediately go to red alert when he smelled hot, musky woman and saw the body of a goddess mere inches from his own.

"That's all right. It's a little late for a bath."

He breathed a mental sigh of relief and nodded.

"But I should probably put something on these. Do you have peroxide?"

She held up her hands, showing him the cuts and sores. They'd had a first aid kit at her office, and she'd washed the cuts and bandaged her torn nails. Unfortunately, some of the abrasions from the gravel were right on her palms where no bandage would possibly stick. Right now, they looked red and sore, still shadowed with dried blood, and Jake felt his own blood begin to boil all over again. *Sonofabitch who did it is gonna pay.*

"Let me help you clean those up," he insisted, gently grabbing one of her hands and pulling her into the bathroom. He waited for her to resist, but she didn't, smart enough to realize she would have a difficult time tending to her right hand with her left, especially since it was scraped up and she had bandages on the tips of three fingers.

"Thank you," she murmured.

Getting a washcloth, gentle soap and peroxide, he went to work on her poor hands. Leanne didn't make a sound, though he knew she had to be in pain. The only time she even winced was when he had to dig around with tweezers for a tiny bit of gravel that wouldn't wash out.

"I'm so sorry," he mumbled, looking up from her hand into her face.

"Go ahead. It doesn't hurt too much."

"No. I'm sorry you were assaulted. Sorry somebody hurt you." He lowered his voice to a growl. "Believe me, I'd like to hurt them back."

"Me too," she said, her tone dry. "I'm just glad I'd left my most important work notebook locked in my desk at work. If I'd lost that, I'd be a whole lot more depressed tonight."

"What's in it?"

"My dreams." She licked her lips and looked away. "I mean, well, just a lot of ideas, but they're some of my oldest, most personal, creative ones."

"About curtains?"

She laughed softly. "Yes. About curtains."

"Good to know it's safe," he teased.

"More than you can imagine. The book contains a little bit of everything, from pencil sketches to printouts of graphic designs I've spent a lot of time on. Snippets of fabric, photographs, ideas for projects I'd like to work on. Everything from the rooms in my own fantasy house to ones I came up with for the Governor's Mansion competition."

"Pretty important stuff."

"Definitely. I feel like I've put a part of my soul into that book, as crazy as that might sound to you."

"That doesn't sound crazy to me. You just sound like somebody who cares a lot about what she does."

"Yes, I do."

"So what's your fantasy house look like?"

She tilted her head and closed her eyes, apparently picturing it. "It's in the country, with a huge yard with rolling hills, maple trees and forsythia bushes. The house is two-stories. A renovated Victorian with an actual turret, a wrap-around porch, painted pale yellow."

He was catching the vision, able to visualize as she word-painted the place.

"It'll have four bedrooms upstairs, a bathroom with a claw-foot tub. There'll be a huge kitchen with washed pine cabinets and hardwood floors."

"You've got this all planned out, huh?"

"Pretty much."

"Based on anything in particular?"

She opened her eyes and looked at him. "Just all the things I wanted as a kid that I never had."

That surprised him. "Really? I kinda pictured you as a doctor's kid, growing up in the burbs in a house much like the one you're talking about."

Her mouth twisted into a tiny sneer. "Not even close." She hesitated for a moment, and then explained, "I actually had a very poor childhood. Single mom, moved all the time. My wardrobe came from Goodwill and my meals came from food stamps. Or sometimes trash cans."

More than a little surprised, Jake stopped what he was doing, staring down at her. Her words had surprised him, but the intensity in her voice told him how important they were. And, maybe, how hard it was for her to admit them.

"I'm sorry, I didn't mean to…"

"It's okay. I'm fine now. Actually, I was fine then, for the most part. I had a parent who loved me. She did the best she could, and I'm okay."

Knowing that having one right parent was better than two wrong ones, he could only nod. His mom, too, had done the best she could. Unfortunately, her best wasn't always good enough when she came up against her husband's brute strength and bad temper, but Jake knew she tried as hard as she could to keep him away from the flying fists and screaming obscenities. Eventually, when he got old enough to fight back, both of those things stopped landing on him with such stunning regularity.

"I'd say you are more than fine," he replied. "You're pretty spectacular."

"Thank you."

Their stares met, locked, for a moment, and he found himself thinking about all the hidden depths there were to this woman. He'd gotten to know the surface—the face she showed the world. She appeared all power female, strong, beautifully dressed, utterly in control of her life. Now he was seeing a glimpse of the powerhouse underneath who made sure nobody ever saw where she really came from or how hard she'd struggled to get here. The true picture only made him admire her more.

"Okay, just about done here," he said as he gently wiped off the fresh blood from where he'd had to poke around to get the gravel. He left some adhesive bandages and antibiotic ointment on the counter. "You should probably wait until after your shower to finish up. Let me know if you need me to help you get them on."

"I should be fine," she murmured, thanking him again.

With nothing left to say, other than, oh, *Want me to scrub your back?*, Jake left her alone and went into his room, closing both doors behind him. Firmly. Not that a closed door was going to be enough to shut out the mental images of sweet, soft, pretty Leanne getting out of her clothes just one room away. As he began to strip off his own, tossing his shirt into the hamper and unfastening his belt and the button on his jeans, he imagined what she was doing in there. He closed his eyes, visualizing her slipping out of the jacket, the blouse, the tweed pants. Kicking off those sexy, high-heeled fuck-me shoes. Sliding a tiny pair of panties—God, please, a thong—down those slim thighs. Unfastening a bra and freeing what were undoubtedly perfect tits. Pulling back the shower curtain to turn on the water, and…

"Oh, fuck!" he exclaimed.

Because he had just remembered something.

Uh, something major.

"Leanne, wait. I forgot to clear out the tub," he called, yanking his door open and lifting a fist to bang on the bathroom one.

But she apparently didn't hear him. Not soon enough to stop herself from pulling back that shower curtain, anyway. Her sharp, shrill scream confirmed that.

"Oh, hell," he groaned, knowing what she'd found in the bathtub.

"Jake! Help me!"

"Calm down, Leanne," he yelled. "It's tame, I promise, just let me in to get it."

The knob jiggled and the bathroom door flew inward. Jake had about one second to appreciate the mouthwateringly perfect naked woman on the other side before said mouthwatering woman swung her fist and punched him in the gut.

"Ow," he said. "What was that for?"

"You asshole! Why didn't you warn me?" She apparently still hadn't noticed she was naked, so he did the ungentlemanly thing and took a look. His heart stopped, his cock went on high alert, and he suddenly couldn't remember why he'd burst in here.

She was absolutely perfect. Just exquisite, from the top of her head to the red-painted tips of her toes. The in-between was a sea of wonders that would rival any treasure chest. The woman had a slender neck he wanted to lick his way down. Her breasts were works of art—full, high, round—with pink, puckered nipples he was dying to suck on. He clenched his hands into fists, the thought of cupping her, squeezing gently, plumping that warm flesh, making him a little dizzy. Her creamy skin was completely smooth, not a single blemish. He couldn't resist letting his gaze fall down to her slim waist, her flat tummy, toward a small tuft of blond-brown curls between a pair of amazing thighs. No man alive could have seen them and not imagined them wrapped around his hips.

Christ, he wanted the woman. Even after she'd punched him. *Especially* after she'd punched him—she was sexy, gorgeous, feisty, smart. The total package.

And you can't have her. Not that reminding himself of that did a damn bit of good.

"I can't believe there's a goddamn snake in your tub!"

And a fucking anaconda in his pants.

"A snake!? Seriously, you couldn't warn me about a snake?"

Oh, yeah. Right. Real snake. Not trouser dweller. "I'm really sorry about that, I remembered Chester and tried to knock right around the time you two met." Forcing himself to look away from the most glorious female body he'd ever seen, he walked over to the tub and pulled the curtain all the way back.

"Chester?" she groaned.

"Yeah."

"That thing is huge. His name should be Eater-of-Worlds."

"Don't exaggerate," he said, reaching in and retrieving the reptile, which was curled up near the drain sleeping. "He's a ball python, and not a terribly big one. They're not venomous, and he's super-sweet."

"Yeah, okay, but why in God's name is he in your bathtub?"

"Remember how you were cat-sitting for Sam and Eve? Well, a buddy of mine is doing a thirty-day stretch in county, and he needed somebody to snake-sit."

She shuddered as he held the snake in his arms, petting it and allowing it to curl around his forearm. Leanne backed away, until her bare ass hit the wall, trying to put room between herself and the creature.

Jake knew he had to get it out of here; she obviously wasn't a snake lover. Then again, he hadn't been either until he'd met Chester and realized what a nice critter he was. Maybe they could be friends. Or maybe he was just stalling since she hadn't remembered she was naked, and he found himself in less of a hurry.

"But why isn't it in a…a cage or something?"

"He doesn't really like his aquarium, which is in the living room. For some reason this is his favorite spot, so I let him stay in here when I'm at work." He saw her starting to calm down, and added, "He's not at all dangerous. He's a constrictor, so he's not venomous."

Wrong thing to say. She shivered again. "I somehow don't think that would be much comfort if he makes himself comfortable around your neck."

"He's just being affectionate."

"Oh." She continued to stare, not looking quite as terrified now. In fact, she seemed more interested than anything else, because her eyes were glued to the snake that was sliding up his arm to his bare shoulder.

Then he realized it wasn't the snake she was fascinated by. No, the way her eyes darkened and the lids half-dropped over them, she'd found something she liked a whole lot more.

Him.

She was eating him up with her stare, reminding him that he was bare chested, wearing only a pair of unbuttoned jeans. Of course, he was still a whole hell of a lot more clothed than she was.

They were heading into dangerous territory here, even if only one of them realized it. No way could he resist a woman who looked at him like that. Especially when she was stark naked, utterly gorgeous, and had a mouth he'd had long, erotic dreams about. One more second and his half-hard cock was going to burst out of his pants and say hello.

He needed to snap her out of it, and though it pained him, also needed her to put some damn clothes on.

"You want to hold him?" he asked, his voice a silky purr.

"Definitely not."

"He might feel nice against your skin."

She shuddered, shaking her head, rubbing her hands up and down her naked arms. Which was, apparently, when she actually heard what he'd said and realized what she was wearing. Or, uh, wasn't wearing.

"Oh, my God!" she shrieked, immediately grabbing a towel off the rack. "You could have told me."

"I've already apologized for that."

"I don't mean about the snake. I mean about me being naked."

"Yeah, uh, *why* would I do that, exactly?"

She glared. "It would have been polite."

"I'm not always known for being polite."

"I've noticed."

"And people usually know when they're naked."

"You mean, you thought I knew and just didn't care?"

He shrugged, lightly scratching Chester's head. "Could be."

"Well, you're wrong," she snapped.

"If you say so."

"Would you just get out of here with that big, scary *thing*?"

He almost asked, "Which thing?" but decided against it. Instead, he said, "Aww, you're hurting his feelings. But yeah, I'll put him to bed."

He hid a smile as he left the room, half-relieved, half-disappointed that he had accomplished his mission to make her cover herself, and put up some barriers. He noticed the way she edged back, practically tripping into the toilet to avoid the brush of the snake on her skin, and knew she wasn't thinking happy thoughts about his bare chest anymore. That was punctuated by the slamming of the bathroom door behind him.

Chuckling, Jake went downstairs to the living room and got Chester squared away. As he did, he realized how lucky it was that Leanne had her guard up and wouldn't be flirtatious with him anymore tonight. Because he wasn't going to be able to just ignore her, go to bed and try to get the thought of her warm, shapely body out of his head. He had to go back into that bathroom and clean out the tub for her.

"So much for Mr. Clean," he muttered, mentally kicking himself for being so cocky about how immaculate his place was. Nothing like a little snake in the tub to throw off the desire for a long hot shower or bath, and he knew she badly needed one or the other.

Hopefully he'd be able to take care of cleaning up and getting back out without any further temptation. She was mad about Chester, and about him not letting her know she'd sort of forgotten she had no clothes on. So she wouldn't be welcoming any personal attention, which was a good thing. If she were approachable, sexy, vulnerable and friendly, he might do something stupid like touch her, and then all bets—and restraints—would be off. He'd forget who she was, how they'd met, and why he needed to steer clear of her. Now, though, she was annoyed enough to put up barriers and keep them there. Best thing for both of him.

Returning upstairs, he saw her standing in the hallway, waiting for him. She'd slipped into a robe that matched her nightgown.

Jake swallowed hard. The material was very thin, meant more to drape than to actually cover, and the soft peach color was just a shade or two darker than her skin. Her still puckered nipples were pressed against the silky fabric, and he couldn't help but imagine how it might make her feel if he covered one with his mouth, suckling her through the material. He knew how it would make *him* feel, and that was dangerous enough to think about.

"I'm not an animal hater," she said as soon as she spotted him, as if she'd been waiting to defend herself. "Just because I don't like snakes or Sam's cat…"

"Nobody likes Sam's cat."

"Well, I happen to like animals."

"But only furry ones?"

"Something like that," she said, watching as he walked toward her.

"Yeah, I like soft, fluffy things that are nice to pet, too," he said, knowing the words were dangerous as soon as he thought them. He cleared his throat, and shook his head. "And again, I really am sorry I forgot to warn you."

"But not sorry you forgot to suggest I put on some clothes?"

"I might be chivalrous enough not to let a woman who'd been mugged go home by herself," he said, rubbing his jaw as he looked down at that body in that robe. "But no man alive wouldn't have enjoyed that view, lady."

"So, a chivalrous horn-dog, hmm?"

"I'll cop to that." Shit, he'd just admitted he was horny for her. *Smooth move, bonehead.* "Now, Chester is all settled. You wait here a minute and I'll go in and clean the tub for you."

"You don't have to..." Her words trailed off as she remembered why he was cleaning the tub. "Oh, okay, yeah, you do have to. Thanks."

Laughing softly, he went past her into the bathroom and grabbed the cleanser from under the sink. A quick scrub and the porcelain was sparkling and bright, and, hopefully, good enough for an interior designer to bathe in. He'd just pulled a towel off the rack to dry off his shoulders, which had gotten wet from the spray of the shower, and from the quick wash he'd given his arms, when she walked back into the bathroom.

"You can take a shower first, if you want to."

He slowly drew the terrycloth square over his shoulder and down his bicep, shaking his head. "It's okay. I washed any snake-trail off already, though Chester doesn't shed nearly as much as Sam's cat."

Glancing up, he expected to see her smiling, but instead saw she was watching his every move, that same hungry look on her face. Those amazing eyes of hers were almost a platinum color now, and sparkled with interest. More than interest.

Desire.

Jake froze, holding the towel against his arm, not making a sound. Neither did she. But when her pretty pink tongue flicked out to moisten that incredible mouth, he couldn't contain a tiny groan.

The woman was killing him here, gobbling him up with her eyes, now licking her lips like she wanted to taste every inch of him. He tried not to respond, but he was only human. He'd been fighting all evening to keep at least a mental distance between them, to focus on being professional and courteous. But now, well, he was losing the battle—big time. The very idea of her using that pretty tongue of hers on his body sent his libido from Defcon three straight to launch-the-missiles. And considering he wasn't wearing underwear, that meant his missile pushed up out of the top of his still unbuttoned jeans.

"Oh," she whispered, her attention dropping down his body.

Silence fell between them, so thick he could almost hear his pulse pounding in his veins. He waited for her to say something—to spin around and storm out, to avert her gaze, something.

When she finally did react, it was his turn to whisper, "Oh."

Because, without a word, without a warning, pretty Leanne dropped her robe to the floor.

And all his good, noble intentions went right down the drain.

Chapter 5

OVER THE PAST ten years, with her three best friends, Leanne had become used to being thought of as the sweet one. The nice one. The quiet one. With a bombshell like Eve, a ballbuster like Diana and a ditz like Ruthie, what other role was there for her to play?

Nice. Sweet. Quiet.

Now, though, as she searched for those qualities within herself, she realized something: The nice, sweet, quiet Leanne had left the building.

The one who remained didn't want to be nice, sweet or quiet. She wanted to be wild, wicked, and loud. She wanted to take something for the sheer pleasure it would give her, to hell with the consequences or with what anybody else thought.

She wanted *him*.

Which was why she'd untied the sash of her robe and dropped it to the floor, knowing by the way he'd looked at her earlier—not to mention by the unmistakable proof bursting out of his pants—that he wanted her, too. "And I thought Chester was big," she muttered, unable to take her eyes off the massive, rigid hunk of deliciousness.

She'd never thought much about penises, considering them all pretty much the same, believing it was the person connected to it that really mattered. Now, though…good lord. She had been wrong. Completely wrong.

"I want that," she admitted, her voice low, but not shaking. She'd never felt more confident in her words, never more sure of what she was about to do. "I want *you*."

He remained silent, watching her, his mouth open, his breaths audible. Every inhalation made his broad chest expand, and sent ripples through the muscles flexing down over his stomach. His body was just spectacular, every inch of him hard, with powerful shoulders, thick, strong arms, and that amazing chest with a dark swirl of hair that trailed down his belly, dissecting a mouthwatering six-pack. His jeans hung loosely from his hips, and as his cock grew even thicker and longer, they sagged lower, revealing all of him.

Leanne grabbed the counter, steadying herself on suddenly-weak thighs. Yes, she wanted, she hungered, she lusted. But the man was more than a little intimidating.

"That would probably be a bad idea," he admitted, sounding reasonable, even as his body told her he wanted her just as desperately as she wanted him.

"I'm aware."

"You had a very rough day."

"I know that, too. But you made it better," she whispered, releasing the counter so she could approach him. Her steps were tiny; she saw the uncertainty in his expression. He was torn between wanting to push past her and leave, and wanting to push her up against the wall and screw her brains out. Frankly, she was more than hoping for option B...she wouldn't accept anything less.

"My point is, only a scumbag would take advantage of a woman who might be a little out-of-sorts after having been mugged a few hours ago."

"I've never been more in-sorts," she insisted, moving to block his path to the door. She lifted a hand and slid a ponytail holder from her hair, letting the long, thick strands fall loose over her shoulders. A few dangled over her breasts, and even the sensation of her own soft hair on her nipples gave her an unexpected jolt of pleasure.

She'd never been this utterly in tune with her senses before. Never been this aroused at just the thought of being with someone. They hadn't touched, hadn't kissed, he hadn't even consented. But the sexual tension roaring between them was unlike anything she'd ever experienced.

He edged back an inch. "Sam would kill me."

She edged forward. "It's none of his business."

Another inch. "*Eve* would kill me."

"Actually, she might give you a medal. She's been hoping I'll meet someone." Someone who wasn't Ned. Although she'd never said so, Eve obviously disapproved of Leanne dating her colleague, who, per Diana, sounded like someone with a stick planted firmly up his ass. Which was sort of true.

"I'm not relationship material," he said.

She shifted closer, until her bare feet were touching his, and his rough jeans scraped against her calves. Lifting a hand, she traced her fingertips along his collarbone. When she reached his shoulder, she gently dug her nails in. She played the seducer like she actually knew what she was doing, when, in truth, she was going purely on instinct here. "I'm not looking for a relationship. I'm more interested in a...a fling."

"I'm not fling material, either."

Stubborn man. "What type of material are you?"

He groaned, covering her hand with his own, forestalling her movements. "I'm the type who would fuck you until you couldn't remember your own name tonight and not call you tomorrow."

She sensed he was being intentionally gruff, trying to scare her off. If so, his strategy had backfired. His words had turned her on even more, if that was possible. Never having been with a dirty-talking man, she had never realized how powerful and sexy such rough language could be.

"I don't think I've ever had amnesia," she mused, more than a little interested in the idea of forgetting her own name.

A tiny hint of a smile. "You're asking for it."

"I'm begging for it," she admitted, not even hesitating. Leanne wasn't always reckless and daring, but now that she'd set her mind on a course of action, and had a goal in sight—one heated night with the sexiest man she'd ever met—she wasn't going to relent.

"One night, huh?"

"Yes. As long as you think once would get me out of your system," she purred.

He barked a laugh. "You're sure you're in my system?"

"Judging by the way you look at my mouth every time you see me, I suspect you've been having some very naughty thoughts about me."

His eyes gleamed. "You think so?"

"Oh, yes."

A brief pause, and then he admitted, "You might be right."

Relief and excitement roared through her. "Tell me," she urged.

"You want to hear I've thought about you sucking my cock?"

She swallowed hard and nodded.

His hand tightened on hers. "Yeah. I've thought about it. From the minute you pursed those lips at me at the wedding, I've pictured them wrapped around me."

She licked her lips, unable to help it. Leanne had certainly sucked a few in her day, but more out of a tit-for-tat sense of obligation. Now, well, she was thinking very seriously about dropping to her knees before him, like a harem girl, and gobbling him up just because she wanted to know how he tasted.

"I've jerked off thinking about you, right here in this shower.

Came so hard I thought I was gonna pass out," he finally admitted.

"Oh," she whispered.

"Have I shocked you? Are you saying you haven't had the same kinds of thoughts?" he asked. "Are you telling me that after the way we kissed, you didn't once think about it?"

She laughed softly. "I'm telling you that after the way we kissed, I laid in my bed and fingered myself, imagining it was you touching me."

"Oh God," he muttered, his hand tightening. Jake's voice lowered, thickened. "I've pictured you lying on top of me, 69-style, your thighs on either side of my head so I could eat you out while I fucked that pretty mouth of yours."

"Oh, my," she groaned, feeling a wave of warm, liquid want surge to her sex. Barely a touch and she was aching for him, wet, swollen and ready. "Is that the only part of me you want to…to fuck?"

He moved slowly, stepping closer, sliding one jean-clad leg between her bare thighs. Releasing her hand, he lowered his own, tracing a path down her body, his knuckles brushing the sides of her breasts as he moved between them. By the time those fingers reached her groin, she was whimpering, and when he tangled them in the curls between her legs, she let out a tiny sigh.

"This would be good, too," he admitted, sliding one strong finger between the lips of her sex. "I've dreamed about being in your pussy even more than I've fantasized about your mouth."

She gasped with pleasure as he circled her clit, stroking her with exquisite precision, before moving deeper. Leanne parted her legs a little to accommodate him, wanting him inside her more than she wanted to live to see the sun rise again. And he gave her what she wanted, gently moving between her folds to drive a finger into her.

"You're so wet," he said with a guttural groan as he added another finger, slowly plunging them both into her and setting a steady rhythm.

"Wet enough to take everything you've got to give me," she said, almost crying at how good she felt. He'd shifted so his hand cupped the front of her groin, and he pressed hard on her clit with his palm as he continued to make love to her with those strong fingers. Leanne had to reach out to put her hand on the wall behind him in order to steady herself. Her energy seemed to be draining away, along with thought and inhibition.

She was dying for him. And he still hadn't even kissed her.

"Take me, Jake. Take me so hard I can't even remember my own name, much less what happened to me tonight."

He slowly withdrew his fingers, pulling his hand out from between her thighs, which made her want to scream in frustration. "I can't..."

"Yes, you can," she insisted, reaching up to pull his face closer to hers. She was dying for his lips, his tongue, his body. "You're worrying too much about other people."

"No," he said as he reached up to tangle his hand in her hair. "I'm worrying about you."

"Well don't. I'm absolutely fine."

"But will you be tomorrow?"

"Maybe I don't even want you to call me tomorrow," she retorted, remembering his words.

One brow went up. "Words meant by no woman, ever."

She flushed. "Look, I have someone to take me out to a fancy dinner every week."

He stiffened the tiniest bit. "The one who didn't bother coming to check on you after you cancelled tonight, and didn't call to make sure you got home safely?"

Nice of him to point those things out. No, she hadn't told Ned she'd been mugged, but it might have been nice for him to at least ask why she couldn't make it, or call her later at home to see if something had happened. Funny that Jake could immediately zero in on what had been so wrong about her supposed boyfriend's disinterest in her well-being.

"That probably shows you what a lack of intimacy there is between us. I have no interest in him physically. We've never…"

"Good," he said, cutting her off. "Any real lover who couldn't hear the tension in your voice tonight and know something was seriously wrong would deserve to be beaten."

"Can we please stop talking about him?"

"You brought it up."

"I did, but only to make you understand that I'm not looking for more than you want to give. I'm not thinking about tomorrow. Tonight is all that's on my mind."

"It's already tomorrow. Do you know what time it is?" he said, throwing up false arguments.

"I don't care, and neither do you. I promise you, I won't regret it. I'm fine with one night of pleasure that remains our secret." She rose on tiptoe to brush her lips against his, flicking out her tongue to taste him, to tempt him. "Give me tonight and I won't ask for anything else from you, ever again." She wrapped both arms around his neck, pressing herself hard against him, loving the way his wiry chest hair scraped against her nipples and that big, hard cock pressed against her belly. "No one will ever know."

He pressed his lips against her temple and breathed deeply, rubbing his slightly rough, unshaven cheek against her hair. She could feel his resistance easing, along with his rigid stance.

Other parts of him remained very rigid, indeed. Fortunately.

"Please, Jake," she whispered. "I need you."

She'd admitted it to him, and to herself. She *did* need him. Leanne needed his kiss and his touch. She hadn't had a lover since her ex had broken her heart more than eighteen months ago, and every night of those eighteen months seemed to now be taunting her with all the sensuality she'd missed out on. She didn't regret not having those nights with her ex. Because, oh, God, she had no doubt Jake would erase the memory of every other lover from her mind. His touch would set a high bar, that she knew, but it was a risk she was willing to take.

"Make me yours. Just for tonight."

"Mine," he said with a guttural groan. And finally, stopped resisting.

Cupping her head in his hand, he caught her mouth in a fiery kiss. His tongue plunged deep, demanding her utter surrender. She gave it, gladly, every molecule in her body on fire for him. Wanting every bit of him she could get, she tilted her head, meeting each of his thrusts with a hot, wet one of her own. Their tongues tangled and twisted, and she was vaguely aware that he was shoving his jeans off his hips and out of the way.

Very glad he was the kind of man who went commando, she lifted a leg, wrapping it around his bare thigh, arching her groin toward his.

"You on something?" he muttered as he grabbed both of her hips and lifted her high, his cock nudging into her slick lips.

"Yes," she said, very glad about that. "And if you say we don't need a condom for other reasons, I trust you."

"Ditto," he replied, catching her meaning.

"Then take me," she commanded, gripping two handfuls of his hair. "Right here and now, the rest of it can come later."

She wanted everything—all the sensuality she could get, including those oral delights he'd mentioned earlier. But right now, she just wanted him to fill her up.

"Hold on," he ordered, backing her against the wall as he gripped her thighs and spread her open for him. She held her breath as she felt that warm, silky cock begin to glide into her. His movements were slow and easy, which was not what she wanted, so she groaned and pushed against him, demanding more.

"You want to be fucked, is that it?"

"Until I don't remember my own name. Keep your promise."

"Consider it kept," he growled, thrusting into her, hard, deep, fast and merciless.

She threw her head back and let out a long, low moan of satisfaction. He was buried inside her, to the hilt, filling every bit of her, and nothing in the world had ever been so right.

"You're so tight, Leanne," he said, burying his face in her hair and staying very still, as if giving her time to catch up and adjust.

"I can take it," she insisted, flexing all her internal muscles, squeezing him, demanding more.

It was his turn to moan as he drew out of her and then plunged deep again, carving a place for himself deeper inside her body than anybody had ever been. Leanne gasped at the sensation, breathing heavily as she adjusted to the sheer size of him.

He thrust again, and again, and she arched to meet him every time. Their mouths crashed together, teeth banging, tongues mating wildly. Each breath was shared between them and the small bathroom grew steamy and hot. The skin beneath her fingertips grew slick with sweat as he pounded her into the wall, and she dug her nails in, scratching him, driven wild with sweet, rough passion.

"Gonna make it up to you," he muttered as he sped up, draining her, filling her, over and over, faster and hotter and harder. "But I've got to…"

"Yes," she demanded, knowing he'd make good on his promise. They had the rest of the night—this one wicked, wild night—to do lots of sinful things, and she looked forward to doing every one of them. But now, right at this second, she just wanted him to lose the last remnants of his control and come inside her.

"Come with me," he ordered.

She couldn't, not at this angle, and was about to say so. Before she could, however, he swung her around to sit her on the edge of the counter. She hissed at the feel of cold marble pressed on her ass, but couldn't bring herself to mind. Because the position gave Jake one of his hands back, and he dropped his thumb to her clit, flicking, stroking, urging her on. He continued to kiss her, his tongue thrusting in time to every deep, hard thrust of his cock and each firm swirl of his thumb.

In seconds, she was flying, pulses of warm delight surging from her pussy throughout the rest of her body, each pounding beat of her heart sending the pulses further along her neural pathways. She was shaken to the core by it, never having been aware of just how good she could feel, as wave after wave of heady, delirious, gorgeous pleasure washed over her.

Only after she threw her head back and screamed with the perfection of it did Jake let himself follow, driving into her one last time, shouting as he came. And then, not removing himself from her body, he scooped her up, carried her into his bedroom, and collapsed with her on his bed.

HE HAD ONE night, only one, and Jake intended to take advantage of every second of it.

After that first time in the bathroom, they'd fallen into a brief sleep on his bed, sheer exhaustion overwhelming them. But when he awoke, glancing at the clock to see it was after three a.m., he realized he wasn't going to waste another minute of the time he had.

So while Leanne slept, he began to explore her body. With his hands, with his mouth, with his tongue. She was soft all over, her skin scented with something flowery and fragrant. Jake buried his face in her throat, breathing her in, loving that fragrance that was uniquely hers—a combination of lotion or something, plus sweet, sexy Leanne.

Tasting her, licking her, biting her lightly, he moved down her body, stopping to enjoy those beautiful, shapely breasts, sucking her nipples until she cried out and came awake beneath him.

"I didn't mean to fall asleep," she whispered, her voice a throaty purr, tangling her fingers in his hair.

"It's okay, you don't have to wake up on my account. I'm doing just fine here."

"Yes, you are," she said with a soft laugh, arching toward his mouth as he continued moving down her front. He kissed her midriff, rubbed his cheek on her stomach, dipped his tongue into her belly button. Leanne was moving restlessly beneath him, obviously anxious for him to reach his final destination.

Which was why he took his damn sweet time getting there.

Instead of burying his face in her crotch and thrusting his tongue into her warm, wet depths, he kissed his way down her body. He paused to explore the soft skin at the back of her knee, then her calves, right to the tips of her toes. Every inch of her was silky smooth, and by the time he worked his way back up the other leg, his mouth was watering for a taste of her most intimate secrets.

"Oh, please, Jake," she said, her words coming on tiny gasps as his mouth brushed across the soft nest of curls at the top of her thighs.

"Please what?"

"You know what."

"I want to hear you say it." Leanne had thrown off her inhibitions tonight, becoming a sultry, erotic woman he'd never have envisioned when he first met her at the wedding. He liked that edge and wanted to push her as far as he could.

"Please taste me—use your mouth on me."

He continued to hold off. "I think that's what I've been doing."

She groaned. "Paybacks are hell, you know."

He considered the way she might pay him back. "Actually, I think they can also be heaven."

"If you want to visit heaven, then please, give me what I need."

He bit her inner thigh. "What is it you need, Leanne? You gotta ask if you want to receive."

She whimpered. "I need your mouth. Your tongue."

"Where?"

"You know where."

He moved to her drenched lips, licking between them, loving the taste of her. "Here?"

"Oh yes."

"You have to say it," he commanded.

"Say…"

"Tell me what you want. Make me believe you really want it."

She groaned and dug her fingernails into his shoulders. A heartbeat—he knew she was shucking off the last of those good-girl instincts—and then she snapped, "Eat my pussy, Jake. Please, lick me, fuck me with your tongue and make me come."

Her words inflamed him; he wanted to applaud as the last of her reservations melted away. He wanted nothing proper between them, wanted the earthy, sexy, sensual woman he was fast becoming addicted to, and at last he'd gotten her.

"My pleasure," he murmured.

Knowing how to drive her wild, he slid his tongue into her tight channel, pleasuring her slowly. She began to tremble, then to shake. And when he moved up to gently suck her clit, her hips rose off the bed.

Fingering her to orgasm had been fantastic. But this...controlling her pleasure as he savored the taste of her, was beyond amazing. Her tiny whimpers of helpless delight were music to his ears, and he knew she was close to climaxing when she tightened her thighs around his neck.

"Come in my mouth," he ordered her. "Right now, Leanne."

Another flick of his tongue on that sensitive, pretty, little nub, and she did exactly that, crying out as shudders rolled through her body. Jake didn't even wait until they'd died from her lips before he slid up to catch her mouth in a kiss, sliding his cock into her in one slow, easy thrust. She was hot and wet, so fucking tight. He'd only had her once before, but already equated sliding into her willing body as something like coming home.

She wrapped her legs around his hips, gripping him tightly, and rocked up to meet him.

"You taste good," he whispered, kissing her face, her jaw, her neck.

"I want to be able to say the same," she said with a tiny pout. She sucked on his bottom lip, reminding him of how she'd promised to use her mouth on him. He thought about pulling out and letting her, but frankly, she felt too damn warm and heavenly to even think about leaving her.

He swallowed hard. "Next time."

"How many times will there be?"

"As many as I can get in one night."

She nodded, and then words failed them as they thrust and rocked, gave and took. It went on and on. He eventually rolled over onto his back, and she straddled him, riding him. He loved the sensation, but also loved looking up at her beautiful face, cupping those swaying breasts, tweaking her nipples.

He couldn't say how long it went on, or how many times and in how many positions they'd done it. He just knew that, by the time the sun shone into his face and awakened him the next morning, after they'd slept and had sex several more times, he felt entirely drained, not only of energy but of cum. She'd wrung him out completely. Honestly though, waking up to find her curled in his arms was one of the best moments of his year, almost better than the sex. Almost.

She yawned sleepily, but didn't open her eyes. Somehow sensing he was awake, she mumbled, "What time is it?"

"It's after nine."

"Uh-oh. I'm late for work."

"Me too."

"Aren't you self-employed?"

"Yeah, and my office is downstairs. But I still like to keep to my schedule.

Sliding an arm around his waist and a leg between his thighs, she said, "Where's room service with our coffee?"

Jake kissed the tip of her noise. "Your wish, babe." Getting up, he grabbed a pair of gym shorts and pulled them on.

"And bring me some of those Girl Scout cookies," she said. "You promised me thin mints."

He laughed. "Breakfast of champions."

"Or at least Girl Scouts."

A broad smile on his face, he went downstairs to put the coffee-pot on. He had no idea how she took hers, so he threw some milk and sugar on a big cookie sheet that would have to double as a tray, along with nearly-filled mugs and a sleeve of cookies. Before he could carry everything back upstairs, however, he heard someone knocking insistently at his front door.

Rubbing a hand over his eyes, trying to remember if he'd forgot-ten a morning appointment, he left the loaded cookie sheet on the counter and walked out of the kitchen, down the short hallway to the door. A quick look out the peephole revealed a face he'd never expected to see.

Disengaging the locks, he pulled the door open. "Sam? What are you doing here?"

His brother didn't wait for an invitation, pushing past him to enter the house. It wasn't the first time he'd come over, but he never stopped by without calling first. Jake supposed that was kind of what brothers did, and part of him didn't mind so much. Another part— the part anxious to get back upstairs to Leanne and to protect the secret of her presence—wasn't so sure.

"Have you talked to Leanne Weston since last night?"

Feigning nonchalance, he crossed his arms over his chest and leaned a shoulder against the wall, watching as his brother paced the small entranceway. "Why do you ask?"

"Because her place was robbed."

"Oh."

"*Oh*? Is that all you have to say?" Sam stopped pacing and glared at him.

"How did you hear about it?"

"It was in this morning's crime blotter on the local paper's website."

"That was fast."

"Yeah. Fortunately, Eve hasn't seen it yet. I immediately tried calling Leanne and couldn't get her on her cell…"

"That was in her purse. It's gone."

"I couldn't reach her at home or at work either. They said she hasn't come in yet, and she hasn't called," Sam continued. "I need to find Leanne and make sure she's okay before my wife finds out and loses her mind. So what do you know?"

"Leanne's fine."

Sam visibly relaxed. "You followed her all the way home last night?"

"Right to her door. And I stayed with her for the next few hours while the police did their investigation."

"Thank God," Sam said, the tension easing out of his rigid form. "Okay, I can breathe now. Where is she?"

"Does it matter?"

Sam frowned. "Of course it matters."

Jake thought of her upstairs in his bed, warm, naked, sated. But they'd agreed last night would be their secret. He didn't particularly want anybody in his business, including his brother. And if Leanne wanted Eve to know where she'd slept last night, she'd tell her friend herself.

"She realized there had been a spare key in her bag—she'd meant to give it to Eve."

"Oh, shit."

"Yeah, bad luck. That's how the thief got in. Anyway, there's no way she could stay there until she gets her locks changed, so I had her pack up a few things and I followed her to someplace safe for the night." He shrugged, completely comfortable with his words, since they weren't actually lies. "I'm sure she'll call Eve and fill her in later."

Sam nodded slowly, accepting the explanation, but his brow was still furrowed, as if he couldn't quite figure something out. Without saying a word, he turned around and walked to the window beside the front door, peering out at the parking lot in front of the row of townhouses. Jake thought about Leanne's car, parked nearby, but didn't worry too much. It was a very typical gray sedan, nothing really unique about it.

After a long moment, Sam turned around, and came closer. His green eyes—so like Jake's own, were narrowed, and his frown had deepened. Before Jake could open his mouth to try to throw off suspicion again, his two-days-younger brother shocked the shit out of him by forming a fist and swinging it at Jake's jaw.

The punch landed. Hard. Jake's head jerked back, and he immediately lifted a hand to rub his jaw. "Dude, what the hell?"

"If Leanne is not upstairs in your room, you feel free to punch me back," his brother growled.

Jake eyed Sam warily.

"Actually," Sam added, "I still owed you that after the shit you pulled at the wedding, so if Leanne is *not* upstairs in your room, let's call it payback for the way you kissed my wife, and believe me, it's not half as much as you deserve."

Having been hit by his brother before, Jake knew Sam had pulled the punch, not swinging at him with his full strength. That was a good thing, since Sam was a brawny, powerful guy, and could probably dislocate Jake's jaw if he gave it his all. And something that serious might require Jake to hit back. Wouldn't be the first time, but he'd really rather not.

"Now, you gonna tell me why I just punched you?" Sam asked.

"I'd think you'd be better equipped explain that."

"I mean, confirm it for me," Sam snapped. He jabbed an index finger in Jake's face. "Tell me you did not bring a sweet, vulnerable woman—my wife's best goddamn friend—back here last night and take advantage of her."

Considering she was the one who'd dropped her robe and initiated things, he could honestly shake his head. "I did not take advantage of her."

Sam groaned, obviously reading between the lines. "Semantics." He thrust a hand through his blondish-brown hair. "How could you, man?"

"I wasn't going to leave her there. I offered to sleep on the couch at her place, but she wanted to go. She had no cash, no credit cards, no ID, and it was midnight. She didn't want to wake you guys up."

"So you couldn't resist dogging on her, huh?"

"You know she's not my type," Jake said, still hedging around the truth. "She's an ice princess, bro, a total stick. I like my women with a little hot blood in their veins. Having sex with her would be like boning a statue."

He could have spoken those words the day he'd met Leanne, but having gotten to know her in the ensuing weeks—and having spent one amazingly hot night in her arms—he knew they weren't true anymore. Sam, however, didn't need to know that.

"She's also gorgeous," Sam snapped, not believing him. "And if she actually slept in the spare room, I will call you friggin' Sir Galahad, but I somehow suspect she didn't."

"Does that make you Lancelot?"

Hearing Leanne's firm, steady voice, Jake jerked his head and saw her descending the stairs. She was wearing a pair of pressed khakis and a red sweater, and her glorious hair was looped up into a loose bun. She looked fresh and fine, totally safe, and not at all the subject of a long, full night of his erotic obsession. He could only think how easily the clothes made the man—or the woman. Because nobody would guess that beneath those clothes were red marks, abrasions from his bristle, love bites...he'd devoured her and had most definitely left his mark.

Curse his brother for showing up before he could leave some more.

"Hello, Sam," she said.

"Lee—thank God you're all right. I heard about what happened." Sam went to meet her at the bottom of the stairs, taking her hand and squeezing it. "Are you sure you're okay?"

"I'm fine, thank you. Jake was very nice to offer me a place to stay. I just didn't want to bother you and Eve at such a late hour."

"You know we wouldn't have minded."

"I know that. But I was exhausted and just wanted to collapse someplace, without having to talk about the robbery with anyone else."

"I'm so sorry about everything that happened last night."

"Me too," she said with a heavy sigh. "I'm going to have a lot of phone calls and paperwork to deal with today. I just called my landlord and he's going to have a locksmith meet me at my place in a little while to change out the locks."

"Good," Sam said. "Take Jake with you."

He wouldn't have it any other way. "I'd be happy to…"

"No," she insisted, cutting Jake off. "It's really not necessary." She looked at him, those cool gray eyes of hers revealing nothing, not a hint of the passion, the sparkle, the secrets they'd revealed during the long night hours. "You've done quite enough for me, Mr. Montez, by offering me your spare room and bringing me here. I couldn't trouble you further."

Mr. Montez? Seriously? Was this the woman whose pussy he could still smell on his cheeks? The one to whom he'd given orgasm after orgasm during the long, lust-filled night? She obviously hadn't been kidding about wanting to pretend their sex-fest had never happened, and not giving the slightest hint about it to anybody else.

He understood, of course. Sam's arrival here couldn't have come at a worse time. Of all people she wanted to keep their one-night-stand hidden from, it would be his brother and her best friend. He got that, totally.

But still, something inside him tightened and throbbed at how easily she'd gone back into her aloof, professional mode.

One night. That's all you wanted, that's all you get.

Meaning he had to be as cool as she was, had to pretend it hadn't mattered a damn, or that it hadn't even happened. Which was why he looked at her, shrugged, and said, "Whatever."

Sam shot him a glare. "The least you can do is check over her place and make sure it's secure. I'd do it myself, but you're the expert."

"She's getting new locks." He cast her a questioning glance. "Deadbolts?"

"Yes, the landlord is very accommodating."

"Then that oughta do," he said, crossing his arms over his bare chest. "I'm sure Miz Weston is smart enough to check a few window locks."

She stiffened the tiniest bit, that sharp little chin coming up. If he weren't so certain she didn't want anything else to do with him, and wanted to pretend she hadn't spent last night in his bed, he'd think she was hurt. Jake was hit with a punch of regret for having sounded so uninterested, when, in truth, he was very anxious to make sure she was okay. He just hadn't wanted Sam to know that. Or her, to be honest.

Still, maybe it was for the best. If she was a bit hurt, or if he was, it would be easier to let last night go, to leave it as a one-night-stand they could both forget about. Leanne was already on her way to doing that, judging by how calm and distant she appeared to be. More than words, her very body language told him how little she wanted his involvement in her life.

So be it.

"Thank you again for coming to check on me, Sam," she said, sounding so formal they might as well be in a courtroom. "Please let Eve know I'm fine and I'll call her later." Glancing at Jake, as expressionless as she'd been toward his brother, she explained, "I really need to get going. I want to stop by my office before heading home. So I won't be staying for coffee."

No coffee in bed. No lazy morning sex. No intimacy at all.

The ice princess was definitely back.

Fine. Great. Go.

He tried to believe he wanted her to do just that, but he'd never been very good at lying, at least not to himself. So the most he could manage was a mumbled, "Okay."

Their stares met and locked. He searched for a gleam of warmth, of humor, of a shared secret. But he saw nothing. Just…nothing.

Jake had never before met a woman who was so good at hiding— or compartmentalizing—her feelings. She'd said she would be fine with one night and no subsequent phone call, and judging by her expression and utter lack of emotion, she'd been right.

Most guys would probably be singing hallelujah at that. Jake knew he should be. But right now, all he felt was…numb.

"I just need to get my things. Goodbye, Sam," she said, turning around and ascending the stairs.

Jake walked to the bottom of the staircase, dropped a hand on the bannister, and watched her go. Gone was the erotic angel. Her spine was ramrod straight. Those curvy hips and that beautiful ass didn't wiggle in the slightest, as if she were a soldier marching in formation. Any softness or longing she'd allowed herself to display during the night was firmly in check. He'd like to think it was because she knew Sam was below, possibly watching. But he suspected, instead, that it was merely Leanne's way of maintaining control, from the top of her head to the bottom of her feet, not showing an ounce of vulnerability.

You agreed to this. One night. You didn't want anything beyond that any more than she did.

True. But right now, he was wondering if he'd made a mistake. A *huge* mistake.

He cleared his throat and turned around to face his brother, intending to show him to the door and then go upstairs to make sure Leanne was okay—that she hadn't frozen up for any reason other than Sam's arrival. God, he hoped she hadn't heard his words to his brother before she'd come downstairs. But he quickly shrugged off that worry. It wouldn't have mattered if she had. She had to know he'd been trying to throw Sam off the scent by claiming he wasn't attracted to her because he liked women with blood in their veins. After the night he and Leanne had shared, he knew damn well how hot-blooded she could be, when she let herself. And she had to know how much he had wanted her.

Still, he would talk to her, just to make sure they were clear, on that score at least. Whether they ever saw each other again, she had to know last night was one for the record books as far as Jake was concerned.

But first, he needed to get rid of Sam. "Okay then, are we…"

He was about to say *good* when he saw his brother's fist flying toward his head again. This time, seeing the anger in Sam's eyes, and realizing the other man probably wasn't holding anything back, Jake ducked and twisted out of the way. Throwing a hand up, he grabbed his brother's fist. "What the fuck was that for?"

Sam lowered his head like a bull and stepped closer until they were almost nose-to-nose. "That was for the scratches on your back, you lying son of a bitch." He threw Jake's hand off, turned and stalked toward the door, shaking with anger. It was as if he knew he had to get out before they really did have a knock-down, drag-out fight on the floor. "And for whatever the hell you did to make Leanne freeze up like that."

Without another word, without allowing Jake to speak in his own defense—and really, what could he say?—Sam yanked the door open and stormed through it.

Leaving Jake to wonder just how much ground he'd lost with his brother when he'd decided to take what the beautiful woman upstairs had so readily offered him last night.

Chapter 6

LEANNE WANTED TO go straight home after leaving Jake's place. She was in desperate need of a hot shower, and had been unwilling to stay at his house long enough to take one. But her landlord had called her back this morning, saying the locksmith couldn't get there until almost noon. So she headed for the office, knowing anyplace was better than Jake's.

She just couldn't spend the morning with him. Couldn't have coffee with him. Couldn't remain calm and cool and emotionless. Not after the night they'd spent together. Not now that she had been slapped with the white-hot face of reality with the morning sun.

Sam's arrival had been poorly timed. Her descent down the stairs to hear Jake's conversation with his brother had been even worse. Even now, an hour later, she couldn't get his comments about her out of her head.

Cold. Stick. Ice queen. Statue. All other ways of saying she was frigid.

After Sam had left, Jake had come upstairs and told her he'd just been trying to throw his brother off-track, to pretend he wasn't even attracted to her. He'd insisted the night they'd spent had been amazing, one he'd never forget.

She'd believed him, for the most part. No man could have made love to her the way he had if he didn't enjoy being in her arms. And the night had definitely been one *she* would never forget.

Yet, when he'd been talking to Sam, Leanne had heard something in his voice that rang a little bit too true. He might have been thinking off the top of his head, but he hadn't had to go too far in his thoughts to figure out what to say about her to his sibling. Maybe last night had shown him she was capable of thawing out and heating up, but *before* last night, she'd bet he really had believed her to be all those things. Cold, frigid, unbending, unfeminine.

That's what he'd thought of her. That's also what Ned obviously thought of her, considering he had never once even tried to get her into bed. And that's what her ex, Sloan, had said to her face a year and a half ago when he'd dumped her for somebody who—how had he worded it?—actually knew how to let loose and have a good time.

Which, apparently, Leanne did not.

"Well you sure did last night," she reminded herself as she pulled her car into her parking space at the office. Of course, Sloan had never given her multiple orgasms or performed the kind of intimate acts on her that Jake had last night. Nobody ever had.

The thought of those acts was enough to make her shake in her seat. She had to remain in the car, clutching the steering wheel, for a few minutes before going inside, just to allow herself to process the long, erotic hours she'd experienced.

Sitting there, heat rushing through her body despite the fact that the interior of the car was growing colder by the second, she realized something. As much as it had hurt her to realize Jake had met her and seen something lacking, as other men before him had, she couldn't regret last night. Even if she'd had to talk him into it—to practically beg him to have sex with her, dropping her robe the way she had—she couldn't be mad at herself, or at him. It had been an amazing, remarkable, once-in-a-lifetime erotic marathon.

No, she had no regrets. Even if, in the brutal light of morning, she'd been reminded that she wasn't the type of warm, sultry, sexy woman men lost their heads over. Throughout those long, heated hours, she'd been enough for Jake Montez. She'd been *more* than enough. Not cold, not frigid, not unyielding. She'd been utterly on fire, and he'd burned up right along with her. And that truth would console her through any long, lonely nights in the future, with Ned or with anyone else.

Not Jake, though.

No, not Jake. She'd told him she would expect or ask for nothing beyond one night, and she intended to keep her word. Not that she didn't still want him, but she knew, in the long run, that it wouldn't be wise to go back for seconds. Or fiftieths. She might have been enough to satisfy a man like him for one night, but she'd never be enough to hold his interest for very long.

Because, in truth, she probably was the controlled, cold, ice princess he claimed her to be. She had goals, personally and professionally, and would never allow her emotions—or her sex drive—to interfere with them. Having grown up with one hand in a garbage can and another reaching for the stars, she knew better than to allow feelings to win out over intellect. She loved her mother— adored her—but there was no way in hell she would ever follow in the other woman's footsteps.

And frankly, her emotions were already too in a whirl when it came to Jake. He could anger her with a look, arouse her with a touch, infuriate her with a smirk, and intoxicate her with a kiss. The more time they spent together—in bed and out of it—the more she would want him, while his interest would almost certainly cool.

No, she had to be happy to have had her one night and never think about anything more. It was better that way. Safer. For both of them.

A tap sounded on her window, startling her, and Leanne looked up to see Sherry, the office secretary, standing beside her car.

"Hey, are you okay?" the woman asked.

She opened the door. "I'm fine."

"I've been watching you out the window and I was getting worried."

"Oh, sorry, just have a lot on my mind."

"I'll bet you do!"

Leanne turned to grab her purse. Then she remembered—she had no purse, no wallet, no money, no anything. God. "I, uh, sorry, it's been a crazy morning. I just wanted to come by and talk to Ned. Uh…something happened last night."

"He knows. We all do. Are you okay?"

"I'm fine," she said, a bit worried, but also relieved that she wouldn't have to explain everything to Ned. "How did you find out?"

"The police officer who was here with you came by this morning to check on you. He told us you'd been mugged in the parking lot last night. Ned was pretty upset."

Leanne allowed a tiny smile to pull at her lips as she exited the car. Maybe she'd misjudged the man she'd been dating.

"He had us all go through the building, top to bottom, to make sure there was nothing wrong inside and nobody had tried to jimmy any windows or anything."

He'd been worried about the office. Not about her. Deflated, she mumbled, "Oh."

She told herself her disappointment was unfair, that he might have been tearing his hair out with worry for her, especially since he wouldn't have been able to reach her this morning. She was late for work, she hadn't called, she no longer had a cell phone, and she hadn't been at home. He was probably worried sick and had set the staff to work to distract himself from his own fears.

Of course, when she walked into the office and saw the way he stiffened and frowned at her, she began to suspect she'd been indulging in a little wishful thinking.

"You're late. Where have you been?" he snapped.

If his words had been accompanied by a stalk-over so he could grab her into his arms and hug her, she might not have been quite as angered by his tone.

"I had a bad night."

"Yes, I heard. The police said you were mugged in the parking lot. I assume you walked through the building to make sure all the doors and windows were locked?"

She gritted her teeth. "Yes, of course. And I double-checked the security system when I left."

"Good," he mumbled. "I can't imagine why anybody would target us when there are electronics stores up the street, but you never know."

Us. The business. Not her. The victim.

"The officer said it was a crime of opportunity." Then, her tone pointed, she added, "Apparently *I* was just in the wrong place at the wrong time."

He must have heard her tension. "Yes, of course. Uh, are you okay?"

She nodded, lifting her hands to show him her still-swollen, scratched up palms. "My nails might not recover anytime soon, but this is about it for injuries."

He smoothed his suit and straightened his tie. It took her a moment to realize he was intentionally busying his hands, perhaps so he wouldn't reach out to touch her, with even a consoling brush of his fingers on hers, in front of staff. Good lord.

"Well, I'm glad you weren't seriously hurt," he said, so fussily she wondered if he truly had an aversion to offering sympathy to anyone, or if it was just directed at her, the woman he was seeing. "I don't know what we would do without you around here."

"Thanks," she murmured, noting the coolness, the calculation of his reaction. God, was this how people—how Jake saw *her*? Would she remain so utterly emotionless to a friend, much less somebody she was dating, if she knew he'd been the victim of a violent crime?

No. There was such a thing as propriety. And then there was such a thing as humanity. Ned was all about propriety, while Jake probably didn't acknowledge the word's existence. As for humanity, the gruff, motorcycle-riding bad boy had shown more of it last night than Ned had in the eighteen months she'd worked for him.

How strange. How very strange.

Just because she was curious about how far he would take this we're-not-at-all-personally-involved bit, she cleared her throat. "I'm not staying. I just came in to get something out of my office," she said. "I have to go back to my place to meet the locksmith to change the locks on my apartment door."

He frowned. "I thought the officer said the robber didn't get your keys." He immediately stared at the front door to Longotti Lines. "Don't tell me we're going to have to re-key the whole building! Do you have any idea how much that will cost?"

Bristling, she admitted, "I had a spare key to my apartment in my wallet. He didn't get my office keys."

Ned nodded, visibly relieved. "Oh, all right then."

"Unfortunately, however," she went on, struggling to keep the sharpness from her voice, "the mugger found that key and robbed my place last night."

Sherry gasped and leapt from her chair, behind the reception desk. "Oh, no, honey!"

Ned actually took a few steps closer, finally putting a hand on her shoulder and displaying what might be genuine concern. "Seriously?"

She nodded.

"Were you there?"

"No, it happened while I was still here with the police. I went home and found my place in a shambles."

His hand squeezed a little, the fullest display of emotion and concern he would allow. A Sir Galahad he most definitely was not.

She thrust that thought out of her head. She didn't want to think about Jake playing Sir Galahad, because that reminded her of Sam's accusing words. And Jake's response to them.

Cold. An ice princess. A statue. A stick.

"I'm sorry."

"Thank you."

"That must have been quite a shock." He cast a glance at Sherry, who was watching wide-eyed, and stepped away, crossing his arms over his chest. "Did you, uh, call someone?"

IE: Did she call someone other than him, the man she was supposed to go out with last night? "A friend was with me," she replied. "My best friend's brother-in-law is a private detective, and she made sure he followed me home, so he was there when I discovered the robbery. He stayed with me during the police investigation."

And she had stayed with him afterward.

"Excellent," he said with a nod. "What better protection?"

"Indeed."

He didn't ask more about the man who'd escorted her home. Because he didn't believe she might actually attract the interest of another man? Because he didn't care? No clue. She only knew that, as Sherry went over to pour her a cup of coffee and then brought it and pressed it into Leanne's cold, shaking hands, Ned drew away, regaining that boss/employee distance he tried so hard to maintain around this place.

"Well, you take as much time as you need," he said, offering that little supercilious smile he usually gave to clients. "If you don't have enough vacation hours on the books, I'm sure we can work something out. Advance you some comp time or something."

"That won't be at all necessary," she said, really not believing he was going there. He was going to dicker over how much leave time she had? First, she'd been attacked in the parking lot of this building. And second, she hadn't even asked for any time off, beyond this morning. But his mind had gone to vacation hours and unpaid leave?

"That's good. It would probably be difficult to loop someone else in on the trade show. With it opening just a week from now, I'm sure we'll be very busy. Do you think you'll be up to working tomorrow?"

"I'm certain I will," she replied, keeping her tone cool, even as she clenched the coffee mug so hard she worried she'd break the damn thing. "But my laptop is gone. I'll need you to re-send me some of the files and documents."

He frowned. "Stolen?"

"Yes. It was taken from my apartment."

"How much material did you have on it? Anything proprietary to Longotti Lines? Mother wouldn't be happy to hear that."

"It was my personal laptop, so no, it was mostly my own designs and notes." And thankfully, not all of those, since most of the good stuff she did by hand and kept in her dream book. "But there are a few things. The files I worked on at home the night before last are gone."

"How unfortunate."

A familiar I'm-not-happy crease appeared between his eyes. Seeing it, Leanne was suddenly struck with a realization so sharp and profound, she almost dropped her mug.

She didn't like this man. She didn't like him at all.

She worked for him, and with him. She'd dated him. She'd kissed him. She respected him, in a lot of ways.

But she truly did not like him.

"Wow," she muttered, a little stunned at the realization. Perhaps it had been lurking in the back of her mind all along. Maybe that's why she'd never pushed things romantically, never tried to seduce him as she'd so quickly seduced Jake last night. She'd thought it had been because theirs was a relationship of common interests and intelligence, not physicality. Now, though, she realized the truth: She didn't want to sleep with the man, because he was an ass.

She never wanted to go to dinner at Josephine's on a Wednesday night again. Never wanted to be told she had to wear a dress, or low heels. Never wanted to feel she was less important than some files on a laptop, or locks on a building. Never wanted this man to touch her or kiss her again. And would never in a million years consider marrying him.

Suddenly, she just wanted to get out of here. She had to get away from him before she bluntly told him what she was thinking. Unless she was ready to start looking for a new job, that probably wouldn't be a great course of action.

"I have to go," she said, feeling a little light-headed. Her thoughts continued to spiral and swirl; she hadn't felt this confused and unsure of herself since God only knew when.

"Of course," he said.

"You sure you're okay to drive, honey?" asked Sherry, who looked back and forth between Leanne and Ned, as if catching some undercurrents. "You don't look so hot."

"I'm fine," she insisted, then handed the other woman the half-empty mug. "Thank you for being concerned, *Sherry*. Nice to know somebody's worried about me."

Let Ned make of that pointed comment what he would. Frankly, she didn't give a damn what he thought. Not anymore. Their relationship was going back to one of strictly business. Whatever else Jake had done for her, she definitely had to be grateful for one thing. He'd made her realize she wasn't going to be satisfied with a passionless, emotionless existence. She might have been telling herself for years that all she wanted was security, commitment, a home, and people who stayed. But the truth was, if those things didn't come with somebody she genuinely liked and respected, she'd probably be better off just living alone.

Which meant it was time to return to her own apartment. Even with its unsafe locks and all the cleaning to be done to make up for the invasion of last night, she'd be better off there than she would in a mansion with somebody who was more worried about company files than he was about her physical safety.

And even if she had nothing else to thank Jake Montez for, she would always thank him for that.

ALTHOUGH JAKE TRIED to get Leanne off his mind after she left Thursday morning, he just couldn't do it.

He threw himself into his work—even making himself send out some bills, one of his least favorite parts of the job, and something he always put off as long as possible. He went to the site of a construction company that wanted him to investigate possible employee theft. He stopped by The Slaughter House to see if his buddy was having any more gang problems. He dropped off some photographs of a very healthy former city employee out bowling with his buddies...while on disability for a bad back. But at the end of the day, he was still thinking only of Leanne.

"She's not okay," he told himself that evening as he unlocked his front door and went inside his house. "You know she's not."

This morning, before she'd left—minutes after Sam's unexpected arrival and departure—she'd sworn she was fine. She'd proclaimed herself ready to go back to work, to her apartment, to her real life. Ready to leave him and the night they'd spent together firmly in the past.

But he'd seen something in her eyes. They'd been clouded, stormy, perhaps hurt. And he couldn't stop thinking about what she might have overheard as she came downstairs that morning, when he'd been talking to Sam by the front door. She hadn't admitted to hearing anything, and she'd acted as though she believed him when he told her he'd made up some bullshit story about not being interested in her. She *had* to believe him when he said last night had been one of the most amazing of his life. If getting hard for her at least a half-dozen times, and having sex with her for hours on end couldn't convince her he was attracted to her, nothing could.

Still, he'd known when she left that something was seriously wrong. It wasn't just the slight discomfort of the morning-after departure from a one-night-stand. She was upset about something, and he wasn't going to be able to relax until he figured out if he'd caused her upset.

Which was why, when he went into the guest room and saw the forgotten hairbrush on the dresser, he immediately decided to return it to its owner.

Grabbing it, and a few boxes of cookies he thought she might enjoy, he headed out, heading for her neighborhood. He didn't call first, figuring she'd just tell him she could replace the brush. He needed to see her, to make sure she was okay. And, all right, for his own sanity.

You agreed to a one-night-stand.

Yeah. He had. But that didn't mean he was happy about it.

Reaching her part of town, he spied a pizza joint and decided dinner might be a good peace offering. Glad he was driving his truck, and not his motorcycle, he ordered a large pepperoni and went next door to grab a six-pack of beer to go with it. Though he knew she was probably more of a wine drinker, he certainly didn't have the expertise to pick something out.

Armed with food and beer, he headed for her apartment. Not entirely to his surprise, the front door of the building—which had been unlocked last night—wouldn't open. Apparently the landlord was more serious about security tonight. Good. Hopefully all the residents were a little more alert. He didn't think it was likely the thieves would come back—they had to know she would have had the locks changed. Still, better safe than sorry. Especially when it came to Leanne.

Seeing her buzzer, he pushed the button. Her car was in the lot; he knew she was home. He only hoped she would let him up when she heard his voice.

"Yes?"

"Hey, Leanne, it's Jake."

Silence.

"Jake Montez?"

He heard her sigh. "I figured that."

"Yeah, well, you forgot something at my place this morning. Thought I'd drop it by."

"Really?"

"Yep," he said, hoping she didn't ask what she'd forgotten. Brushes were easily replaceable, as far as he was concerned. Five bucks at Wal Mart and you're done, and hers was on the far end of well-used. Which probably meant he was gonna look stupid for having spent more on gas and pizza to bring hers back.

But...whatever. Another chance to see her made even the pro-spect of looking stupid worthwhile.

Clearing his throat, he added, "I figured you might not have gotten a chance to throw out all your food and go to the grocery store, so I brought some dinner."

Another long moment of silence. Then he heard a click and real-ized she'd remotely unlocked the door to the building. A smile on his face, he shifted the pizza to his other hand, held the six-pack under his arm, and went in. Taking the elevator up, he went to her door and knocked sharply.

"Jake?" she asked from within.

Good girl for being safety conscious. He'd noticed she didn't have a peephole and made a mental note to get her one and install it. Screw the landlord if he didn't like it—he was lucky Leanne wasn't the suing type, given how the main building locks hadn't been in use when she'd been robbed. "It's me."

"Hi," she said, opening the door to greet him.

Jake quickly looked her over, to gauge her mood and see if she was okay. She looked fine—more than fine, she couldn't help but look beautiful. Even dressed in jeans and a sweater, with her hair looped up in a ponytail, a smudge on her cheek, and a vague scent of cleanser wafting off her skin, he still found her incredibly sexy.

"Doing some cleaning?"

She nodded.

"I promised I'd help you with that."

"I didn't really expect you to."

"Well, I'm here now. Bearing food."

"That was very thoughtful," she said, eyeing the pizza box in his hand, and the beer under his arm. Finally, she stepped out of the way to usher him in. "But you really didn't have to do it."

"It's no trouble."

Heading into the kitchen, he put the pizza and the six-pack on the counter, along with the bag containing the cookies and the hairbrush, and looked around. Two large trash bags were on the floor, each filled with packages of food. She hadn't been kidding about throwing out everything the thieves might have come into contact with. Not that he blamed her.

"What did I forget?"

He grabbed the plastic bag and retrieved the brush. As he held it out, he tried to keep a straight face and hide the fact that it was slightly ridiculous for him to come over here tonight just because she'd forgotten something so minor.

"Oh, thank God," she said, grabbing it from his hands.

He brazened it out. "I, uh, didn't know if you had a spare."

"I have a dozen," she said, clutching the brush to her chest, "but none like this. I can't believe I forgot it."

It took him a second before he realized she was not shitting him. She really looked thrilled and appreciative about an old-looking, black-handled hairbrush that was missing more than a few bristles. "Seriously?"

She nodded, licking her lips. "This was my grandmother's. I use it every night."

Oh, wow.

"She died when I was little. I actually lived with her for a year in elementary school, during one of my mom's really bad phases." She ran a fine, fragile fingertip along the edge of the raggedy old brush, blinking rapidly, as if on the verge of tears. "I can't believe I forgot it. This is the only thing of hers I have."

Wishing he'd put it in a case or something, rather than tossing it into an old Acme bag, he stuffed his hands into the pockets of his jeans. "Uh, don't beat yourself up about it. Last night was pretty rough."

"Yes," she said, walking over to put the brush into what looked like a brand new purse.

"So was this morning," he added, his voice low, his tone holding the barest hint of a question.

She quickly glanced at him out of the corner of her eye, and then walked past him to the dishwasher. Ignoring the comment, she said, "Let me get some plates. I've run this thing four times already—

washed every dish, pot and pan I own."

He let her get away with the subject change. "How many loads of laundry have you done?"

"Seven," she admitted with a laugh. "I know, it's probably stupid. But I just couldn't stomach the idea of drying my hands on a towel some creep might have touched, or, God forbid, putting on any of my clothes—my underthings—and finding they'd been...."

"Gross," he snapped, knowing exactly what she was getting at.

"Tell me about it."

"You do realize the thief was probably in here for no more than ten minutes, grabbing electronics and jewelry, looking for cash, and then getting back out?"

"Logically, yes, of course I know that. But logic wouldn't have helped me get into my bed tonight, wondering if somebody else had touched my sheets. I washed them twice."

"Surprised you didn't throw those out with the food."

She grunted. "I would have, but they're Egyptian cotton."

He wouldn't know Egyptian cotton from Martian cotton, but figured it was expensive or something. "Gotcha."

"Let's eat," she said as she put two plates on the counter and went to grab some napkins. She also retrieved two large mugs.

"Bottle's fine for me, thanks," he said.

She nodded, but poured her own beer into a glass. He watched approvingly as she lifted it to her mouth and swallowed deeply. She didn't exactly belch for ten-points afterward, like some guys he knew, but she obviously appreciated it. So she wasn't always the wine-drinking lady he'd once imagined her to be.

Hell, who was he kidding? She'd proved last night that she was a wild woman. Drinking a beer now and again would be nothing for a woman who knew how to use her mouth the way this one used hers. Jesus, she'd sucked him so hard he felt sure he'd lost a little of his soul between those sultry lips.

"What are you thinking about?" she asked, eyeing him over the glass.

Jake opened his own bottle and turned away to flip the cap into the nearest trash bag. "Nothing," he muttered, not ready to look her in the eye yet. He wasn't the blushing sort, but if he were put on the rack, he might admit his own face felt a little hot. "You hungry?"

"Starving," she admitted as she served up slices of the steamy, cheesy pie onto two plates, and carried them to her small kitchen table.

"I also brought desert," he said, gesturing toward the bag. "Cookies."

"Oooh."

"The peanut butter ones."

"My favorite!"

"I thought you liked the mint ones."

"Only because I didn't know you had the peanut butter ones," she said with a smile that was bright and unworried. "You were holding out on me."

"Not anymore, I brought you my entire stash." He'd have brought her cases of the damn things if only to keep her looking happy and unstressed.

"My hero. Thank you. And thanks for the pizza—you were quite right, I didn't have a chance to go to the grocery store."

"Not surprised, with all the cleaning and laundry you've been doing today." More curious than he cared to admit, he—casually, he hoped—asked, "Did you have any help?"

"Help?"

"Did anybody come lend you a hand with all these chores?"

"Oh, no, it was a work day. I couldn't ask Eve or Ruthie or Di to take a day off to clean with me."

"You know they would have." He'd met the fabulous four at the wedding, and had heard Eve wax poetic about her three besties. Sounded like the four of them had a sister-like bond.

One thing was sure, he wouldn't want to get on the wrong side of that quartet. He knew what they'd done, or at least tried to do, to Sam. Before Sam and Eve had fallen in love, his brother had been scheduled for humiliation and heartache, all because of that dumb book he wrote about how to avoid commitment. One of the four friends had been dumped by some jackass who'd quoted Sam's book. He couldn't remember which. That had launched the scheme.

He suddenly found himself very curious about that, the big plan to "bring down" his brother. Which of the friends had been dumped? And why did his gut—not to mention his heart—twist at the idea that it might have been Leanne?

"I'm sure you're right, and they would have dropped everything to come over. But I didn't want to bother them."

She didn't like being in anybody's debt, this one. He'd already noticed. The fact that she'd gone to his place with him last night, rather than inconvenience one of her possibly-sleeping friends, had told him that. Not that he was complaining. Oh, *hell* no.

"And there was nobody else you did feel comfortable asking?"

"Not really," she said, lifting her glass to sip from it.

Unable to get the answer he was looking for by the sideways route, he asked head-on. "What about the guy?"

Her hand shook the tiniest bit, sending a small amount of beer sloshing over her fingers. "The guy?"

He nodded, pretending not to have noticed her unease. "Yeah. The one who takes you to fancy dinners once a week."

She swallowed visibly, her throat working, and then put her glass down. Reaching for a napkin, she dried her hand, mumbling, "He knows what happened. I went by the office—he's a colleague."

Huh. A guy who picked out curtains for a living just didn't sound like he would be man enough to satisfy the wild woman he'd had in his bed. No wonder they'd never had sex and only had boring weekly dinner dates. He wondered how on earth Leanne had ever believed that would be enough for her...and if her opinions had since changed.

"And he couldn't come over here to help you out?"

She laughed, but not bitterly. He heard genuine amusement there. Which told him all he really needed to know about fancy-dinner-guy. Not just a prig, but a thoughtless asshole.

"No, suffice it to say it would never have occurred to him to help me clean out my refrigerator." She gestured toward the plates which she'd just placed on the table. "Nor would he ever have thought about picking up a pizza. You'd better watch yourself, Jake, or you're going to start living up to that four-letter word you dislike so much."

"Which word would that be? Jerk?"

"Now why would you dislike that one? I thought you enjoyed being a jerk. You do it so well."

"Is that any way to talk to the guy who brought you pizza and cookies?"

"Kidding. The four-letter word I was referring to was nice," she murmured, a tiny smile on her pretty lips, warmth gleaming in her eyes. "You keep doing things that make me think you're nice."

"Well," he said, reaching for his own beer, "I'll have to be more careful about that in the future."

"You do that," Leanne said as she lifted a fork and knife and cut into her pizza, as delicately as if she were having tea with the queen.

Lowering his bottle, he eyed her, disbelieving.

"What?"

"You seriously eat pizza with a knife and fork?"

"It's hot," she said, a little defensively. "I don't want to burn the roof of my mouth."

He'd happily kiss it to make it better, but didn't figure he should make that offer right now. She hadn't entirely relaxed around him, and there was still that stupid deal they'd made for a one-night-only relationship. He was already regretting that one, and had been since shortly after he'd agreed to it.

"Uh-huh, sure," he said, taking a big bite of his own slice, which was just the right temperature.

"What? You think I'm too prissy to eat with my hands?"

"Babe, I know you're not prissy."

She eyed him warily, as if realizing he wasn't finished.

"You're just very proper," he said with a smile. "All cool and ladylike."

She dropped her knife and fork and glared at him as if he'd called her a bad name. "I am not."

"Sure you are. You could give lessons to Miss Manners."

Steam practically came out of her ears, though he didn't know what he'd said that was so offensive. He was just calling it like he saw it—Leanne was an adorable blend of ladylike formality and earthy sex-goddess. How could he not see, and admire, both?

She apparently didn't view it that way, and jabbed an index finger toward his face. "So I'm cold? Frigid? Was I cold and proper when I was sitting on your face twelve hours ago? Huh? Was I?"

Jake dropped his slice onto his place. He gawked at her, shocked, and, yeah, a little turned on. Or a lot. But he saw how heat flooded her cheeks, until her face was flaming. Her mouth rounded into a horrified "o" and her eyes were just as round.

She couldn't believe she'd said it. *He* couldn't believe she'd said it.

Silence, thick and tense, filled the air between them. Her words echoed in that silence, and he had no doubt she was vividly remembering, as he was, all the things they'd done together during the night. Such amazing, powerful, fantastic things.

He wanted to do every one of them again. Right the fuck now.

"No, you definitely weren't proper then," he finally said with a wicked smile. "Or when you begged me to eat your pussy."

The temperature in the apartment was comfortable, but he'd swear it suddenly spiked up ten degrees. This fire between them had been banked all day, but the embers had sparked back to life with just a few words. He knew nothing would douse them except doing more of what they'd started the night before.

"I think you should leave," she finally whispered.

Jake shook his head, slowly. "That's not what you're thinking."

"How do you know?"

"I can read you like a book."

"You don't even know me."

"The hell I don't."

She licked her lips, gripping the edge of the table. "One night. That was our agreement."

"Ever heard of a modifying clause?"

She blinked, tilting her head in confusion.

Jake pushed back from the table, slowly rising to his feet. "Let's modify the terms of our agreement."

"How so?"

"Thirty-six hours. Not a one-night stand, a day-and-a-half stand." He kept his tone light, almost teasing. Thirty-six hours would never be enough, but he was willing to play this dumbass game her way if it got him—both of them—what they really wanted.

She pushed her chair back, too, looking up at him. Her pulse was fluttering wildly in her throat, her lips trembled, and her lids were dropping over her eyes, as if to shield the unmistakable desire he saw in their depths. "Just tonight. And that's it?"

"If you say so."

She gulped. "I do."

"You sure?"

A pause. A nod. Finally, "Yes, I'm sure." She cleared her throat. "In fact, I want your promise. I want to go into this knowing there's an end date, so I don't have to stress about it, worry about it, think about it. One more night, Jake. That's all."

Yeah, he'd believe that when it happened. If she went a week without finding a reason to get in touch with him, he might actually start to think she was sincere. Of course, that didn't mean he couldn't find a reason to get in touch with her.

"Okay," he said.

"You promise? You'll let this go after tonight?"

"I promise I won't push you," he said, and that was as far as he was willing to go.

She stared up at him; he could practically see the thoughts churning in her head.

"This is a bad idea," she mumbled.

"Remind me of that later," he said, reaching for her hands and pulling her up out of her chair. When she was standing in front of him, he cupped her face in his hands and bent close. "You can tell me all about it tomorrow."

They'd done enough talking. Actions spoke much louder than words.

Without another word, his mouth was on hers, and he was kissing her with savage hunger. She held herself stiff and unrelenting for half a second, then melted against him, sliding her arms around his neck, twining her fingers in his hair. Jake groaned into her mouth, thrusting his tongue deep and hard, tasting beer and pizza before finding that ineffable flavor that was so uniquely hers. She tasted like every good thing he'd ever experienced in his life, all rolled up together. Sweet. Perfect. Intoxicating.

"God, I want you," she mumbled against his lips. "It's crazy how much."

"You're not alone in that," he said, already reaching for the bottom hem of her sweater and pulling it up.

He scraped the tips of his fingers across her midriff, skimming the fabric up and off her, freeing her loose ponytail and letting her hair fall free. Leanne arched against him, pressing her chest against his. He cupped one soft, curvy breast in his hand, dying for a taste. Bending, he kissed his way along the lace, licking her nipple through her bra before pulling a strap down to reveal all of her.

"So pretty," he mumbled before taking one pebbled tip between his lips and sucking. As he suckled, he squeezed her, plumped her. She gripped his hair, tugging him even closer, and he pulled the other strap down to give attention to her other nipple.

Leanne was moaning softly, rubbing herself against him like a cat needing a scratch, and he was just the tom to give it to her. He was already hard, thick, and ready for her, wanting nothing more than to lose himself in the heat of that tight little body.

When she reached down into his jeans to find him rock-hard, she groaned and admitted, "I've been thinking about this all day."

"So have I."

She quickly unfastened his button and unzipped his jeans, taking his cock into her soft hand and squeezing. He arched into her touch, loving it when she moved down to stroke his tight balls.

"Your hands are amazing," he muttered. "But don't do anything to hurt yourself again."

"I'm fine. Thank you for caring," she insisted. Then, with a tiny smile, she added, "Still, maybe I'd better give them a rest."

He kicked himself for a fool for a moment, before realizing she intended to substitute her hands for something else. Leanne pulled away from him, dropping to her knees onto the linoleum floor. He looked down at her, at the perfect face, the mass of hair tangling around his fingers, and watched as she leaned close enough to breathe on his erection. The warm exhalation felt shockingly good in the cool air, but he knew her mouth would feel even better.

"Tell me what you want," she said, a note of challenge in her voice. "You have to ask if you want to receive."

Jake rarely asked for anything. He'd learned from a young age to take or else do without. But this kind of gift was beyond precious, as he remembered from the way she'd pleasured him before.

"Well?" she whispered with the barest scrape of her lips on his skin.

"Please, Leanne, suck my cock," he groaned.

"Now, was that so hard?"

Her warm, wet tongue slid out and curled around the head of his dick, dipping to taste the cum already seeping from its tip. Jake shuddered, his hands tightening reflexively in her hair. He didn't pull, didn't try to change the pace or demand more, he was just holding on for the ride.

"I love how you taste," she whispered.

Then words died and she focused only on making him feel so goddamn good, licking and kissing all nine rock-hard inches of him, from tip to base. He was shaking, both at how good it felt, and at how much more he wanted to do with those nine inches, preferably between her thighs, and definitely soon.

As if reading his mind, sensing he was about to pull away, pick her up, and plunge into her tight pussy, she mumbled, "I want to swallow you down."

With that, she opened her mouth wide and drew him inside, sucking hard. Her hand tightened carefully on his balls, and she began to make love to him in earnest, swallowing as much as she could, setting a heartbreakingly intense rhythm.

"Christ, baby," he groaned as she draw him closer and closer to the edge. "Back off."

She reached around to grip his ass, holding him in place, continuing to eat him like she feared she'd starve if she let go. Knowing how much she wanted to take him all the way was enough to send him over the top, and with a low, guttural groan, he warned her he had reached the point of no return.

She didn't move away, didn't even hesitate. Instead, with a few more powerful pulls, she drew his climax out of him. He threw his head back and groaned as he came a gallon into her warm, willing mouth, both utterly satisfied, and incredibly turned on by her erotic generosity.

It took a few long moments for him to calm down enough to even open his eyes and look at her. And when he did—when he saw the cat-who'd-licked-the-cream expression on her face—he started getting hard all over again.

No woman had ever looked at him like that after doing something so intimate. Leanne might be proper when it came to eating pizza, but she was a fucking wildcat when it came to sex. And as he dropped to his knees in front of her to kiss her into sheer oblivion, Jake came to a realization.

He was wild for her—for both sides of her. The lady, and the wildcat. His spicy, sexy ice princess.

Jake was falling hard for a woman he'd never dreamed would want him. And even if she was totally out of his league, destined for guys who took her on proper weekly dinner dates, he was going to savor every single minute he could get with her until the day he had to give her up.

Chapter 7

AFTER A LONG day at work Saturday—to make up for the hours she'd missed on Thursday—all Leanne wanted to do was hang out with her friends, have a few drinks, and relax. Which was why Eve's invitation to come over to dinner to finally see the honeymoon pictures came at a perfect time. The rest of the gang would be there, too, and she could not think of anything that would improve her mood more than hanging out with her gal pals. And one token guy—Sam.

It was four o'clock, and she was heading out of the office, happy to leave behind Ned, the trade show, the Governor's Mansion competition, and all the stress. The closer they got to the show—and the lucrative contest—the more tense things were getting at the office. Today's drama had been, again, over the décor and staging pieces for the master bedroom.

The furniture would be delivered to the convention center next week—exhibitors were allowed to start setting up on Tuesday. The show opened Thursday and ran through the weekend. But the accessories, art and fixtures were all being delivered to the office, to be stored upstairs.

When the boxes from a New York supplier had arrived yesterday, Leanne had braced herself for battle, and, as expected, she'd gotten it. Ned threw a shit-fit, his mood awful and his patience stretched thinner than she'd ever seen it. So, once again, she'd spent her day trying to mollify a guy who insisted that yellow freaking pillows were going to cost him first place. And today things had started all over again when he'd uncrated the fixtures for the master bath and lost it over the delicately painted porcelain handles for the sink.

Frankly, Leanne was ready to tell him to take his damned dark, burgundy linens and flat brass handles and shove them up his ass. He'd probably be shocked if she raised her voice, and if she used bad language, he'd surely collapse. But oh, lord, was it tempting.

Funny, though, he hadn't had much of a reaction when she'd told him she was no longer interested in their Wednesday dinner dates. He'd looked annoyed more than hurt, saying they would discuss it later—after the show, after she was past the shock of her mugging. She'd tried to tell him she wasn't going to change her mind. As usual when the subject was something he didn't want to hear, however, he didn't listen.

"How on earth could you have ever envisioned yourself married to the guy?" she mumbled as she drove home, the drive taking mere minutes in late Saturday afternoon traffic. On weekdays it was three times as long. "You'd have eventually wanted to smother him in his sleep...or jump off a bridge."

She'd been thinking of the partnership of marriage, not of the intimacy of it. She'd imagined them working together, not actually living together. Now, she couldn't envision either one. She most definitely didn't want to be intimate with him, and was getting pretty darn tired of working with the man too.

She'd like to think her change of feelings had absolutely nothing to do with Jake, but she knew she was fooling herself. No, she wasn't crazy enough to imagine what they were doing had any kind of future. A few romps between the covers did not signal happily-ever-afters, especially with a guy as rugged, independent, and sexy as Jake Montez. He was having fun now—as, of course, was she. But eventually, those accusations he'd jokingly thrown at her wouldn't seem like jokes anymore, to either of them. Someday soon he would see her using a knife and fork on a slice of pizza and again conclude she was a major priss, a cold, frigid ice princess. Only that time, he'd no longer be interested in fighting the battle to warm her up.

The thought made her unutterably sad. She didn't want to be cold, distant or aloof. Deep inside, in her heart, she knew she was capable of warmth, emotion, even love. But a lifetime of being self-protective wasn't easily discarded. The lessons she'd learned as a child about not relying on other people, never letting your emotions take control of your intellect, had been seated deep within her psyche. In that respect, her ex, who'd called her rigid and unlovable to her face, might have been right.

Having a fling with Jake wasn't going to change that.

"And a fling is all it is," she reminded herself as she changed her clothes and prepared to go back out. She barely spared a glance for her bed, where Jake had slept with her Thursday night, doing the kinds of wild, erotic things she'd only ever imagined or read about in sexy books. Perhaps the fact that she hadn't heard word one from him since yesterday morning, when they'd both left for work, should have been enough to make her stop thinking about him. But, of course, it wasn't.

She couldn't be angry, though. He was just doing what she'd insisted she wanted—letting it go after their thirty-six hours. One night had stretched into two, for which she should be grateful. More, though, just that brief affair had been enough to change something inside her. Jake had showed her what she was capable of sexually, and she didn't want to settle for less than that. Which was, at the end of the day, probably the reason she'd dumped Ned.

Not *for* Jake. But because of Jake.

Stopping to buy a bottle of wine and some flowers, Leanne arrived at Sam and Eve's building and knocked on their door. One more thing to love about Sam and Eve being married—Eve had gotten a new teaching job in the city and moved here. She used to be about an hour outside of Philadelphia, and Leanne only ever saw her on their occasional Tuesday night outings. It was nice to have her practically in the neighborhood.

When the door opened a moment later, and she saw a familiar frowning face, framed with shoulder-length, jet-black hair, she had to chuckle. "What's wrong?"

Diana, who was the balls-to-the-wall hardass of their group, stepped back and gestured her in. "I'm gonna skin that animal."

Knowing immediately who Diana meant, Leanne looked around for Quigley, clicking her tongue and calling for him.

"Little bastard's hiding," her dark-haired friend said as she took the wine from Leanne's hands and carried it into the kitchen. "As he should be. He bit my ankle!"

"Yeah, he does that," she replied. "Mine are scarred."

"I'm surprised you didn't leave him to starve while they were on their honeymoon."

"Nah, I just learned to always wear boots."

"And he didn't move to scratching your face?"

"Oh, we came to an agreement," she said with a laugh. "He eventually deigned to let me feed him and clean up his poop, and I let him not terrorize me the minute I walked in the door."

"Stop talking about my baby," Eve said as she joined them in the kitchen. The cat in question was in her arms, all fluffy and adorably cute—deceptive, that. As she cuddled him like an infant, he purred so loudly the wallpaper might have started peeling off.

"I see you've finally made friends," Leanne said. Quigley hadn't been so sure about Eve when Sam first started bringing her around, either.

"Of course we have," Eve said, cooing and scratching the hell-beast. "Him'um just needs a widdle wuv."

"I'm going to puke," Diana said.

Eve—dressed in simple jeans and a sweatshirt that did not one thing to take away from her drop-dead, cover-girl beauty—snickered and put the cat down. He hissed at Diana and made grudgingly calm eye contact with Leanne, like they were a pair of enemy generals meeting at the site of their last battle, which had ended with no clear winner. Then he took off through the apartment, looking for a place to hide, or to defend voraciously, as the case may be. Woe to anyone who stumbled onto him when he didn't want to be found.

"Ruthie's not coming, unfortunately," Eve said as she popped open the bottle of wine and began pouring. "Her trainee chef called in sick tonight, and they're really busy."

Although Ruthie's family-owned hotel restaurant wasn't typically very crowded, they were enjoying a bit of a renaissance thanks to a renovation. So Leanne wasn't terribly surprised...though she was disappointed.

"Oh, but there will still be five of us for dinner. Hope you guys don't mind, Sam's brother is joining us."

Leanne immediately stiffened, her hand clenching on the stem of the wine glass. Fortunately, Eve had dragged out the good stuff, obviously wanting to show off her wedding presents, so the thing didn't immediately snap in her hand.

"Ooh, the bad-boy motorcycle dude?" asked Diana, appearing surprised. "The one who came to the wedding?"

Eve nodded. "Yes, Jake."

"Is he bringing his whole m.c.?" Diana asked.

"You've been watching too much *Sons of Anarchy*," Eve said with a roll of her eyes.

"I know. Netflix binge. Just wanted to try out the lingo."

"He's not in a motorcycle club, and he's not as bad as he seems." Eve gestured toward Leanne. "Ask Leanne—he even helped her out this week."

Leanne nodded and mumbled something appropriate, not getting into the story of the robbery. She imagined that would come later. Right now she was just too frazzled, and couldn't take her eyes off Eve. She couldn't tell whether her friend knew anything, suspected anything, or if Eve was merely offering a meal to her brother-in-law to be nice.

One thing she did know—she was suddenly very glad she'd worn cute, cropped black slacks and a sexy blouse, and hadn't changed into jeans and a sweatshirt. She was not a former supermodel and could never be mistaken for one.

"So, any particular reason for the invite?" asked Diana. "If you're planning a fix-up, shove him onto Leanne. I've got my eye on a new guy in my building. He's a cop. I'm hoping he'll hear strange, terrifying noises coming from my bedroom one of these nights and burst in to rescue me from my boring orgasms."

Eve laughed. "Are you really that lonely that you're making terrifying noises in hopes of rescue?"

Diana shrugged. "I'm making terrifying noises in hopes of climax. Believe me, it's not so easy when you're alone. Still, alone's better than with the great cheating accountant."

Diana's ex, Pete, had seemed like a good guy for a while, and their friend had seemed happy. Then came the cheating. *Bastard*.

"I do miss him in the sack, I must say. He was pretty good in bed. If only he hadn't been a totally untrustworthy prick." Diana crossed her arms over her chest. "I sort of hope he gets a visit from Mr. Mayhem."

"Enough with the *Sons of Anarchy* references," said Eve, obviously getting it. Leanne, having never watched the show, did not.

Diana shrugged. "Okay, then I sort of hope he gets hit by a bus."

"Me too," said Leanne, loyalty to her friend driving her own troubles out of her mind, at least for the moment.

"If he does, you could solve your problems with that new dildo I read about," said Eve with a totally wicked smile.

Diana and Leanne both just looked at her.

"It's made to hold a small amount of cremated ashes," Eve explained, somehow managing to keep a straight face. "So you can keep your loved one…close."

"Ewww!" Leanne and Diana said in complete unison.

Diana dropped into a chair. "You totally just made that up."

"Nope, dead serious."

"That is disgusting," Leanne said, shaking her head hard to drive away the mental images. She didn't think even a thorough brain bleaching would do it.

"Imagine if it broke," Diana mused.

Eve was snorting with laughter. "I dunno, it sounds kind of…sweet?"

"I think demented is a better word," said Diana. Then she cleared her throat. "As pleasant a subject as that might be, let's get back to the point. What's the deal with the brother?"

Leanne immediately tensed up again. She hadn't quite put Jake out of her mind, and now had to confront the thought of him again. How strange it would be to interact with him in front of her friends, and his family members. Could they really pull it off, act like they had only a passing acquaintance and barely knew each other? Behave as if they hadn't burned up the sheets at his place, and then at hers, until they were both left weak-legged and breathless?

How could she face him? Damn him for not calling to warn her he'd be here!

"He called a little while ago and told me he wanted to stop by with the bail money he owes you, Leanne," Eve explained, not really looking over as she went back to preparing a salad for dinner. "I guess he told you he'd get it to us to give to you?"

Her heart pounded in her chest, and her mouth went dry. Managing to mumble, "Yes," she lifted her glass to her lips and took a deep sip of her wine, needing to stall for time while she tried to figure out what to say. More—how to feel.

Why would Jake feel the need to give the money to Eve and Sam? Did that mean he *really* didn't intend to see her ever again, didn't want anything else to do with her? Was the passed-along money meant to be a message to say, "So long, it was fun, thanks for the memories?"

She felt sick and gripped the back of the nearest chair. Jake hadn't called her since he'd left her yesterday morning. After two nights in a row of amazing, phenomenal sex, there'd been utter radio silence.

The truth finally sank in. She'd been telling herself it had been a short-term fling, but the truth was, deep down, a part of her had expected it to continue. She hadn't had nearly enough of him, and the way he'd made love to her for those two nights had made her believe he felt the same way.

But he didn't. And now, he was doing what she'd asked him to— what she'd made him *promise* to do. Staying clear. They'd had their modified one-night-stand agreement, and he was out. Just as she'd demanded.

She'd never considered herself a stupid woman, but right now, she was prepared to doubt not only her intelligence but her sanity. Like a complete idiot, she'd demanded that promise. Still, he had worded his response in a way that left him a way out. And left *her* a way out.

And she'd been counting on that way out ever since.

Hell.

Bad enough he wasn't calling her, he was actually going out of his way to avoid her by sending the money along like she was a stranger who'd lent him a buck for a cup of coffee. He probably had no idea she was going to be here, and the thought that they'd be face to face any minute was enough to make her want to throw up. He'd probably see her, invent an illness, and leave without so much as taking off his coat.

"What's this about bail money?" asked Diana, bringing Leanne back to the moment at hand.

"Ask Leanne," Eve said, waving her hand as she turned to wash some celery to go in the salad. She'd made a roast, with all the trimmings, which smelled delicious. Except, unfortunately, Leanne was feeling too nauseous to appreciate it.

"It was nothing," Leanne explained. "He got picked up for fighting when Sam and Eve were away. I heard the message and bailed him out."

"Sam said the charges were dropped," said Eve, absently.

Leanne immediately jerked to attention. "Really?"

"Yeah, apparently the cop in question had a personal history with the hooker Jake was defending. He'd already been warned about harassing her. Jake really was a hero that night."

"Oooh, a barroom brawler who takes on corrupt cops? He's Batman! I think I like this guy," Diana said, wagging her eyebrows.

Leanne frowned at her, a flash of jealousy hitting her hard in the dead center of her chest. Diana was tall, lean, and seductive looking. Nobody would ever call her cold. Or frigid.

"He's not available," she said, before she could think better of it.

She regretted the words the minute she'd said them, and saw Diana's eyes widen. Eve turned around from the stove, looking equally as stunned.

"I mean," she stammered, "he doesn't seem like the dating type."

"What type is he then?" asked Diana, one corner of her mouth curling up.

"The...the play around type. Not serious. He's not interested in relationships or anything like that."

"And you would know this, how?" asked Eve as she pulled a pair of brightly-colored oven mitts onto her hands.

Leanne forced a shrug. "I guess we talked a little."

"About relationships?" Eve's tone couldn't have been more disbelieving. "You and my hard-ass, tough-guy, Harley-riding brother-in-law sat and had a heart-to-heart about love and romance?"

Leanne felt heat flaming up into her face. Her pulse was racing, her whole body tense. She needed an escape, but Diana was blocking the door, and Eve was circling closer. So she could do nothing except gulp her wine, finishing the glass in three big sips, then lowering it onto the kitchen table.

"Well, fuck me gently with a chainsaw," said Diana with a broad smirk.

Leanne threw her hand up and shook her head. "Oh, God, please not 80's movie quotes."

"You banged him," the brunette said, not the least bit apologetic.

"Shut up."

"You tapped that boy, admit it!"

Eve was waiting for an answer, too, her chin resting somewhere in the vicinity of her chest. "Lee?" she prompted. "Is it true? Did something...happen between you and Jake?"

"She did him."

"Shut up, Diana," Eve said, coming closer to put a hand on Leanne's shoulder. She had looked shocked at first, now she appeared worried. "Was it the other night?" Her jaw jutted out a tiny bit. "Did he take advantage of you after the mugging?"

Diana actually laid off with the sexy teasing and gaped. "Mugging? You were mugged? Why does nobody tell me these things?"

"I was going to, tonight," said Leanne. "I'm fine. It happened as I was leaving work Wednesday night."

"And then you were robbed, I mean, your apartment was," said Eve. "Sam told me about it this morning. I can't believe you didn't let me know."

"I would have, of course." Did Sam tell Eve where he'd found her? God, she hoped not. "I'm fine, insurance claims are in, all is well."

Her two friends simply stared. They'd known her for years— since they'd all been college freshmen—and she knew they weren't easily palmed off with the old *I'm fine* answer. They wore matching expressions of worry, each of them likely envisioning all the bad things that could have happened to her. But she'd done enough of that herself over the past few days. She didn't particularly care to take a step back. She'd begun to heal, to move on, and letting them fuss over her was not going to help.

So she said something that would most definitely get their minds going in a different direction. "And to answer your question, yes, I banged him. Meaning tonight's dinner might be just a little bit awkward."

JAKE HAD WRACKED his brain since yesterday morning to figure out a good reason to get back in touch with Leanne. As soon as he'd left her apartment, he'd begun to miss her. Thinking of the two nights of sexual bliss they'd shared only made things worse.

He'd thought about just showing up at her door again, maybe with a toothbrush, claiming he'd found it in the bathroom and thought it was hers. She'd see right through that gambit, of course. Jake suspected he could cajole her into forgiving him.

Something held him back, though. She'd been so insistent on

laying down guidelines from the start. She'd been absolutely determined that she wouldn't want anything more than one hot night in his bed, and he suspected she had worked hard to make herself believe that.

Yeah, she had been flexible enough to extend their fling by another night, for which he'd forever thank his lucky stars. Yet, Friday morning, as they got up and got ready to split up for their work days, she had slowly reverted to cool, aloof, distant, unavailable woman. She'd actually presented him with her cheek when he'd moved in to kiss her goodbye, though there was no way he was letting her get away with that. Only after his tongue was in her mouth and his hands were full of her ass did she relax and kiss him back.

But the moment had been just another brick in the wall that she kept firmly in place to prevent anybody from getting too close. She'd begun rebuilding the damn thing, and he had to think that she really wanted it there. So just showing up at her place seemed…pushy.

Now, if they just so happened to be invited to the same place, on the same night, for dinner, well, that wasn't his fault, was it?

Jake was still smiling at how things had worked out when he got to Sam and Eve's place. He was also still very thankful he'd called his brother about something today, and had heard that Eve was having her gal-pals over for dinner and a vacation slideshow. It had taken Jake all of ten minutes to come up with a way to get himself invited. As expected, when he'd called Eve to tell her he wanted to give her the bail money to give back to Leanne, she'd asked him to join them.

It had been a little sneaky. But…fuck it. He wanted to see Leanne, but didn't want to push her too hard. This seemed like the perfect way to do it.

Unfortunately, however, when he saw her brittle smile and the flat, non-sparkling gray of her eyes, he began to worry he'd made a mistake.

"So, Jake," said his sister-in-law as they all sat down around the dining room table shortly after he'd arrived. "What's this I hear about you and Leanne having more adventures after we left you Wednesday night?"

He had just reached for his beer, but slowly lowered the bottle to the table. His eyes met his brother's, but Sam merely shrugged, silently saying, *You're on your own, dude.* As for Leanne, well, she wouldn't look at him at all.

"Yeah, I guess we did," he replied, noting the other friend, introduced as Diana, appeared very amused about something. "Did Leanne tell you she'd forgotten she had an apartment key in her stolen bag that she'd meant to give to you?"

Eve gasped and drew a hand to her heart. "Oh, God, no, it was my fault?"

"Don't be silly," Leanne said.

"It was only the fault of the person who robbed her," Jake said, his tone brooking no argument. "And he did a pretty good night's work."

"Yeah, but did you?" Diana mumbled.

Jake caught the glare Leanne cast the other woman, and his suspicions were aroused. But considering how pink Leanne's cheeks were, he didn't push it, not wanting to cause her any more embarrassment.

"Did the thief take anything irreplaceable?" Eve quickly asked, after she'd sent a quelling look at her dark-haired friend.

Leanne shook her head. "Not really. I needed to upgrade my laptop, anyway. And my jewelry wasn't very valuable. There were some files and stuff that might be a pain to replace."

"Good lord, tell me he didn't get that book of yours," Diana said.

Sam tilted his head, curious. "Book?"

"That big scrapbook thing she used to cart around everywhere she went," Diana explained. "And still does."

"Her dream book," Eve said, her smile a little gentler than the brunette's. "It's safe, isn't it, Leanne?"

She nodded. "Yes, I had it locked in my desk at work. Thank goodness."

She had mentioned something about the book the other night at his place, but it hadn't hit home to him just how serious she'd been about it. If her friends knew she valued it above all her other possessions, she had to be pretty attached to the thing. Kinda funny, considering it sounded like not much more than a bunch of sketches, but he guessed for a creative person, it would be sort of like losing a limb. Sam, a professional writer, had once told him that when his hard drive had gotten fried and he'd lost four unsaved pages of a project, he'd nearly cried.

"Leanne used to buy little tiny pieces of fabric, yarn, lace, wallpaper, anything that caught her eye, and stick it in that book," Diana explained. "She'd even dab paint on some pages. It was massive and was falling apart by sophomore year."

"I've retired that one," Leanne explained. "Actually, all my college ones are in storage. The new one's just from since I turned pro."

"And it's already massive, I'll bet."

Leanne shrugged. "I'll have to start a new one, soon."

Sam jumped in. "What is this dream book for?"

Leanne, who was a soft, quiet light between the two other flashy women at the table, murmured, "Just my ideas. Things I'd like to have, or make. Designs."

"She talked about nothing else except her Victorian dream house when we were in school," said Diana. Then, her gruff, sarcastic tone softening, added, "Leanne is the most creative person I've ever known, a regular artist with color, light, fabric. Everything."

Leanne ducked her head, obviously not used to being the center of attention when her friends were around. If he had his way, she'd never try to hide her light under a barrel again.

"I get it honestly, I suppose," she admitted. "My mom's very creative."

"Is she a designer, too?" asked Sam. "Or an artist?"

Leanne smiled, and then cut into her dinner, eyes down. "Well, she's a *con* artist."

They all laughed. All except Jake. She'd told him she had sometimes eaten out of garbage cans as a kid, and had spent a year with her grandmother when her own mother was unable to take care of her. He doubted she was joking.

He assumed Eve and Diana knew some of her history, too. How could they have been best friends for more than a decade without sharing secrets? He wasn't sure, however, if they realized just how affected she still was by that background.

Did they know—as he'd already come to—that she built walls around herself for protection, because, growing up, she hadn't known if there would be any walls, or a home, around her at all? He couldn't say for sure how he'd already figured that out, but didn't doubt it was true. Leanne's demeanor, her calmness, her I-don't-need-anyone attitude, had been forged during her rough childhood.

Maybe it took one to know one.

His own childhood had made him a reckless, angry, aggressive, physical man.

Hers had made her a guarded, self-controlled, quietly-determined woman.

Different pieces of clay, but they'd come from similar fires and similar kilns. Perhaps that explained their immediate connection.

They continued to enjoy the meal, making small talk, mostly about Eve and Sam's wedding, and about the house they were considering buying. Jake didn't say a lot. Nor, he noticed, did Leanne, who was sitting directly across from him, but still wouldn't look him in the eye. That made for an uncomfortable meal. It also, however, allowed him to study her face—to stare at those lips he'd kissed so thoroughly, to note the sweep of her long lashes against her high cheeks, and remember how that soft skin felt against his own.

She caught him once and her jaw tightened, as if she were gritting her teeth. She quickly turned to Diana and started a conversation about the magazine the other woman worked for, intentionally excluding him.

He knew she was mad, probably resenting his intrusion on her night with her friends, and he felt like an ass for having foisted himself on her.

She doesn't want you around. How much more clear could she make it?

"So, Jake," said Eve when they'd all just about finished eating, "since you're here, and Leanne's here too, I guess that means you can just give her the money you owe her in person. That *is* why you wanted to come by tonight, isn't it?"

He glanced at Sam's wife, seeing her pointed stare. Had Eve figured out why he'd wrangled an invitation for himself tonight? Given Leanne's stiff-necked tension, and Diana's mumbled snark, he had to think the women had been doing a little talking. Hell. This was going to be uncomfortable, and judging by his brother's smirk, Sam knew it, too.

"Yeah, uh…right."

"You could have just mailed me a check," Leanne snapped, her chin going up. Finally, some emotion out of her.

"I also could have just knocked on your door," he said, his tone even.

She licked her lips—God, those lips. "But you chose to leave the money with Sam instead."

She sounded…hurt? Now why would that be? "Were you afraid I

wasn't going to pay you back?"

"That thought never crossed my mind."

"Good. Because I don't welch on debts. And I don't make promises I don't keep."

He stared at her intently, hoping she would hear the words he wasn't saying. He was trying to remind her she'd wanted his promise that he would be content with just a modified one-night-stand. And he had not given her exactly what she'd asked for. He only wondered if she still wanted it.

"Well, good for you," Leanne said with an eye roll that wasn't at all like her.

"Is there a problem?" Sam asked, his brow furrowing.

"No, not at all," Leanne said. She lifted her glass to her lips, finishing her wine in two gulps. It was, he thought, her third glass. Maybe that explained the color in her cheeks, the tremble on her lips, and the sudden sparkle in her eyes. "I mean, far be it for me to think your brother might have, I don't know, wanted to show up at my door to give me the money back. Oh, no, he had to pass it through you, heaven forbid he have to see my face again. Well, message received, loud and clear. Do you want a receipt?"

Diana coughed into her fist, and Eve and Sam exchanged surprised looks. Leanne didn't even appear aware that she'd stunned everyone at the table with her outburst, which was so out of character for her. Jake merely smiled. He wasn't shocked. He knew better than most that the supposedly sweet, demure woman was capable of fire, heat, and passion. Hell, hadn't she almost shoved him into a fountain, and then practically broken his toes, the day they'd met?

And now he knew something else.

He knew why she was mad.

If they hadn't been at such cross purposes, he could have laughed about it. She was pissed-off because she thought he'd wanted to send the money through Sam so he could avoid seeing her again. When, in truth, he'd used the money as an excuse to get invited to dinner…just so he could be with her. It was like one of those stupid rom-coms, where the couple just needed to have a conversation to straighten out the problems between them.

Well, the time had come for them to have one of those conversations. And he didn't really give a damn where they were, or who heard it.

Leanne stood up, grabbing her wine glass. "Is there more?" she asked Eve.

Eve nodded, starting to rise, too, but Jake held up a hand, palm out. "I'll help her," he said, picking up his own dishes, and a few of those around him, and following Leanne into the kitchen. The others remained at the table.

The apartment was small. Eve, Sam and Diana would undoubtedly hear every word. Still, he wasn't going to leave things like this. Whether Leanne liked it or not, she was going to hear his explanation.

"So, you think I was avoiding you, huh?" he asked as he scraped the plates into the sink.

"Weren't you?" she said as she dug in the fridge for another bottle of wine.

He brushed by her and pulled out a bottle of water instead, twisting off the top and giving it to her.

"I don't want water."

"You don't really want more wine, either. What you want is a bottle you can smash over my head."

A lopsided smile pulled at her mouth. "Now that you mention it…"

"Wanna tell me why?"

Her smile faded. "I was joking."

"No you weren't. You're pissed at me. I'd like to know why."

"I don't know what you're talking about." She sipped the water, and then turned her back, going over to the sink to start washing dishes.

Jake followed, moving close behind her, putting his hands on her shoulders. She flinched beneath his touch, and he reminded himself to go slow and easy. She'd built up a fine head of steam, and he was going to have to convince her she was entirely wrong in her conclusions.

"I came here tonight for you," he murmured, his lips close to her soft hair.

"Sure you did."

"I knew you were coming," he insisted. "I made up an excuse about the money so Eve would invite me to join the party."

Her whole body stiffened as she finally heard what he was telling her. The glass she was washing fell from her hand back into the sink full of soapy water. "What?"

He turned her around to face him. His fingers brushing her cheek, he tilted her chin up so she had to meet his stare. "You are the only reason I am here. I heard what you said the other night, and I was trying to give you what you wanted—space. No morning-after unpleasantness, no uncomfortable phone calls."

"Did I say that?" she murmured.

"You did. And I tried, Leanne, I really tried." He brushed his thumb against her lips, desperate to kiss her, but not quite there yet. "I couldn't break my promise. But I couldn't let you go, either. So, call me a manipulative bastard, I made sure I'd get to see you tonight."

"Really, Jake?"

"Really."

One more second, and then she finally relaxed against him. Her whole body went soft, all her curves melting into his angles. She licked her lips, silently asking for the kiss he so desperately wanted to give her. And finally their mouths came together. There was no frenzy, no wild thrusting. Her lips parted, their tongues met and gently tangled and twisted. It was slow and easy, sexy but sweet, too. Just like Leanne.

She wrapped her arms around his waist and he curled his around her shoulders and they kissed and kissed and kissed. At one point, he kind of thought he heard somebody else moving around behind them in the kitchen, but didn't really give a damn. Maybe if she hadn't had a few glasses of wine, she would have. Fortunately, she didn't even seem to notice.

Eventually, after several long, drugging, mind-numbing kisses, they drew apart.

"Why don't you let me drive you home?" he whispered.

She smiled up at him. "I'd like that."

A clank of dishes from the dining room suddenly pierced the erotic lethargy between them, and she quickly backed up a step, out of his arms. "But, uh, we have to do the slideshow thing first."

"Yes, you do," said Diana, who came barging into the kitchen carrying a stack of plates. "If I have to sit through nine-hundred-and-eighty-six pictures of beaches and flowers, so do you. Now where's the damn wine?"

Jake grunted, not having given much thought to that part of this evening's gathering. Watching somebody else's vacation photos slide by on a big-screen TV didn't sound like his idea of fun. But thinking about who he would be taking home afterward made it worth sticking around for.

"Stop bitching, you haven't seen a single picture yet," said Eve, who'd followed Diana into the kitchen. "It'll be great...and I got dessert."

"Does it contain chocolate?"

"A little."

"If it's not dripping with the stuff, I'm not interested."

Eve went to the refrigerator, opened it and pulled out a box with the logo for a popular downtown Italian bakery. She popped the lid open and flashed the box to them. "Cannoli."

"Yum," said Leanne. "I love those. That place makes the best in the city."

"Don't think I've ever tried one," said Jake.

They all stared at him. "Seriously?"

He shrugged. "Hey, my last name's Montez and I grew up in Houston. You wanna talk about dessert? Bring on the Sopapillas and Tres Leches cake."

"You gotta try these, man. They're my new favorite food," said Sam as he joined them.

Eve giggled. The girlish sound was unusual coming from the super-sexy woman. When Jake stared at her questioningly, her face pinkened the tiniest bit.

"Something you want to share?" asked Diana, obviously noticing too.

"It's nothing," said Eve.

"Like hell," her husband said, sliding an arm around his wife's waist and pulling her close. He kissed the side of her head. "Eve read this book, you see. That's how we got introduced to cannoli."

"A cookbook?" asked Leanne.

Sam's laughter deepened. So did Eve's blush.

"No," Sam explained. "It was one of those hot romance books with the red covers."

"What's that got to do with cannoli?" asked Leanne, looking adorably confused.

Jake, seeing Eve's blush and his brother's smirk, was already starting to get the picture.

"Oh, food sex?" said Diana with a bored shrug. "Whatev."

"You don't understand," said Eve, shaking her head. "This was…well, let's just say that book wins the award for most creative use of a pastry."

Diana at last looked interested, and Leanne's eyes had rounded to silver dollars in her face. She looked at the box containing the tube-shaped, cream-filled confections, and then cast a surreptitious glance at Jake.

He couldn't help it. He grinned broadly, not giving a damn that his brother was smirking and his sister-in-law was giggling and Leanne was staring. All he could think about was that Leanne's walls were coming down, promises were being rewritten, agreements were being modified, and one-night-stands were becoming something far, *far* more important.

Which was why he said, with perfect confidence, "Wrap two up. We're taking ours to go."

Chapter 8

FOR SOMEBODY WHO had always thrived on being in-control, who'd always known what was coming next and been sure of what she wanted, Leanne was having a fine time being utterly reckless.

She'd never have guessed it a few weeks ago, before she'd met Jake, but now, she just couldn't imagine going back to her dull, sedate life, and her completely normal routine. Jake constantly surprised her, and her delight in that was a surprise to herself.

They had left Sam and Eve's late Saturday night, after the interminable slideshow and a quick game of Cards Against Humanity, which had been hilariously raunchy. Jake, usually so tough and stoic, had grumbled that he felt like he was in an episode of Friends, or in a beer commercial, but he still played. When he had paired, "Why am I sticky?" with "Being awesome at sex," he'd immediately been proclaimed the winner and they'd grabbed their dessert and taken off.

Saturday night, back in his bed, had been…well, every bit as good as Wednesday and Thursday nights. Maybe even better, because this time, neither of them were putting time limits or definitions on what they were doing.

It was sex, but, for the first time, it was perhaps a little more than that.

When he woke her up Sunday morning, saying he wanted to take her to his favorite restaurant for breakfast, she'd never in a million years imagined that would mean getting onto the back of his motorcycle and riding with him all the way down to Wilmington. It had been her first time on a bike, and she'd been more than a little intimidated. But he'd put a helmet on her head, wrapped her in his spare leathers, and promised her he'd drive carefully. With her arms wrapped snugly around his waist, her front pressed to his back, her legs encircling his lean hips, she'd found herself loving every minute of it.

Gone was the safe, demure, in-control Leanne. In her place was someone who liked adventure, wanted to try new things, go a little crazy.

They'd spent all of Sunday together, as well as Sunday night, but when morning light crashed in Monday morning, she'd buried her head under her pillow and groaned. "No. Don't make me."

He started to get up, pausing only to kill the alarm. She scooted closer, cajoling him back down by sliding a leg across his hips and an arm across his waist. She cuddled against him, sucking up his warmth. Damn, this was a cold winter. She'd never realized how drafty her apartment was until she'd started counting on his body heat to sleep at night.

"Playing hooky?" he asked her, kissing the top of her head.

She nodded, yawning. "Sounds good to me."

"I'm game." Another soft brush of his lips on her temple. "But don't you have that big show thingie this week?"

Yeah. The big show thingie. The event she and everyone she worked with had been focusing all of their time and energy on for months. The one that was going to give her a nervous breakdown, or see her in jail for having beaten up her demanding, aggravating boss. Ugh.

"I suppose I have to go," she grumbled.

"Are you going to be able to take a lunch break?"

"Probably, but it will be my last of the week. We move over to the convention center tomorrow and then it'll be crazy-pants time until Thursday's opening."

"I like crazy-pants time," he said, sliding his hand down her belly to her hip. "But I like no-pants time better."

Leanne quivered in his arms, loving the way his warm, calloused fingers felt on her body. He'd touched her again and again in the past several days, but she couldn't quite get enough. Especially when he went slow and easy, seducing her with soft, deliberate caresses. As he was right now.

She arched toward him, leaning up for his kiss, and their mouths came together in a long and lazy exploration. He kissed like he made love—with precision and dedication. She'd never been with a man who so enjoyed kissing, who got off on the brush of lip on lip, on the seductive mating of tongues. Jake did. And as the kiss continued, along with his tender, gentle strokes on her body, she forgot all about the time, and the job, and the alarm and the cold.

Jake made her hot. He made her flame.

"I can't stop wanting you," he said as he kissed his way down her throat. He paused to lick the hollow, and scraped his teeth along her collarbone. Then he moved down, kissing his way across the upper curves of one breast, and then the other, before finally taking a nipple into his mouth.

Leanne cried out, twining her fingers in his thick, glossy black hair. He suckled her, the steady pulls of his mouth sending waves of sensation clattering, careening, soaring throughout her body. When he moved away, she whimpered, but was relieved to know he was merely going to pay equal attention to her other breast.

"I love these," he muttered as he licked her aerola, tasting her as if she were as sweet as ice cream. He caught her nipple between his teeth, biting lightly, bringing an exquisite mix of pleasure and a tiny hint of pain.

Leanne shifted restlessly beneath him, sliding her legs up along his, loving the feel of his wiry hair against her much smoother skin. Every inch of him was firm and rough, so masculine, and she was reminded of the wonderful differences between masculine and feminine every time they came together. Where he was hard, she was soft. Where he angled, she curved.

Where he touched, she quaked.

He slid his hand up her inner thigh, until his fingertips brushed the lips of her sex. She arched up to meet his hand, wanting his caress, and cooed when he slid a finger in to test her wetness. She was slick, totally ready for him, and welcomed him inside her. His hands were big, masculine, and strong, and he slid another finger inside, making slow love to her with both. She began to whimper when he dropped his thumb onto her clit and gently stroked.

"You are so responsive," he whispered as he kissed his way back up to her face.

"Only with you," she admitted, doubting he'd believe it. But it was true.

She'd had lovers before. None, though, had ever made her feel like this.

Like she was…perfect. Adored. Worshipped.

Capable of absolutely anything. Including reaching the most impossible heights of physical sensation.

He moved between her thighs, and she parted them easily, welcoming him. They'd had sex many times by now, enjoying four full nights of the most erotic scenes she'd ever fantasized about. But this was different, somehow. Slower, gentler. It was easy, lazy, warm and wonderful. As he slid inside her, she sighed, taking him into herself, and not just physically. She was welcoming his body even as she welcomed his very intrusion into her previously well-ordered life.

She didn't know where they were going, didn't know where it could possibly lead. But for now, she was ready to go with him. Be with him. Savor him.

"I love being inside you," he whispered, his lips brushing her earlobe.

"I love having you there," she replied, meaning it. He filled her to her very core, but didn't pound or thrust. Pounding and thrusting was wonderful; she loved it. But this slow, tender rocking was almost unbearably sweet.

He was taking his time, savoring her, and she loved him for it.

They gave and took, with touches as light as moonbeams, kisses as lazy as summer days, and such tenderness as she'd never known. And when he finally neared his climax, he reached down to touch her, making sure she could come with him.

It was perfect.

Nothing—absolutely nothing—could make this day anything less than perfect.

Or so she thought.

Because, just four or five hours later, when she was standing almost nose-to-nose with Ned, arguing over the goddamned yellow pillows for the thirtieth time, Jake and his body and his lovemaking had never seemed more far away.

"I'm sorry, Leanne, but I simply can't risk it. I've had the burgundy set on order for weeks. Now that the yellow is here, I'm very glad of that fact."

They were standing in an upstairs storage room, where Leanne had gone looking for some fabric samples for a client. When she'd found the large boxes, addressed to Ned, with a slew of familiar-colored fabrics spilling out of the top, she'd gone looking for him, demanding he come up and explain himself.

And he had. Just not to her satisfaction.

"I was given the job of accessorizing this suite, Ned," she said, carefully biting out each word from between her clenched teeth. "We're supposed to be a team, both our names are going to be on the entry form. You had no right to go behind my back and negate everything I've done."

He shrugged. Spoiled mama's boy. "I'm sure you'll agree once you see the set I chose."

"I've seen it," she snapped. "It's right there in the box."

"I mean, once you see it on the bed."

"How can you be so sure the set I've chosen won't work, when we haven't even seen it with the furniture, either?"

"I just know," he insisted, so patronizing she wanted to scream. "Now, because there's no time to replace the lampshades, we'll have to do something else on the night tables. I've gotten in touch with a local florist."

"Flowers?" she groaned. "Ned, those lamps are perfect with the furniture you picked out."

"But the shades…"

She grabbed two fistfuls of burgundy sheets from the box. "I'll find the damn color and make new ones myself," she snapped before storming out of the room and heading back to her office. Her pounding footsteps down the stairs had to announce her anger, and she got several glances from behind half-closed office doors of her colleagues. She also got more than a few commiserating glances.

Everybody knew how hard she'd been working.

Everybody also knew, had probably always known, that Ned wasn't going to do what mommy had told him to and accept any ideas other than his own. Everybody except Leanne.

"I hate this job," she muttered as she flung open her office door.

"Oh!" a woman's voice said.

Startled, since she'd fully expected the room to be empty, as it was when she'd left it fifteen minutes ago, Leanne drew up short and stared at the redhead behind her desk. "Noelle?"

Noelle Singleton, who'd worked here until a couple of weeks ago, rose from behind Leanne's desk, a broad smile on her face. "There you are!"

"What are you doing here?" she asked.

"I had an appointment nearby and thought I'd stop by to say hi to everybody."

Well, that answered part of her question, but not the main one. "I mean, what are you doing in my office?" *Sitting at my desk?*

"Sherry told me what happened to you last week," Noelle explained, her expression somber. She came around and grabbed both of Leanne's hands. "I'm so sorry, that must have been awful."

Leanne nodded slowly, still more than a little confused. She and Noelle had never been friends—more like rivals. In fact, once Leanne's designs had been chosen over Noelle's for the trade-show competition, Leanne had felt genuine dislike from her. That had eased up once Noelle had gotten another job offer and no longer felt they were competing, but still, they were not buddies, and never had been. So finding the woman sitting here, waiting to console her over last week's mugging, was a bit strange.

"Anyway," Noelle said as she scooped up her coat from a nearby chair, and her big, baggy purse from Leanne's desk, "I must run. I just didn't want to leave without seeing you, to tell you how sorry I am that you were hurt. And, uh…well, how sorry I am about how nasty I was toward you."

That came as a surprise. "Excuse me?"

Noelle laughed softly, her smile softening the sharp lines of her not unattractive face. "You don't have to be polite, I know I was a jealous bitch toward you. I thought since I was working here for a few weeks before you got here that I should get some kind of perks."

Leanne shrugged, knowing full well that the only person in this building who got perks for anything other than their talent and their ideas was Ned Longotti.

"It's been bugging me," said Noelle. "Now that I'm so happy, working for Custom Craft, I felt like it was time to bury the hatchet."

Custom Craft was one of Longotti Lines's chief competitors. They were a great firm, with a stellar reputation. She hadn't realized that's where Noelle had gone, and was frankly a little surprised. Michael Craft was internationally known, and very picky. Only the top designers got hired at his company, and, to be honest, she had never thought much of Noelle's work.

"Well, great seeing you," said Noelle. "Let's do lunch sometime!"

"Sure," Leanne murmured, probably looking as confused as she felt. She watched the other woman leave, thinking about what she'd said, and decided to take her at her word. Maybe getting out of here, to a more even-keeled workplace with a more reliable, professional boss, had changed Noelle.

Maybe it could change Leanne, too.

It bore considering. Lots of things bore considering, actually. Since the day she'd met Jake, she felt like she had been thrown onto a twirly ride at a carnival. The last few weeks had left her spinning. And while she'd never been the type to enjoy thrill rides, right now, she couldn't think of anything she'd rather be doing than going on this adventure with him.

It would never last. Eventually, the midway lights would blink out, the thrilling rides would slow and come to a stop, the popcorn would grow stale and the cotton candy become nothing but a sticky mess.

In the meantime, though...oh, in the meantime, she intended to ride and laugh and spin and eat her fill.

There would be time enough later—hopefully not too soon—for

the morning after when the carnival packed up and went away, and reality set back in.

HEARING THE STRESS in Leanne's voice when he called her Tuesday night to see how she was making out, Jake realized she was in desperate need of a break. Or at least a distraction. Maybe even some food, since he doubted she'd taken time for dinner.

So, without asking her, he went to a deli and picked up some sandwiches, then parked in a lot on Arch Street, right by the PA Convention Center and the Reading Terminal. The place had ubdoubtedly been buzzing with activity earlier in the day, when the vendors were allowed to start coming in to accept deliveries of furniture and the like. Right now, though, it was pretty quiet. It was after nine p.m., and most workers had gone home, probably intending to do the bulk of the work tomorrow.

That's what Leanne should have done, too. Instead, she'd informed him when he'd called, she was still at the Longotti Lines booth, trying hard to make herself like the changes her boss had made to it, and to fix what could be fixed. Alone.

The guard at the entrance to the center recognized Jake, who'd done some private security for big events in the past. He smiled as he let Jake in, looking up Leanne's company name so he could direct him to the right section on the right floor. The place was massive, with more than a million square feet of space, and her company's spot was on the second level, on the south side.

As he walked through the center, past half-constructed booths with everything ranging from sofas to dinette sets to designer bidets and fancy toilets, he couldn't help but think about this world Leanne lived and worked in. To him, a house was a house. He'd been happy enough to have a bed to sleep in as a teenager, knowing his stepfather would have happily kicked him out for the slightest reason. The thought that people spent thousands of dollars on stuff like lace tablecloths and dishes was pretty eye-opening.

In the grand scheme of things, he never thought stuff like this mattered much. But having gotten to know Leanne, to see things through her far softer, more artistic vision, he'd realized why it did, to her at least. Being able to surround herself with beautiful objects was one thing; he knew that would appeal to someone with such an artistic temperament. But more important was her ability to be creative and artistic while designing a place in which people would live, love, be happy and raise families. She was creating spaces she'd always dreamed about and longed for, but had never had. It wasn't just about pretty wallpaper or pictures, it was about building a *home*. And that, he imagined, was the most important word in Leanne Weston's vocabulary.

As his boots tapped on the tiled floor, Jake began to realize just how shadowy this place really was when empty. He had passed a few people working in their own spaces, but as he reached the far end of the hall, he realized there was absolutely nobody around. That didn't make him happy, thinking about Leanne being here all by herself, and he wondered how she was feeling about it. Given the attack on her last week, she had to be a bit edgy. So, not wanting to frighten her, he began to whistle as he drew closer to the aisle where her booth was set up.

She obviously heard. She stepped out from behind a partition about ten feet away, looking curious. When she saw him, her curiosity quickly changed into visible pleasure. A broad smile creased her mouth and her eyes absolutely lit up.

"Jake! What are you doing here?"

"Thought you might be hungry," he said, lifting the bag of food. He reached her and cupped her face in his hand, bending to kiss her hello. "How are you doing?" he asked once they drew apart.

"It's been a long day," she admitted, rubbing a hand over her eyes. "Very long."

"Anything I can do to help?"

"Did you bring any patience pills with that food? Because I'm going to need them this week."

"I think those are the kinds of things you have to buy on dingy street corners," he said with a laugh. "But how's turkey on rye sound?"

"Heavenly," she said with a happy smile, grabbing the bag and plopping down to sit on the carpeted floor of the display area.

"Can we eat here?" he asked.

She shrugged as she dug out the food. "Ned decided he wants brown carpeting, so this stuff's going tomorrow anyway."

He eyed the booth, which was loaded down with an entire master bedroom suite. Almost every inch of the space was filled with the dark-wooded furniture. There was a massive four-poster king-sized bed replete with those weird, old-fashioned pineapple base decorations carved in. Plus a dresser with attached mirror, a bureau, a TV armoire, two nightstands, and a vanity with a stool. The place looked like a furniture store on crack.

One thing was for sure, the guy probably should've decided on the carpeting before all this dark, heavy crap had been put into place. He didn't envy whoever was going to have to move it all out of the way again tomorrow.

"A little crowded in here, isn't it?"

She grumbled something, shaking her head in disgust as she took a bite of a sandwich.

Jake dropped to sit beside her on the floor. "I take it that's a sore subject?"

"Definitely. I can't even begin to describe how differently I would have done this," she said as she wiped her mouth with a napkin.

"I have no doubt it would have been a lot better."

"It's like throwing money away. Who is going to see this room and want to hire our firm—or me, specifically, since my name is going to be on that placard along with Ned's—to do anything in their homes? And there's no way we'll have a shot at a prize for the governor's mansion redecoration contest."

"No way you can talk him into changing it?"

"I've tried til I'm blue in the face. That's why I'm here alone— Ned got really pissed off and left a couple of hours ago because I threatened to call his mother, who owns the company."

"Maybe you should."

"That's so childish," she said, finishing off the sandwich and licking the tips of her fingers.

She might knife-and-fork pizza, but she certainly ate her sandwiches the right way. He loved seeing that tongue flick out against her skin, mainly because he had so many glorious memories of it doing the same thing to his.

"I just can't believe we can't have a rational, adult conversation," she added. "Adults ought to be able to do that."

He shifted uncomfortably, having been guilty of avoiding those kinds of conversations himself. Of course, his relationship with his sperm-donor father couldn't be compared to hers with her asshole of a boss.

"I'm thinking it might be time for me to put out feelers with other firms," she said. "I only wish I'd done it before my name was attached to this monstrosity."

"I doubt they'll judge you based on one ugly bedroom."

"They might. Though, honestly, one of my former co-workers landed a job with a great company, and, in all modesty, she's not as good as I am." A frown pulled at her mouth. "It was weird, she came by to see me yesterday, saying she'd heard about the mugging. Now

I'm wondering if she just wanted to rub-in her good news or something. We were certainly never friends."

He'd like to say she was probably wrong, but couldn't. Human nature being what it was, he didn't doubt somebody would be that snotty.

Leanne reached up and rubbed her neck, tilting her head from side to side. Seeing the signs of sore muscles, Jake shifted around behind her on the floor. He put his own hands on her shoulders and began to knead and squeeze.

"Oh, God, that's heavenly," she mumbled.

"You're so tight."

He thought he heard the faintest giggle before she replied, "That's what you said this morning."

Warm hunger swept through him. "Yeah. I did. And I meant it then, too."

She leaned back against his chest, and he kissed her temple, scraping his lips down her jaw and then to the side of her neck. He nibbled on her earlobe as he continued to massage her, feeling her relax beneath his hands. The tension oozed out of her and she dropped her head back onto his shoulder.

Sliding his hands down her arms, Jake continued the gentle massage, stroking away all the bad moments of her day, right down to the tips of her fingers. His hands then drifted to her middle, and he moved one up, and one down, caressing her midriff, and also her pelvis.

"Oh, God," she whispered with a heavy sigh.

He knew he should stop. She was technically still at work. There were other people in the building, though they were few and far between.

But he couldn't. That sigh, that softness, that longing in her called to a part of him that needed to answer. So without a word, he tugged her blouse free from her slacks and pulled it up, letting his bare fingertips stroke her belly and then move up to cup her breast. His other hand dropped down between her legs, cupping her moist heat, evident even through her clothes.

She wanted him. She was aroused and ready. And he wanted her, too.

He unbuttoned her pants, and then unzipped, giving himself access to that heavenly spot in which he'd lost himself so often. Caressing her curls, he dipped lower until he could glide into her creamy crevice, teasing her clit and then slipping one finger into her. She squeezed him in welcome, taking him easily, and he reached deeper, adding another finger, stretching her, filling her, moving in and out. All the while, he continued to toy with her breast, and to kiss her throat. The scent of their arousal filled his breaths, and the air, which had been cool, grew steamy and hot.

"Take me, Jake," she whispered, curving her hips to thrust toward his steady hand. "Take me right now."

He looked around again, still spotting no one. They were engulfed by silence, emptiness, in a world defined by shadows of furniture and half-walls and pseudo rooms. But no people.

"I don't care where we are," she mumbled as she turned around in his arms to face him. "I want you badly."

She rose to her knees, and then to her feet. Jake looked up at her, seeing the glitter of want in her eyes. She began to unbutton her blouse, sliding each button free with erotic, deliberate slowness. When she'd finished, she shrugged it off her shoulders, dropping it onto his lap. Jake wrapped his hands in its silkiness, content to watch for now as she moved up to unfasten her bra. He swallowed hard as she freed those beautiful breasts, the tips hard and pink and begging for his touch.

"Aren't we lucky there's a nice big bed close by?" she said, gesturing toward the interior of the booth in which she'd been working. It was open to the corridor, but had walls on three sides, and provided a bit more privacy.

"Are we allowed to play on the merchandise?"

She smiled as she pushed her pants down her hips, taking a pair of tiny panties with them. Her shoes came off with the rest of her clothes, and she was suddenly gloriously naked, all warm skin and hot woman. "Those are some sheets we decided against," she said with a wicked smile. "Let's break them in before I strip the bed."

"Your wish is my command," he said, unable to resist her when she was so damned sexy and inviting. There was an edgy quality to her voice, she liked that they were flirting with danger, and wanted to do it some more.

He'd never had a problem with danger. And even if he had, she was so completely worth the risk.

He got up, tearing his shirt off and unzipping his jeans, watching her as she sauntered to the bed, her hips swaying, the curves of her ass pale in the dimly-lit building. He followed her, tossing his jacket and shirt to the floor and unbuttoning his jeans. And then, just to drive him even further out of his ever-loving mind, she crawled onto the bed on all fours, lifting that ass enticingly. She looked back at him over her shoulder, giving him a smile as old as womankind herself, inviting him to take her from behind.

"Christ," he muttered, his hands trembling as he shoved his jeans down. His cock sprang out, rock-hard, and he encircled it in his own hand as he moved to the edge of the bed. He didn't bother stripping any further; he couldn't wait, and sensed she couldn't, either.

She proved it by backing up to meet him, spreading those legs, giving him the kind of view that would make any red-blooded man howl at the moon and thump his chest like a savage.

"Take me," she purred.

"Yes, ma'am."

He grabbed her hips, pulling her closer, widening those slim thighs. Staring down, watching as his cock slid into that slick, soft opening, was enough to make him groan, and the want only increased as he felt her take him in. She was so hot, so ready, so sweet, he could not stop himself from gripping her tightly and plunging balls-deep.

"Oh, God, yes!" she cried, throwing her head back and crying out in ecstasy.

He pulled back, pounded into her again, and she caught his rhythm, matching him stroke for stroke. Jake was lost to everything else—time, place, possible audience—able to focus only on how beautiful she was, how good she made him feel, and how fast he'd grown addicted to the kind of wild and wicked games they played together.

Leanne was everything he'd ever fantasized about in a woman. Brilliant, beautiful, tender, so sexy. And as he pumped into her, filling her with his cock and then his essence, he knew that he'd gone and done it for the first time in his life.

He'd fallen in love.

It probably wasn't smart, and he doubted she could really love a guy like him in return, but it was true. He loved her. And he was going to do whatever it took to make sure he got to keep her.

Chapter 9

L EANNE HAD THOUGHT Tuesday was bad. Wednesday proved to be even worse.

When moving the furniture so the booth could be re-carpeted, one of the workers had accidentally dropped a nightstand, snapping off a leg and a large corner piece. He'd then proceeded to stagger into one of the portable walls, which fell over, hitting the vanity, and cutting a long gouge in the wood.

Ned nearly lost his mind.

Everyone on the convention floor had to have heard him screaming. Heads popped out from other booths, security came to see what was happening, and the poor workman was almost sobbing during the public reaming-out. Leanne tried to calm her boss, putting a hand on his arm, but the temperamental designer threw her hand off so hard Leanne actually stumbled out onto the showroom aisle and fell to her knees.

Ned didn't even notice, not until she snarled from the floor, "Would you please stop proving to the entire city what a complete fucking asshole you are?"

He froze, mid-tirade, looking over to see Leanne clambering to her feet. She wasn't sure whether he was more shocked that he'd actually knocked her over, that she'd dropped the f-bomb, or that she'd called him an asshole. Or maybe he was just stunned by the fury she couldn't hide from her face.

"What did you say to me?" he said, each word drawn out slowly, between hissed breaths.

She brushed off her clothes, glanced around to see the avid expressions of onlookers, and sighed. There was no graceful way out of this now. "You heard me. You're embarrassing yourself, Ned. Just calm down and let's figure out how to deal with this."

He followed her pointed stare, looking around and seeing the attention he had drawn. In the corner, the workman, who looked barely old enough to drive, was sniveling. The nightstand was lying on its side, the wall half-collapsed, the entire booth a shambles. And Ned, to her shock, didn't say a word. He merely spun around and marched away, striding through the center aisle toward the exit. Leaving her alone to clean up the mess.

"God help me," she mumbled as she rubbed a weary hand over her eyes.

"He might not be available, but is there anything I can do?"

Spinning around, she saw a well-dressed, silver-haired man, eyeing her sympathetically. He glanced toward the booth and winced, though because it was a wreck or was so poorly designed, she couldn't say.

"That's very nice of you," she said. "But unless you're a master carpenter who can fix broken furniture and scratches, probably not."

A tiny smile appeared on his face, and he reached into his pocket and pulled out a cell phone. Without consulting her, he called someone named Fitz, asking him to come to her booth. When he was finished, he ended the call and dropped the phone into his pocket.

"There now."

"Did you seriously just call somebody who can fix this?"

The man's smile widened. "Well, he can't fix ugly, but he can fix broken and scratched."

That startled a laugh out of her. She stuck out her hand, saying,

"Good enough. I'm Leanne Weston. Thanks so much for your help."

"Michael Craft."

She sucked in a surprised gasp. "Oh my God, I can't believe I didn't recognize you." Not letting go of his hand, she added, "I so admire your work."

"Thank you, Miss Weston. I admire yours too. That is, as long as you didn't have anything to do with...that." He waved toward the booth.

Embarrassed, she admitted, "My name might be in the program, but I can't claim credit."

"I didn't think so. I saw the work you did at Emily Foster's country house. It's exquisite."

Remembering the job, she nodded in appreciation, thrilled that he'd seen it. The job had taken months, the wealthy Philadelphia socialite being very picky about the old farmhouse she'd bought and renovated. Leanne had loved how it had turned out and now, knowing it had brought her name to the attention of Michael Craft, loved it even more.

"Thank you, I appreciate that. I really enjoyed that project."

"It showed. I'd love to see more of your designs some time."

She almost opened her mouth to say she just so happened to have her dream book here with her, inside the new satchel she'd picked up over the weekend, but that seemed a little pushy. Besides, she had a lot to do.

"I'd love that." Then, suddenly remembering something, added, "One of my former co-workers recently came to work for you. Noelle?"

"Oh yes, Miss Singleton. We're thrilled to have her," Craft said. "She's remarkable."

Leanne wondered how on earth she'd missed that. If Noelle was talented enough to draw the eye of Michael Craft, she must be very special indeed. Yet Leanne had never seen a single thing Noelle had done that smacked of originality or creativity. Talk about hiding her light under a bushel, she must have been hiding it under a cement truck.

"She actually designed our master bedroom entry here."

Leanne's jaw fell open. "Seriously?"

"Yes," he said, obviously seeing her surprise. "She's young, and she's new, but I saw some of her designs, one in particular, and knew we couldn't do any better."

"I'll have to come and see it."

"You do that. It's downstairs, booth 107, I believe. We have several rooms in that vicinity."

She would imagine so. Craft's was a much bigger company; they could afford to enter several rooms in the contest, and sponsor several in the home show. She made a mental note to check them out later, and extended her hand. "Thank you again, Mr. Craft, I truly appreciate your help."

"You are most welcome." Glancing again at the Longotti booth, he sighed heavily. "And good luck to you." He didn't add, "You're going to need it." It was understood.

Nodding pleasantly, he walked away, pausing to look at what was happening in nearby booths. Checking out the competition, she supposed, not that he would have much.

True to his word, the guy Mr. Craft had sent up, Fitz, was a true genius at furniture repair. He had the vanity scratch fixed and buffed to invisibility within an hour. The nightstand he had to take with him, but he promised to get it repaired and have it back to her by tonight. So all would be the way it should be. Well, not the way it should be, but at least the way Ned wanted it to be.

For the rest of the day, Leanne busied herself with lots of other small touches—swapping out a painting that didn't work, putting decorative items on the dresser and designer perfume bottles on the vanity. She also finished the whimsical lampshades she'd designed and made herself. Ned would probably hate them, but, oh well. He didn't bother to come back for the entire day, dumping all the work on her shoulders, so she was going to do what she thought was best.

Fitz called at eight p.m., saying the repair was taking longer than expected, but he hoped to still have the piece back to her by tonight. When she heard it would probably be at least ten before he could get here, she felt her whole body sag. Still, it couldn't be helped. They needed the nightstand, if only to keep Ned from trying to cause more trouble for the poor kid who'd dropped it. So, although she was exhausted, mentally and physically, she agreed to wait for him.

Which meant calling Jake and telling him why they couldn't meet for a late dinner as they'd planned.

"Are there still other people around?" he asked.

"It's not as deserted as last night, in case you were thinking we could, uh...."

He laughed, knowing exactly where she'd been heading. "No, that wasn't what I was thinking. Not that I'd mind a repeat."

Neither would she. Good lord, last night had been incredible. She hadn't even realized she was capable of being so brazen, so demanding, so confident. The memories of the wicked things they'd done in that staged bedroom had calmed her down and brightened her mood more than once today.

"Me either," she said, hearing the note of longing in her voice. She just couldn't get enough of the man. She'd become something like a sex fiend, to her complete shock. Sex had always been something she liked, that was a stepping stone in the path of any good relationship. But she'd never been totally addicted to it as she was now.

"You want me to bring you some food?"

"No, it's okay. Security is walking around a little more tonight than they did last night. No way could we risk, uh…"

"I didn't mean for that," he insisted. "I just want to make sure you're fed."

"I grabbed something from the snack bar this afternoon, and you can feed me as soon as I get home. I should be out of here a little after ten."

"Okay," he said, the word dragged out, as if he didn't like saying it. "Just promise me you'll be careful."

"I will."

"That parking garage is pretty dark."

"I'm parked right by the entrance."

"I think I'll give the security guard a call and have him walk you out anyway."

"Don't be silly," she insisted, though she knew why he was being protective. "I'll be fine, there really are other people here."

"All right. But call me as you're leaving for your car, and once you're safely inside it."

"You got it, Dad."

He chuckled, and so did she. After they hung up, Leanne found herself liking that he was worried about her, protective of her. So few people ever had been, certainly not her own father, whose name she'd never even known. Nor any of her previous lovers, who'd all assumed that because she was independent, calm, and steady, she never needed to lean on anyone else.

Jake's protectiveness was a nice change. One of the many things she liked about him.

"More than like," she mumbled to herself as she sat down on the stool in front of the vanity to rest her aching legs.

Yes, she did more than like him. She hadn't wanted to think about it, there hadn't been *time* to think about it. They'd gone from strangers to lovers so quickly, a one-night-stand turning into a wildly passionate love affair, that there'd been no quiet moments of self-reflection.

That should scare her, panic her even. But it didn't. Because she was just enjoying herself too much.

She knew it was too soon, that they were too different, that she would never be enough of a woman to hold onto a guy like that for too long. Sooner or later, he'd get tired of her uptight ways and her cautious personality. He'd stop finding her prissiness cute, would realize she was playing the role of free-spirit by taking those long motorcycle rides and having hedonistic nights of sex in public places. But that wasn't really her. And he'd find that out eventually.

"So what are you going to do?" she asked herself, wishing the place weren't so empty so she'd have somebody else to talk to, something else to focus on.

Work was a great distraction, but there was little else she could do tonight but wait. There had been voices nearby a little while ago when she'd been on the phone, but she'd heard them fade away, along with footsteps, and suspected she was the lone holdout in this part of the building.

Fortunately, before she had to try to come up with an answer to her own annoying psyche, her phone rang. She glanced at the screen, saw Ruthie's name, and immediately felt a little lighter of spirit. Ruthie could brighten anyone's spirits—she was just that kind of perky, plucky woman. A little overweight, a little hysterical, a lot talented, and a lot kind.

"Hey girl," she answered.

"Where are you? I just heard about the mugging. Oh, my God, Leanne, are you okay?"

"Who blabbed?"

"Diana. She said you were robbed, too? I feel just sick. Can I do anything? I know, I'll bake something. Chocolate cake. You want some chocolate cake?"

Leanne laughed softly. As always, Ruthie's mouth moved at a mile a minute. "I'd love some."

"Okay, I'll get to work on it now."

"It doesn't have to be right away," she said, smiling at how thoughtful her friend was. "Unfortunately, I'm at the convention center, so I'm going to have to take a raincheck."

"This weekend?"

"The trade show goes through Sunday. Next week, okay?"

"How about I bring it to Casa Rosada Tuesday night and we'll all have a chocolate feast after our margaritas?"

"That sounds perfect."

"Great. And you can tell me all about the guy. There's a guy, I hear. And I wanna hear all about the guy."

She groaned. "Good grief, doesn't anybody in this friendship know how to mind their own business?"

"Are you joking? Do you not remember you're talking to the woman who got you to show me how to use a condom by sheathing a banana in freshman year?"

"That definitely wasn't me," Leanne said with a snort. "I suspect that was Diana."

"Oh well, the point is, no secrets baby-cakes, and no privacy, either. I can't wait to hear all about your tattooed motorcycle-gang guy."

"He is not in a gang," Leanne said, suffused with helpless laughter at Ruthie's over-exaggeration.

"Tattoos?"

"Well, yes, he does have those." Leanne had found all of them on his delicious, rock-hard body. The military ones always tugged at her heart.

"Okay, come prepared to spill every single bean. And good luck this weekend!"

"Thanks sweetie," she said, ending the call.

Just in time, too, because, when the silence descended again, she heard the squeaky wheels of a furniture dolly, and hoped Fitz was arriving at last with the repaired nightstand. Seeing him walk around the corner, she hurried over to meet him. "Oh, thank you so much, you can't imagine how appreciative I am."

"It was no problem at all."

"Can you just send an invoice to Longotti Lines?"

"Sure thing, I've done work for Eleanor in the past," the old man said. "Not lately—not with that poisoned pill of a son in charge—but I still have all the info."

Leanne made no comment on that. She still couldn't even think about Ned without fuming. He hadn't even checked to see what was going on today, though his secretary had called a few times to keep tabs on her, likely at his behest. Leanne had informed her the repairs were underway, and gotten absolutely no information in response.

The more she'd thought about it, the angrier she'd become, until she'd reached a decision. Today, she'd been given an unexpected opportunity. Michael Craft had been admiring and friendly. He'd asked to see her work. And good things came to those who went after them.

So maybe it wouldn't be a bad idea to call the man next week and make an appointment to talk to him. Noelle probably wouldn't be happy, but Leanne was far more worried about her own future. If she continued to work for Ned, she really didn't think she would have one.

The idea of leaving, doing something different with someone she truly respected, brightened her mood considerably, and she was smiling as she told Fitz where to put the nightstand. Although the huge banks of overhead lights had been turned off earlier tonight, there was still enough perimeter lighting to illuminate the piece, so she could see Fitz had done a good job.

After he put it into position for her, she shook his hand, thanking him again. Once he was gone, she gently wiped down the furniture with polish, buffing it to a glossy sheen, and then began to pack up her things to go. It was well after ten, and all she wanted was food, man, and bed, in that order. Or, if they still had any cannoli left, all at the same time.

In any case, she realized as she yawned widely, she was going to sleep like the dead tonight. *After* she made love with Jake. Because, really, what good was being in a bed with him if she couldn't get a little freaky on the man?

Smiling at the thought, she grabbed her coat, her purse and her satchel and turned to leave the booth. She was about ten steps beyond it when, to her great surprise, the lights in the massive space went off. There hadn't been a whole lot to begin with, just the ones along the perimeter, which didn't always sift through all the corridors created by the exhibitor' display areas. But it had been enough to see by...until now.

"Hello?" she called. "Could you please turn the lights back on, I'm not out of here yet!"

Nothing. No response.

She narrowed her eyes, trying to see where the hell she was. Some exit signs were vaguely visible in the distance, and a few exhibitors had left floor lamps burning. So it wasn't pitch black.

"But close enough," she mumbled, growing more irritated than annoyed. The security guy shouldn't have shut down the lights until he'd made certain no one was around.

"Hello?!" she called again, a little louder this time. Again, she got no response.

Knowing she couldn't just stand here waiting for somebody to come along, she put her eyes on the closest Exit sign, and began to swim through the sea of darkness toward it. Her own footsteps were loud on the tile, and she could hear her own breaths, so thick was the silence.

But then, suddenly, it wasn't.

She heard a noise. Low, furtive. A squeak of rubber shoe on floor. Not too far away.

"Who's there?" she called, her heart picking up its pace in her chest. She tried to stay calm, but after last week's incident, couldn't quite manage that.

Another sound—the brush of cloth against a partition perhaps? And footsteps. Soft. Deliberate.

Leanne drew in a choppy breath, every instinct she possessed going on high alert. She clutched her bags tightly against her side, and picked up her pace. She couldn't flat out run—it was too dark for that, she might slam into something—but she walked quickly, determined not to let fear get the best of her.

Behind her, a heavier footstep, and then another.

She was definitely being followed. Stalked.

And then chased. The sounds of harsh breathing and stomping feet reached her ears.

No more striding. She started to run, eyes on that Exit sign, hearing the footfalls coming closer. Sobs threatened to choke her, but she couldn't waste the energy to let them. She merely focused on escape.

"Stop, bitch," a voice growled in a thick, harsh whisper.

She let out a small scream. This time, she wasn't out in the open, in a parking lot with fistfuls of gravel, but she was in an enormous maze with plenty of places to hide. She thought about darting down the next aisle-way, even as she felt a tug on her shoulder and realized the shadowy attacker was grabbing her satchel.

She screamed again—half in frustration that this was happening to her again, half in fear—and prepared to turn and fight. She fisted her hands that had only just healed from last week, not willing to let herself be victimized again, especially since, this time, she did have her dream book in her satchel. She'd already lost enough and couldn't bear to lose that, too. But before she had to even try to fight off her attacker, she saw a tall rectangle of light appear about forty feet away, beneath the Exit sign.

The door had been opened. A tall figure was silhouetted in the doorway.

One she recognized.

She didn't know why he was here—figuring he'd probably just decided to check up on her—she only knew she'd never been happier to see anyone in her life.

"Jake!" she screamed, lunging toward him, pulling hard away from the shadowy figure who'd gripped her bag.

Jake didn't waste time asking questions, he merely came charging out of the doorway toward her. "Leanne?" he shouted, trying to locate her in the darkness.

"I'm over here," she called, running toward him, feeling the tension on her satchel release as her assailant gave up. She heard his footsteps pound his retreat as he ran in another direction. He'd been willing to attack a lone woman, but not confront a furious, powerful man whose expression screamed bloodlust.

Then Jake was there, grabbing her in his arms, pulling her against his body. "What happened?"

"Someone following...grabbed me...ran off..." She buried her face in his chest, gasping for breaths, trying to remain coherent and not burst into sobs.

His arms swooped around her, hugging her tightly. "I've got you, baby, you're okay. Nobody's gonna hurt you, Leanne, I swear."

Her raging heart slowed. Her breaths became more even. Her panic receded.

The person who'd been after her was probably still somewhere nearby, maybe even waiting for another chance, yet she felt all her tension, all her fear, drain away. Because she believed him. Jake was here, he was holding her, gripping her like he would never let her go.

Nobody would ever hurt her again. He'd see to it.

JAKE WANTED TO hurt someone. Wanted to punch, and pound, and draw serious blood.

As Leanne slowly stopped quaking and shivering in his arms, he found his own fury building, until it was like he was in a cloud of steam, able to see nothing, hear nothing, think of nothing…except pulverizing whoever had dared to frighten her.

"Let's get down to the security desk," he told her. "I want the guard to shut down the building and call the cops."

What he really wanted was to sweep the floor himself, and find the slimy, cowardly bastard before he had the chance to slip out of the building. But he couldn't leave Leanne alone. Not when she so obviously had a target on her back.

He just wished he'd seen it sooner.

The first incident could have been just a random city crime. The second, bad luck due to that forgotten spare key. But three? For her to be targeted by somebody with evil on his mind three times in one week was no coincidence. It was a pattern.

Somebody was after her—or after something she had—and they weren't afraid to stalk her, hurt her, and terrify her to get it. He didn't intend to leave her side until he found out who that was. Now, though, he just needed to get her to safety.

As expected, the security guard felt awful about the incident. He had not been the one to turn off the upstairs lights and said he hadn't seen anybody else coming out. Meaning the assailant could still be somewhere in the huge building. But he could also have left via the maintenance stairs and loading dock, of which the guard didn't have camera views at all times.

The guard had called the police immediately, making Leanne comfortable in his office while they waited for them to show up. She sipped a hot cup of coffee from a foam cup, quietly relaying everything she could remember about what had happened. She'd have to do it all again once the cops arrived, but Jake wanted the details while they were fresh.

"Did anybody stand out as strange to you today while you were working in the booth?" Jake asked, keeping his tone calm and even, in witness mode, glad to see she was calming down, too.

She shook her head. "No, not at all. I interacted with dozens of people. No-one was the least bit suspicious, or unfriendly."

"What about earlier this week, at the office, or at home? Notice anybody watching you? Anybody say anything strange to you?"

She wrinkled her brow in confusion. "Well, no, but what would that have to do with this?"

He hedged for a moment, and then figured she deserved to know what he was thinking. "Look, I don't want to freak you out, but this just seems too big a coincidence to me. You're mugged, your place is robbed, and now you're attacked?"

Her mouth fell open. "You think they're all connected?"

He nodded slowly.

"But, that's crazy! Why would somebody target me? I'm nobody!"

He sat beside her on the guard room's lumpy sofa, dropping a hand onto her knee. "You're definitely not that."

She covered his hand with hers and squeezed. "I mean, I have nothing anybody would want. The few valuable things I had were already stolen."

Maybe. Still, this all smelled wrong to him. Jake had grown accustomed to trusting his instincts. Those instincts told him Leanne was on somebody's radar, and not in a good way. He couldn't say why, couldn't even venture a guess why this very nice, hard-working, decent woman would have drawn the eye of a thug, but he truly believed she had.

Before they could discuss it further, the police arrived to take her statement. After talking to her, they did a walk-thru of the whole convention center, but, to nobody's real surprise, found nothing. The perp was either long gone, or hiding in one of the hundreds of "rooms" on display in the place. He could easily stay all night and then blend in with the crowds come morning. The security cameras in the building were only at the exits, elevators and offices. The main floors were just too massive to make them worthwhile, he imagined. The attacker had chosen a good spot to try for her. It made him sick to think how things might have gone down had he not shown up when he did. He was very thankful his protective instincts had made him decide to come check on her tonight.

Once the police were finished, they told Leanne she was free to go, and he took her straight to his place. He had no intention of leaving her alone, anyway, but sensed she might feel a little safer somewhere other than her apartment.

It was after midnight by the time he got her safely tucked into bed, stretching out beside her. This time, when he drew her into his arms it was with no intention other than offering comfort, and to remind himself that she was okay. He had been tense and on alert all evening, since the moment he'd opened the door and heard her scream. He couldn't remember another incident in his life that had terrified him as much, and didn't think he was going to get over that fear for quite some time.

"You scared the shit out of me, you know," he said, brushing his lips across her temple.

"I was a little scared myself."

"With reason."

"I don't like being afraid," she admitted, her voice thick. "I hate it, in fact. It makes me feel…out of control."

"And control is important to you?" It wasn't really a question, because he definitely knew the answer.

"I guess. Never having had it when I was a kid, always feeling sort of at the mercy of random circumstance, gave me a bit of a phobia. My mother thrived on that lifestyle. I always hated it."

She had talked a little bit about her upbringing, but not much. Tonight, though, she seemed to want to explain, telling him more about her childhood, right here in Philadelphia, or sometimes in Baltimore, or Jersey. He held her in his arms, listening in the darkness. He suspected her close call had opened up a floodgate of memories and figured the best thing to do was just let her talk.

And he listened. Really listened. Even though it was painful to think about sweet little Leanne going through the kind of crap she'd endured.

Although her mother sounded like an irresponsible flake, the tone in Leanne's voice said she loved her. Still, if he ever met the woman, he'd have a hard time being cordial, especially when he heard about the months they'd spent living in a car, or in a shelter, sometimes on the street. One thing was sure, the picture she painted of her childhood was shocking compared to the one she presented now.

"I know people say it all the time, but damn, you are a perfect example of somebody overcoming their rough childhood," he said when she stopped speaking.

"I suppose so. I am self-aware enough to know that's why I've always wanted my dream house. A home, a family. I wanted to be respected and respectable, completely secure financially, to always be safe."

She'd deserved that. If anybody was entitled to be kept safe and secure, to never have to be afraid, or worry about money, or where she was going to live, or if she was going to eat, it was the woman in his arms.

She deserved the world. And she'd hooked up with *him*.

It was almost laughable, in a pathetic way. How the hell could he be the guy to give her what she deserved, what she wanted? He was a high school dropout who ran his own struggling P.I. firm, who she'd already bailed out of jail, who had a few bucks left at the end of every month after making his bills and paying for the tiny house they were lying in. A guy who got in brawls, who had used more women than he would like to admit, who had practically ruined his own brother's wedding. A guy who'd caused calamity in his father's marriage by showing up in the middle of a family celebration to announce his existence. Who'd cried tears of joy when his stepfather had died. Who had no real future that looked much better than the life he was living now.

What the fuck was she doing with him?

More...who did he think he was to distract her from all the things she'd longed for all her life by pushing her into this fling she'd never wanted? She'd asked for a night, but he'd been too greedy for that. He'd pushed her, seduced her, forcing himself into her company, counting on their hot chemistry to carry them along.

Now, though, having seen her in danger and realized how much he cared about her, all he could think about was what a selfish asshole he'd been.

He didn't deserve her, wasn't nearly good enough for her, and knew she could do better. It was only a matter of time until she realized that, too.

He knew what he should do, what would be the right thing to

do: end this. But aside from the fact that he'd rather rip his own guts out than lose her so soon after he'd found her—and fallen in love with her—he also wasn't about to leave her unprotected. He needed to figure out who was targeting her and make sure she was safe. After that he'd allow himself think about what was best for Leanne. Before that, he knew what was best for her: Him.

Hearing a soft sigh and the tiniest of snores, he looked down to see she'd finally drifted off. The moonlight spilling in through the window shone on her face, revealing the tracks of her tears. Whether she'd shed them because of what had happened tonight, or because of all the secrets she'd whispered in the dark, he didn't know. He just knew he never wanted to see tears—or fear—on her face again.

Which was why, the next day, he went with her to the convention center, telling her he wasn't leaving her side for the entire weekend. It was early—six a.m. They'd only had a few hours' sleep, but the home show opened to the public at eight, and all the vendors were buzzing around the place like bees in a hive, getting ready. Quite a change from the shadowy gauntlet Leanne had had to walk by herself last night.

"Jake, honestly, what can happen to me in broad daylight, in a crowded public place?" she asked him as he walked with her, ducking around people moving furniture, hanging signs, and even laying sod for lawn displays.

"Nothing can happen, because I'm going to be here to make sure it doesn't," he said, sliding an arm around her waist to guide her around two guys carrying a long ladder.

"I'm sure you have other things to do. Other clients."

"You're my client. I'm your protection detail."

"I don't need…"

"Yeah, you do," he said, tightening his grip around her waist. "Now stop fighting me on this, because I'm not leaving. If you don't say I can stay, I'll just lurk around the show, wasting the time of people in other booths who think I might actually hire them or something."

Not that his house couldn't use a little work, but he suspected most of these home improvement, decorating, construction, and lawn companies were a little out of his price range.

He was more of a do-it-yourselfer. Or would be, once he'd taught himself how to do-it-yourself.

"All right," she said, "but be prepared for me to put you to work. It might be just me again today if Ned hasn't gotten over his hissy fit."

"Happy to oblige. You tell me which curtains to hang up, and I'll get right on it."

She chuckled, obviously remembering their conversation in the car the day she'd bailed him out. He'd asked if her job title was just a fancy way of saying she picked out curtains. Now he knew she did much more than that. Judging by this place, the sheer number of booths, and the massive number of people who began pouring in as soon as it opened, lots of people were interested in what she had to sell.

He stuck close all morning, watching her chat up the dozens, if not hundreds, of people who stopped by to look at the display. She showed them photos of her other work, which definitely represented her better than the display in which she stood. She gave out business cards, took phone numbers, offered prizes, talked fabric and color and design for hours, always standing in her high-heeled shoes, never looking tired. There wasn't much Jake could do to help, other than be there as moral support, but he did make sure to provide her with fresh water and get her to sit down a few times when there was a rare lull.

It was almost lunchtime when he noticed her entire body grow stiff. Her hands clenched into fists at her sides, her body language screaming tension. Following her stare, he saw a thirty'ish guy dressed in an overly-tailored suit walking toward the booth. He was accompanied by an older, gray-haired woman wearing a Junior League worthy dress, complete with pearls.

The pair stepped into the Longotti Lines display and greeted Leanne.

"You see, Mother, isn't it perfect?"

Mother. Ahh. He knew who this was now. The Ned guy she had talked about several times. The asshole who'd apparently thrown a fit yesterday and abandoned her to finish doing all this work by herself.

"Hello Leanne," the woman said with an air-kiss. "Been busy?"

"Nonstop, Mrs. Longotti," Leanne replied, her smile tight. She cast a hard glance at the dude. "I've been here by myself since yesterday morning."

The woman whose name was written in scroll on a sign over the booth frowned, eyeing her son. "Why is that?"

"Oh, Leanne was on top of everything. I had a million things to do," he replied, the excuse rolling easily off his practiced tongue. "But she obviously managed it all right."

He walked over to look at the nightstand, which Jake knew had been damaged. She'd told him the story, including Ned's meltdown, saying that was why she'd been forced to stay so late last night, to wait for its return. Which just made him hate this guy even more.

"It looks fine," Ned said, patting the dark wood.

"Yes, it does," Leanne replied, probably trying hard not to add, "See, you asshole, you shoulda stayed calm." Instead, she merely murmured, "Crisis contained."

"Barely," Jake muttered under his breath, unable to help it.

But the sharp-eared business owner heard. The woman in the power dress turned to look at him. She gave him a once over, top to bottom, and her eyes widened a little bit, though whether it was in appreciation or immediate dislike, he really couldn't say. "I beg your pardon?"

"I said barely—as in the crisis was barely contained."

"And you are?"

"Call me Leanne's bodyguard." He had been standing in the back corner, out of the way, but now came forward, ignoring Leanne's warning frown. "She needs one because she was here so late last night, completely alone, that someone had the opportunity to attack her."

Ignoring the woman's gasp, and the way Ned swung around, visibly shocked, he put out his hand. "I'm Jake Montez, by the way."

The woman shook his hand, but her son quickly pushed between them, going to Leanne and grabbing her shoulders. "Is he serious? Are you all right?" He dragged her close, hugging her, whispering something. And Jake, suddenly hit with the truth of the situation, flinched.

Son of a bitch. This was the guy. The once-a-week guy. The asshole who took her out for nice dinners every week but couldn't be bothered to come see if she was okay when she didn't show up for one. The guy who'd left her alone last night to be terrorized.

The one she was involved with. Well, when she wasn't sleeping with Jake.

Leanne squirmed a little, pushing the man away. "I'm fine."

"What happened?" Ned asked.

He glanced at his mother, released Leanne and stepped back, suddenly the solicitous boss rather than the would-be boyfriend. Jake assumed mama didn't know about those Wednesday night dates, and that she wouldn't approve.

"Somebody tried to rob me," Leanne admitted. "But Jake was here and scared him off."

Ned immediately looked around the booth. "Did he take anything? Some of these pieces are borrowed!"

Jake couldn't prevent steam from coming out of his ears. His whole body as tight as a wire, he stalked over to the man, put a hand on his shoulder and spun him around. "I think the questions you should be asking are, 'Did he hurt you, Leanne? Are you all right, Leanne? What can I do to help you, Leanne?'"

The other man's eyes widened and he jerked his head back. "Who the hell are you again?"

"I'm the guy who was there for her the three times this week she was a crime victim, when your sorry ass couldn't be bothered."

"Jake, it's all right," Leanne said, laying a hand on his forearm. "Please, you should leave this to me."

Ned sniffed, watching the way Leanne touched him, apparently noticing their easy intimacy. How could the world not know they were lovers? How could anybody see the way Jake watched her, the way Leanne blushed when he was near, and not know they'd had each other way in every way known to man? And woman.

Ned wasn't oblivious. He wasn't stupid. He noticed.

"I think you should leave now," he said, grabbing Leanne's arm, staking his claim as bluntly as if he'd waved his Captain Caveman club and yanked her by the hair. "I'm here now, Leanne is fine. I wasn't aware she was in danger, but now that I know, I'll be responsible for keeping her safe."

"Yeah, you've done a damn fine job so far," Jake snarled, edging closer until they were toe to toe.

Leanne stepped between them, looking back and forth at their faces, visibly angry. "I'm not a toy truck here, okay? You two don't have to argue over who gets to roll me down the hill. I can take care of myself."

"Oh, sweetie," interjected Mrs. Longotti, who'd been watching the scene unfold, "do let them fight over you. It's quite exciting."

Leanne lifted hand to her face, covering her eyes, almost shaking. Her embarrassment was obvious, and Jake suddenly regretted having said anything at all. He'd had no business starting shit with this jackass. Worried about her or not, he knew the real reason he'd confronted her boss was out of sheer jealousy.

The guy was good-looking, obviously rich, educated, and ran in the same uptight, well-off circles Leanne wanted to. He was about as different from Jake as a diamond from a sandstone rock, able to offer Leanne everything she'd always longed for, worked for.

Jake…well, Jake couldn't offer her much other than great sex. And he damn well knew it. Sooner or later, so would she.

"I should go," he muttered.

"Please do," said Ned, apparently not having noticed—or cared about—Leanne's upset, humiliated reaction. "You're causing a scene as it is. Leanne doesn't need someone like you around."

"Just stop talking. No more talking," Leanne moaned. "I'm the one who's leaving."

Without sparing another glance for any of them, she did exactly that, beelining out of the booth and almost immediately getting swallowed into the crowded convention center. Jake lost sight of her before she'd gone five feet, and could have kicked himself.

Because Leanne was out there alone. Angry.

And unprotected.

Chapter 10

S TILL NOT QUITE believing the scene in the booth between Jake and Ned had really just happened, right in front of the esteemed Eleanor Longotti, Leanne moved blindly through the convention center. She pushed through the crowds, not caring where she was going, with no destination in sight. She only wanted to outrun the embarrassment and humiliation.

She could kill Ned, she could slap Jake, and she could kick herself.

How dare they treat her like a toy they could fight over, right in front of a woman she truly respected? And how stupid was she to have put herself in that position by not keeping her personal life completely clear of her professional one?

First, there was Jake. Yes, she could have ordered him to leave the booth as soon as she spied Ned, but she hadn't done it. Involving him in her work had been about her safety, but being totally honest, she'd also just liked having him around this morning.

But the bigger issue was that she'd ever gone out with Ned Longotti. That had been the biggest mistake of her professional career. He obviously hadn't gotten the pretty direct message that she was no longer interested, acting like he still had some kind of romantic claim on her. But it was her fault for having ever said yes to that first dinner invitation. And yes to the second one, even though his kiss had made her feel more bored than excited. She'd been so focused on the fact that he was the right kind of man, the kind she'd always thought she wanted, that she hadn't realized she didn't want *him.*

The only man she wanted was Jake.

She just didn't know if she was going to get to keep him.

"Not if you keep causing him so much trouble, you won't," she mumbled, tears stinging her eyes. Sooner or later, he was going to decide she was more trouble than she was worth, and he'd stop coming around. Now that he'd seen her with Ned, who'd been at his most patronizing, and Mrs. Longotti, at her most entitled, he'd probably lump her in with them, see her as she'd been when they first met: the cold, ambitious, ice princess he'd accused her of being.

But I'm not. Not anymore.

No. She wasn't cold, wasn't an ice princess, wasn't emotionless and driven by only ambition and her own personal goals. She wasn't proper and rigid and self-protective.

She definitely wasn't frigid.

She just needed the chance to prove it to him.

Heading for the escalators, Leanne milled through the downstairs exhibition hall, not really paying attention to anything. She didn't want to go back upstairs to face Ned and Mrs. Longotti, and assumed Jake had already left.

Though she wasn't looking for anyone, at last she did see a familiar face. Across a crowded aisle, she spotted Noelle, and was about to lift her hand to wave hello. Before she could do it, though, she saw the dark-haired woman duck out of sight into a small vestibule between two booths.

Leanne hadn't really wanted to talk to anyone, and was about to go on, when she saw a man follow her former co-worker into the tight spot. She didn't recognize the guy, who not only didn't look like Noelle's type, he also looked completely out of place at this show. The convention center was filled with homeowners and those in the industry, families just starting out and millionaires looking to upgrade, not to mention judges from the governor's staff.

This guy looked like a thug.

He was probably in his mid-twenties, and was dressed in baggy jeans hanging halfway down his ass, unlaced high-tops, and a pulled-up hoody. The way he ducked into the small area after Noelle looked a little creepy.

Remembering what had happened to her last night, and worried for the other woman, she hurried over. She reached the first booth, went past it and peered into the narrow crevice between it and the next. There, in the shadows, Noelle and the guy were having a whispered conversation. So apparently she did know him.

Embarrassed, and feeling judgmental, she immediately backed away, leaving the pair alone. Their conversation had looked intense, and personal, so she doubted the guy was somebody working for Michael Craft and company. But it was none of her business who the older woman made time with, so she quickly walked away, slipping into the crowd.

But having seen Noelle, she was reminded of her conversation with Craft. Now, more than ever, she was thinking about how good it would be to get away from Longotti Lines—and Ned. And, she could admit, she was very curious to see what kind of work Noelle was doing now that she'd gone someplace else.

Remembering the booth number, she headed for a nearby aisle, seeing signs for Custom Craft. They appeared to have the entire aisle, and she paused at each booth to admire a gorgeous sunroom, followed by a living room, a kitchen, and a home theater. She loved everything about the booths, admiring all the little touches that had made Michael Craft and his firm famous, everything perfectly coordinated, from the walls to the lights to the socket covers.

At last, she came to the master bedroom. The room Noelle had designed.

And she froze.

Somebody bumped into her, and she mumbled an apology for having come to a complete standstill in the middle of the aisle. People began to move by her like water around a dam, but still she couldn't move. She could only stare at the Custom Craft master bedroom. The one Noelle had most definitely *not* designed.

Leanne knew she hadn't designed it, because she recognized it right away.

It was Leanne's room, right out of her dream book. The one she'd tried to convince Ned to go with, the one others in the office had thought was so beautiful and perfect. The one Leanne loved with all her heart and had envisioned putting together.

Every detail was there. From the light oak furniture, to the soft blinds with a constructed window lit with false sunny light from behind. The carpeting, the drapes, the pillows, fixtures, artwork, right down to the small wooden jewelry box on the dresser.

All of it hers. One-hundred percent hers.

"You sneaky bitch," she muttered, immediately realizing what had happened.

Noelle had seen the design—obviously seen it very well—and recreated it. She'd then taken it to Michael Craft and presented it as her own.

She wondered if Noelle had realized Mr. Craft would choose her design for the home show. She doubted it. Noelle had known Leanne and Ned would be here, she had to assume it would be seen. No, she'd probably just been using it to show off, to get the job, never expecting that she, as a brand new employee, would actually get a room showcased at such a prestigious event, and on such short notice.

Leanne felt sick, as if she'd been robbed all over again. It was like mind rape, like she'd been plagiarized, violated. She'd never experienced anything like it before, and couldn't quite decide whether to scream or just walk into that room and start breaking shit.

Before she could decide, she looked up and saw the sneaky thief walking around the corner toward the room.

Their eyes met. Noelle's widened, and even from several feet away, Leanne heard her gasp. The redhead looked around quickly, as if making sure her new employer wasn't nearby, and then looked again at Leanne.

And smirked.

"You bitch," Leanne snapped, striding toward her. "You lying, deceitful, unoriginal bitch."

"I don't know what you're talking about," Noelle said, tossing her head and sneering, though her voice shook a little. Sheer bravado was pushing her on.

"You stole my design," Leanne snapped. "Is that why you came to my office the other day?" The minute she said the words, she knew that wasn't possible. In order to have gotten all the items on display, this had to have been set in motion weeks ago, when Noelle first started with Craft.

"That's silly. If it's anything like something you came up with, it's just a matter of creative synergy." Noelle shrugged, gaining confidence, obviously thinking she had the upper hand. "Maybe you'd better run along back upstairs to your ugly little booth," Noelle said with a bitter smile. "I'm meeting with one of the judges from the contest."

Leanne's head was reeling, spinning, and she whispered, "How could you?"

Noelle crossed her arms over her chest. "Some of us don't use our looks to get ahead. You came in the door, spread your legs for the boss, and slept your way ahead of me. You deserve whatever you get."

"I wonder if Mr. Craft knows what a talentless thief he hired."

Noelle took a step back. "You can't prove a thing."

"Oh, yes, I can," she said, thinking of the original drawings, every inch of them identical to this display area, still in her dream book.

Noelle suddenly smiled again. A taunting, confident smile.

Which was when Leanne began to panic. "You didn't."

"I don't know what you mean."

"Tell me you didn't steal those drawings out of my sketch book."

Noelle's eyes glittered, and her expression grew positively wicked. And Leanne feared the worst. If Noelle had, indeed, stolen those drawings rather than just copying them—perhaps the other day when she'd stopped by for a visit—how would Leanne prove she was the true designer? She hadn't registered any copyright, couldn't prove without a doubt that Noelle hadn't merely done something similar rather than identical.

No wonder the woman looked so cocky.

Feeling sick, desperate even, she swung around and raced away. Her satchel was locked in the trunk of her car—she hadn't wanted to bring it in here today amid all the hubbub. Now, she could only think of getting to it, finding out for sure if Noelle had taken the bedroom sketches…or anything else. God, what if she'd stolen more, reached in and helped herself to Leanne's hopes and dreams and passed them off as her own?

Moving against the throng, it took her a while to get out of the convention center and into the parking garage. The place had been so crowded this morning, she hadn't been able to get a spot close to the exit, and she had to take the elevator up a few floors. When the doors swished open and she hurried out, beelining toward her car which was parked at the far end of the level, she was almost at a run.

Getting to her car, she gave thanks that she'd had her keys in her pocket when she left the booth earlier. She unlocked the trunk, grabbed the satchel, and yanked her thick sketchbook from it.

Flipping it open toward the end, where she'd had the bedroom design, she saw the ragged edges of torn pages. Worse, a quick flip through revealed more ragged edges—a half-dozen at least.

"Oh, you evil witch," she groaned, feeling tears well up in her eyes.

Noelle had, indeed, stolen from her. Stolen her dreams. Stolen the proof.

Stolen a little piece of Leanne's heart.

She should probably count herself fortunate the miserable thief hadn't lifted her entire book the other day at the office, instead of tearing out pages and shoving them into her big purse. But right now, Leanne couldn't feel very lucky.

Before she could even think of what to do, who to tell, or how to prove it, she saw something out of the corner of her eye.

A shadow. Long, large. Close.

Leanne whirled around in time to see a fist flying toward her face.

With a shriek, she ducked out of the way, managing to evade the blow. Everything happened so quickly, she was only able to catch a glimpse of a male in a dark hoody, coming at her again as she stumbled against the car, practically falling into the trunk. Her mind reeled, shock setting in that she could be attacked in broad daylight, in a public place. But even without looking, she knew no one was around. The level was completely filled with cars, all their occupants still inside the home show, new arrivals being directed to other floors.

"Please," she gasped, not even sure what she was asking.

The bastard clawed her, grabbing at her, and she suddenly realized he was trying to get the sketchbook.

In a flash, everything fell into place. All of it.

But knowing who was doing this—who had attacked her before, and why—wasn't going to help her now. The hooded creep was on a mission, and this time he didn't intend to fail.

"Get the fuck off her!" a hard voice yelled.

She almost collapsed with relief. It was Jake, who must have been following her, watching over her from a distance. Her guardian angel—her special bodyguard. He'd exited the elevator, seen what was happening, and come at a run.

The thug she'd seen whispering with Noelle a little while ago saw him and took off. He dropped the sketchbook a few feet away, apparently deciding that finishing the job Noelle had paid him to do wasn't worth his teeth.

Or his life.

Because Jake looked ready to kill. He didn't even slow down, simply barreling into the man, diving onto him until they both hit the cement floor, rolling across it. Jake's fists flew and he pounded the guy, who fought back just as viciously.

Leanne watched, her heart in her throat, wishing she'd just let the bastard take the book. She would want to die if Jake were seriously hurt on her behalf. There was nothing she could do to help, except run to the side railing and yell down to some people below, begging them to call security.

Luck was with them. An armed Philadelphia cop who'd been hired as extra security for the trade show was one floor down. He came running up the ramp seconds later, but by then, it was already all over. Jake had subdued the thief, who was lying in a bruised, bloody lump, waiting to be arrested.

The minute the cop took over, Jake came to her, opened his arms, and she flew into them.

"Thank God," she whispered, tears welling up in her eyes. Her whole body was shaking, not with fear for herself, but for him. "Oh, thank God you're okay."

"I'm fine baby. I promise. Are you?"

She nodded and sniffled, unable to let him go, keeping her face buried in his chest. "Yes, yes. I'm totally fine now."

She knew there was a lot to say. She had to tell him what she'd figured out—that Noelle had somehow convinced this guy to steal her dream book. To cover her own theft of some of its pages? Or because she needed fresh—stolen—ideas to impress her boss? She didn't know. But she had no doubt that the man being handcuffed by police was the one who had mugged her, and then robbed her apartment.

But all that was for later. Right now, she just wanted to go home. Screw the show, the contest, her boss, her job.

She needed to be alone with her man. All the rest of the world could wait.

IT WAS SEVERAL hours before Jake felt like Leanne was relaxed enough to talk again about everything that had happened. They were at his house, having come here after having once again gone through the ordeal of a police interview. He'd been sitting beside her throughout it, and had put the pieces together, along with the cops. Still, they hadn't talked about it privately. Because the minute they'd arrived home, she'd told him she wanted him, and had taken him by the hand and led him upstairs to his bed.

They spent much of the afternoon and evening there, making slow, easy love. He'd been tender, careful, worried she carried residual wounds—physical or mental ones—from the attack. She'd been just as emotional, weeping when she admitted how terrified she'd been when she watched him fight with her attacker.

Now, after they'd loved and slept and showered together, he was making her a light dinner in the kitchen. She sat at the table, watching him, wearing nothing but one of his T-shirts. Neither of them said it, but they both wanted to stay close.

"So," he said as he flipped over a grilled cheese sandwich in a buttered pan, "when are you going to go meet with Mr. Craft?"

Leanne rubbed her eyes. "I'm not sure. He told me to come by any time. He was very kind—and very apologetic."

Yes, he had been. Jake had been there, with Leanne, watching as the police came to question Noelle. Her accomplice had ratted on her the minute the cuffs snapped on, admitting he'd been hired to steal Leanne's satchel containing her sketchbook. He'd failed in his every attempt, until today, when he'd seen her going to her car and had decided to follow.

Noelle had ended up in cuffs, too. The police officer had told Leanne she would be charged as an accomplice to assault and robbery. Multiple counts.

Michael Craft had fired her as she'd been led out of the center. Of course, her job was now the least of Noelle Singleton's worries.

"I still can't believe this whole damn thing was about curtains," Jake said, shaking his head.

She laughed softly. "I do good curtains."

"You must. Mr. Craft said he had expected that room to win the Governor's Prize, and that he was withdrawing it to make sure the credit didn't go to the wrong person."

"Maybe next year," she said with a shrug, as if she truly didn't care that her work *should* have won a major prize.

"You're really okay?"

She nodded, rising to join him by the stove, lifting a hand to smooth his hair off his brow. "Jake, seeing you fighting with that guy was one of the most frightening moments of my life. I honestly don't care about anything else other than the fact that you are okay." She cleared her throat, as if working up nerve, and then whispered something. Something that stopped his heart.

"I love you."

He went very still, unable to speak, not sure what to say.

"I know it's too soon, and that you think I'm not the kind of woman you really want, but I do love you, and I want you to know it."

He moved the pan off the burner and turned off the stove, slowly turning to face her. "What the hell are you talking about?"

Her eyes widened. Not the response she'd expected to her declaration of love, he assumed. He quickly explained. "Not the kind of woman I want? Are you crazy?"

"I mean, I know you think I'm an ice princess, that I'm…cold." She swallowed, and her lashes swept down to conceal her eyes. "Frigid."

He threw his head back and laughed, shocked that such a word might ever be used in connection with the woman standing in his kitchen, her sexy bare ass flashing now and again from below his T-shirt.

"Yeah, you're crazy. He hit you in the head, didn't he."

"I'm serious," she insisted. "I know what people think of me. What men think of me."

He gave himself a moment to become enraged that any man could ever make this beautiful, passionate, vibrant woman think of herself as frigid, and then said, "What I think, Leanne, is that you're beautiful, and brilliant, and adorable, and way too fucking good for the likes of me."

She was shaking her head. He didn't let her stop him.

"I mean it. I've been telling myself that I don't deserve you, that I can't give you everything you want and dream of."

"But you're what I want and dream of."

He cupped her face in his hands. "I'm not a rich guy, Leanne. I'll probably never be able to buy you that Victorian house in the country, not unless I accept the money my father's always trying to give me, and I just can't do that. Not even for you."

LESLIE KELLY

"I would never ask you to," she said, sliding her hands up to wrap her arms around his neck.

"It's more than that," he said, trying to resist the urge to just kiss her and say to hell with all the problems. But he owed her more. "I'm not a nice guy. I am not a gentleman. I'm a fighter, and a jerk and…"

"And a hero, and a protector, and an amazing lover, and a wonderful, funny, tender, sexy, smart, noble man," she said, placing her fingers over his lips. Then she said, "Just answer me one question, Jake. Just one."

He nodded warily.

"Do you love me?"

He could lie. For her sake, he probably should lie. She'd be better off without him. She'd probably land a new job with that famous guy she'd talked to today. New circles were opening for her. Her world would widen, she would become famous and touted, winning awards and contracts, fame and wealth. He'd only hold her back.

But he was helpless against that look of longing in her gleaming silver eyes. Though it might damn his soul, he could not say the words that would make her go away.

He could only tell her the truth.

"Yes. I love you."

She sighed the happy sigh of someone who wanted nothing more in the world than to hear those words. So he couldn't possibly regret them.

"You're right, it's too soon, and I've never been in love with anyone before. Which, to be honest, is how I know what this is." He brushed his thumbs across her trembling mouth, wanting so badly to kiss her. "It's love."

Her eyes grew luminous with moisture—happy tears, he thought—and she smiled at him.

"That's all I need to know."

Not giving him a chance to argue, or question how they'd make this work when they were such opposites, she rose on tiptoe and pressed her mouth to his. The kiss was long and tender, a languid mating of lips, and mouth, and tongue. He hungered for her, body, mind and soul. And, he was able to admit, heart.

When they finally separated, he said, "I'm never gonna be good enough for you."

"You're the only man I want, Jake. You're the one person in the world who taught me the lesson I've waited my whole life to learn. That it isn't a two-story house that defines a place as a home, and a balanced checkbook doesn't mean security." She tightened her arms around his neck. "It's the right person who builds the foundation, who creates the walls…"

"Who hangs the curtains?"

She laughed softly, and nodded. "And makes the roof." A soft, sweet, gentle kiss. "You're my home, Jake. Just you."

He couldn't resist her anymore, hearing the genuine emotion in her words, seeing the heartfelt love in her eyes. Miracle of miracles, this woman who he hadn't even known a month ago, loved him with the kind of love he truly believed would last a lifetime.

He believed it…because that's how long he would be in love with her.

Epilogue

Nine Months Later

IT WAS A lovely day to welcome a new life into the world.

As Leanne finished tying a pretty bow on a large package wrapped in blue, she glanced out the front window of the townhouse and saw Jake pulling up outside on his motorcycle. He had run out to the store to get some cigars, wanting to bring them to the hospital to give to the new father. He'd been walking around with his chest puffed out all morning—a proud uncle—ever since they'd gotten the call that Eve had safely delivered a healthy boy overnight.

Eve, her dearest friend, was now a mommy. It boggled the mind. She'd apparently gotten pregnant on her honeymoon, and she and Sam couldn't have been happier. Which made Leanne very happy, too.

"Almost ready?" Jake asked as he came into the house, seeing her sitting on the living room floor, surrounded by pretty paper and ribbons.

She nodded, extending a hand so he could help her up.

She needed it. Because she was a little heavy on her feet these days, too.

He kissed her cheek and patted her six-months' pregnant tummy, bending to whisper, "Hey baby girl, ready to go meet your cousin?"

"We're ready," she replied.

She covered his left hand with hers, smiling at the sight of the plain gold bands they each wore on their fourth fingers, put there just two months ago.

Married. A baby on the way. Deliriously happy.

Had any woman ever been luckier?

Had there ever been a small house that had become as huge a home as this one?

No, she didn't think there had. Because every day she spent with Jake simply made the world—their house—bigger, happier, stronger, more perfect.

She had everything she'd ever wanted, without any of the trappings she'd once believed she needed. All the love she'd ever dreamed of, but never really believed she'd find.

All because of him.

And life had never been better.

Excerpt

Did you miss book 1 of Leslie's "Temptation In The City" series? Here's an excerpt of Sam and Eve's story, BRINGING DOWN SAM, available now!

Prologue

"A single woman's number one goal is to get a ring on her finger. A single man's number one goal is to steer clear of jewelry stores."

—From *101 Ways To Avoid Commitment*

T HE VOICE EMERGING from the speakers of her car was confident, smooth and masculine. But no matter how attractive the sound, the words still made Eve Barret want to punch something. "Sexist jerk," she snarled as she settled for smacking the "off" button.

As she stopped at a red light in downtown Philadelphia, Eve realized she was clutching the steering wheel so hard her palms hurt. She eased up, acknowledging she'd mentally pictured having Sam Kenneman's throat in her grip.

She simply couldn't stand the man. She'd never met him, never even set eyes on him, but she detested him. As did just about every other unmarried woman in America.

Eve took a few deep, calming breaths wondering why she'd paused on that particular station when she'd first heard he was to be this afternoon's guest.

"Morbid curiosity," she muttered, feeling like a highway rubbernecker looking at an accident scene. Only a woman with a sick sense of curiosity would listen to the musings of Sam Kenneman, the author of the latest hit in the book-battle-of-the-sexes, *101 Ways To Avoid Commitment*.

When Eve had first heard of his book, months before, she'd assumed it was a joke. It seemed the hints on avoiding long-term relationships and marriage Kenneman had written about in a series of humorous articles in *His World* magazine had gained something of a cult following. His ideas had achieved huge popularity on the Internet, and publishers clamored for a book.

What reviewers called a humor book, many men called a dating manual. Kenneman's words had become their mantra. Soon, women started complaining that men were taking his words seriously. Eve had heard about his *Good Morning America* appearance, when the author had said it would take a ton of cement stuck to his shoes to make him stand at an altar and say, "I do." Supposedly, the females in the audience hadn't known whether to boo him for his work, or swoon at his feet for his good looks.

Turning a corner, she noticed a covered bus stop near the edge of the street. On the side of it was a poster-sized ad for Sam Kenneman's book. Groaning, she sped past it. She couldn't escape the man! For the past few weeks, each telephone conversation she'd had with her best friend, Leanne, had included his name.

"Dumped because of a stupid book," Eve said, shaking her head in disgust. Eve couldn't believe Leanne had been jilted by a man she loved because of a testosterone-laden humor book.

When she thought of Sloan, Leanne's ex, she conceded the breakup wasn't necessarily a bad thing. The old adage "Good riddance to bad rubbish" definitely applied. The guy had been a schmuck, no doubt, but he'd been *Leanne's* schmuck. And Leanne sure hadn't deserved to be ditched by a guy who wasn't nearly good enough for her. Especially not one who cited insulting reasons right out of Kenneman's book, waving it at her as he walked out.

Leanne was a self-confident, intelligent woman. But she'd been devastated by the experience. Hearing the misery in her voice when they talked on the phone had been agonizing for Eve, and she looked forward to comforting her in person tonight.

She generally saw Leanne, as well as their other two best friends, once a month. But Eve had been busy with end of the year activities at the private school where she taught and hadn't been able to make it last time. So tonight's gathering was long overdue.

Sighting her destination, Eve steered her car into the parking lot of a Mexican restaurant. The lot was nearly empty, as usual, which was one reason they always met here. That and the to-die-for enchiladas. The four of them had discovered this place years ago and were Casa Rosada's most faithful customers.

As she entered the restaurant, she heard one breathy, high-pitched, unmistakable female voice. "Sam Kenneman is public enemy number one of every single woman in this country."

Eve walked through the dimly lit bar area and overheard the angry declaration. Her friends hadn't noticed her yet, and Eve studied them with affection as she approached. Ruthie, the petite redhead whose voice could be heard from the door, sat with her back toward the aisle. Across from her sat Diana, tall, lean, her brown hair cut short and no-nonsense, matching her attitude. She rolled her dark eyes in resignation as Ruthie chattered on. Next to Diana was Leanne, who observed them with her customary cool detachment, though an indulgent smile creased her lips.

"You three look like a TV commercial on *Lifetime*. Three twenty-somethings sitting in a bar griping about men," Eve said as she slipped into the empty chair next to Ruthie.

"You're late," Diana barked.

Eve took no offense. Diana always sounded gruff. She had a gravelly, raspy voice that could make her sound ticked off even if singing *It's A Small World* at Disneyland. Then again, remembering her last trip to Disneyland, Eve supposed anyone would.

"Sorry. Remember, I don't live right here in Philadelphia, like you. Took me over an hour because of traffic."

Before Eve had a chance to slip her purse strap off her shoulder, their regular young waiter was at her elbow, an eager smile on his face. "Your usual margarita tonight?"

After Eve nodded, and the waiter hurried away, Ruthie giggled and said, "At least he didn't drop the entire tray of glasses like he did a few months ago when you walked through the door."

Eve shrugged uncomfortably. "That was just an accident."

Diana's old wise-cracking south Jersey accent slipped out. "Sure hon. Like it was an accident when the guy following you in the park tripped head first into the fountain last year."

"Or when the artist said he was going on hunger strike until you posed for him," Ruthie said.

Eve knew her friends were teasing, but she couldn't hide a frown. Across the table, Leanne caught her eye and gave her a commiserating smile. Of course Leanne understood; after all, she and Eve were the most alike, at least emotionally. They'd both fought to overcome their pasts, though for different reasons. Physically, the only thing they had in common was the blond hair. While Eve's was a long, loose curtain of gold, Leanne's more platinum-colored curls were usually worn up in an elegant twist.

"So, what were you talking about before I arrived?" Eve asked, though she knew the answer.

Ruthie was immediately distracted, as usual. "Remember the musician I went out with, who actually bothered to *ask* me whether I liked blood and guts movies?"

"Yeah," Diana retorted. "And we know you lied through your teeth, then sat through an hour of guck before you barfed up your popcorn and Sno-Caps right into his lap."

"Well, that's right out of Kenneman's book. I just thought I'd *die*," wailed Ruthie, ignoring Diana completely. "To think, the jerk tells men to take women to those shoot-em-up testosterone-oozing movies as a litmus test."

"And you failed big time," Diana said with a smirk. "Just like you would have in Bio-101 if your lab partner hadn't dragged you through dissection hoping you'd set him up with Eve."

Ruth wrinkled her nose at Diana and got a look of disgust in return. Eve hid a grin. The two of them acted just like they had as teenagers. It seemed on these Tuesday nights, when they were together, they all fell back into their accustomed roles.

They'd met in college. Forming a friendship, they'd become roommates in a townhouse…and lifelong friends. Ruthie, the bubbly dreamer, worked as a chef in her family's fine old Philadelphia hotel, and looked the part with her pretty, round face and soft figure about which she constantly complained. Diana, the protective, dark-haired ambitious one, who had nudged them relentlessly through their final exams, was now a magazine executive. Leanne, the reserved blonde who seemed to feel things the most deeply, now satisfied her creative streak with interior design.

Then there was Eve. The former loner, the ex-model, the one who had never had a real, true female friend before that first year of college.

They were an unlikely quartet, perhaps. But there were no three people on earth she loved more.

Eve glanced across the table, noting the tension around Leanne's tightly held smile. Ruthie and Diana didn't appear to notice, leading Eve to wonder if Leanne had told them the details of her recent breakup. She doubted it. Though Ruthie was a complete scatterbrain, even *she* wouldn't have been callous enough to mention Kenneman if she'd known the whole story.

"Well, it serves you right, Ruthie, for going out with the guy again after your first date when he asked you to pick up the tab!"

Diana said with a definite rolling of her eyes.

"He said he was short on funds because he was between gigs."

"Gigs? I bet the closest that loser's been to being a real musician was playing oboe in his in sixth grade band."

Leaning back in her chair, Eve sipped her drink, listening to Diana and Ruthie's banter. She'd missed them in the past months. These Tuesday night meetings kept her connected to the adult world after days of talking to nobody but moody, pubescent kids. These dinners were her chance to be herself with the three people who knew her best in the world.

Eve still wondered what might have happened to her if she hadn't found them. She'd been so lost, so alone, with her father thrown in jail, her money gone, her modeling career over. All before her eighteenth birthday.

They'd taken her into their lives, their hearts. They were her sisters in every way except biologically. They'd bonded to form their own family, and each holiday, birthday, heartbreak or bitching session in her adult life had been spent in their company.

There was *nothing* she wouldn't do for them.

Ruthie rested her elbows on the table and plopped her chin on her fist. "I don't know how you can stand working with Kenneman, Diana," she said. "Though, he is kind of dishy."

Diana crossed her arms in front of her chest, giving Ruthie a look of disgust. "It's been tough enough being hired as a senior editor at *His World*, the only female on the editorial staff. Looking at his smirking face as he talks about his stupid sexist articles and his stupid sexist book make it ten times worse. So I don't care to hear how 'dishy' the guy is."

"Oh, I know," Ruthie said, nodding so hard her red curls nearly bounced into the long-stemmed green goblet the obsequious waiter had just placed on the table. "I'm not really interested of course. I just would love to see someone bring Mr. Big-Shot writer down a peg…let *him* deal with a broken heart for once."

Eve slid her hand across the white tablecloth and pushed against the cactus shaped base of her glass, sliding her margarita out of harm's—hair's—way.

"But what kind of woman could bring down a gorgeous single man who wrote a book called *101 Ways To Avoid Commitment?*" Leanne said softly, so softly Eve almost didn't hear her.

Glancing at her friend, Eve saw a look of melancholy on Leanne's face. The other woman stared at the potted palm next to their table, not teased out of her bad mood by Diana and Ruthie's bickering.

"Yeah, what kind of woman would it take?" Diana said, but her words were speculative. "I mean, who could bring Philadelphia's most avowed bachelor to his knees?"

Eve brought her drink to her lips and sipped it, knowing her friends would move off the topic eventually. The man-bashing never lasted too long. But, for some reason, the silence around the table stretched on. Glancing over the rim of her glass, she saw all three of the other women staring at her. Ruthie's green eyes sparkled in anticipation, Diane's brown ones were purely speculative. Even sweet, sad Leanne looked amused.

"Forget it." Eve shook her head. "Never. Not in a million years. You can't talk me into this, so don't even try."

Her friends had dragged her into wacky schemes before. She still couldn't bring herself to walk into Rusty's Grille because of the time they'd decided to try to save a poor lobster swimming alone in a tank near the dining area. That was during Ruthie's "I'm a vegetarian" stage. Of course, Eve was the one nominated to execute the rescue. Ruthie would never have been able to bring herself to touch something so…icky. Diana swore if she got her hands on it someone had better have some melted butter nearby. Leanne was simply too worried about getting caught. So Eve stuck her hand in, giving the creature a strained smile through the distorted glass hoping he'd know she was trying to help him. She didn't even notice one of the little sucker's claws was unbound. Ouch.

There were other instances, so many she couldn't remember them all. But this time she was standing firm. There was no way on earth she was going to try to set some guy up for a romantic fall. Not on a bet, not on a dare. It wasn't gonna happen.

She told herself that, again and again.

Yet, somehow, two hours later, Eve found herself nodding wearily as they went over the plan one last time. Even Diana, usually the voice of reason, had been sucked in and was agreeing with the ridiculous idea, and she had a lot more to lose than anyone else. Probably because she was also incredibly protective of Leanne.

"So, we're clear," Diana said. "You'll stay in the company condo here in Philadelphia for at least two weeks."

"I still don't see why I have to stay there," Eve said, still wondering how on earth they'd gotten her to agree. It was insane. It was risky. It was just plain stupid and juvenile.

But somehow, they'd gotten her to say yes. Maybe because she just couldn't stand seeing the sadness in Leanne's face any more and her agreement had made her best friend smile. Maybe because she'd had a couple of margaritas.

"Well, he's sure not going to buy you as a big world-traveling model if you stay at the Budget Inn, is he?"

"Probably not. And that's about all I could afford."

"And if you bunk with one of us, he might suspect something!"

"You're sure you're not going to get in hot water for letting me stay at the condo?"

"Absolutely not. The penthouse sits vacant forty weeks out of the year. It's for execs and high-profile visitors the magazine brings in.

No problem whatsoever with you using it."

"Goody," Eve mumbled, reaching for the pitcher.

"I'll do my part. I can make sure Sam first sees you at just the right moment, and under the perfect circumstances." A secretive look crossed Diana's face, and Eve could only imagine what she had in mind. "Ruthie will supply all the aphrodisiacs needed. You get him to take you to her hotel for dinner and she'll be sure to load him up on oysters and chocolate."

"And me on garlic and onions," Eve muttered.

Diana shot her a dirty look. "Eve..."

"Well," Eve insisted, "I said I'd make him want me, not that I'd let him have me!"

"What's my job?" Leanne asked.

"You're on call to be my cheerleader," Eve said quickly, taking Leanne's hand. "And to listen to me whine when Diana works me like a slave at the magazine office."

Diana smirked. "Sure, hon. We all know you just hate the thought of getting in front of a camera again."

Eve didn't know how she felt about that part of their plan. She understood the necessity. If she was going to get Sam Kenneman to fall for her, she had to be the ideal woman—the one he described in his book—no matter how personally unappealing. Playing ditzy model would help with that goal.

"So, Eve, do you think you can do it? Get this guy to go nuts for you, then drop him like a hot potato, in as public a way possible? Preferably with paparazzi witnesses?" Ruthie asked, grinning with wicked anticipation.

"She can do it," Leanne said, her eyes sparkling with humor.

It was the sparkle that made Eve nod her head in agreement. Leanne deserved vindication. So did every other American woman whose man had read *101 Ways To Avoid Commitment* and decided

227

his successful, career-oriented girlfriend was too smart, too witty, too much a real woman to stick with.

Sam Kenneman had better look out. He was about to take a one-way drive straight down to dumpsville. And Eve Barret was going to be the one behind the wheel.

About the Author

Leslie Kelly is the New York Times and USA Today Bestselling author of dozens of books in various genres. She writes romantic comedies as well as dark, suspenseful thrillers, both for traditional publishers, and independently.

Leslie lives in New Mexico with her husband Bruce.

To keep up with her books, please visit her websites: www.lesliekelly.com or www.leslieAkelly.com and sign up for her newsletter.

You can also find her on Facebook at: www.facebook.com/-authorlesliekelly or on Twitter at www.twitter.com/lesliekelly.

Leslie loves hearing from readers—if you have a moment, will you please consider leaving a review of this book?

www.ingramcontent.com/pod-product-compliance
Lightning Source LLC
Chambersburg PA
CBHW070619130626
46556CB00001B/416